T

"Pratchett has now moved beyond the limits of
humorous fantasy, and should be recognized as
one of the more significant contemporary
English language satirists."
Publishers Weekly

"He's arguably the purely funniest
English writer since Wodehouse."
Washington Post Book World

"Humorously entertaining . . . subtly thought-
provoking . . . Pratchett's Discworld books are filled
with humor and with magic, but they're rooted in—
of all things—real life and cold, hard reason."
Chicago Tribune

"Discworld takes the classic fantasy universe
through its logical, and comic, evolution."
Cleveland Plain Dealer

"Pratchett's books are richly textured, and far more
complex than they appear at first."
Barbara Mertz

"Unadulterated fun . . . witty, frequently hilarious."
San Francisco Chronicle

"Truly original . . . Discworld is more complicated
and satisfactory than Oz . . . . Has the energy of
The Hitchhiker's Guide to the Galaxy and the
inventiveness of *Alice in Wonderland* . . . Brilliant!"
A.S. Byatt

Terry Pratchett

Sourcery

A Novel of Discworld®

HARPER

An Imprint of HarperCollinsPublishers

This book was originally published in Great Britain by Victor Gollancz Ltd. in association with Colin Smythe Ltd.

HARPER

An Imprint of Harper Collins *Publishers*
195 Broadway
New York, NY 10007

First Harper premium printing: May 2013
First Harper mass market printing: April 2008
First HarperTorch mass market printing: February 2001

DEDICATION

Many years ago I saw, in Bath, a very large American lady towing a huge *tartan suitcase very fast on little ratty wheels which caught in the pavement cracks and generally gave it a life of its own. At that moment the Luggage was born. Many thanks to that lady and everyone else in places like Power Cable, Neb., who don't get nearly enough encouragement.*

This book does not contain a map. Please feel free to draw your own.

There was a man and he had eight sons. Apart from that, he was nothing more than a comma on the page of History. It's sad, but that's all you can say about some people.

But the eighth son grew up and married and had eight sons, and because there is only one suitable profession for the eighth son of an eighth son, he became a wizard. And he became wise and powerful, or at any rate powerful, and wore a pointed hat and there it would have ended . . .

Should have ended . . .

But against the Lore of Magic and certainly against all reason—except the reasons of the heart, which are warm and messy and, well, *unreasonable*—he fled the halls of magic and fell in love and got married, not necessarily in that order.

And he had seven sons, each one from the cradle at least as powerful as any wizard in the world.

And then he had an eighth son . . .

A wizard squared. A source of magic.

A sourcerer.

Summer thunder rolled around the sandy cliffs. Far below, the sea sucked on the shingle as noisily as an

1

old man with one tooth who had been given a gob-stopper. A few seagulls hung lazily in the up-draughts, waiting for something to happen.

And the father of wizards sat among the thrift and rattling sea grasses at the edge of the cliff, cradling the child in his arms, staring out to sea.

There was a roil of black cloud out there, heading inland, and the light it pushed before it had that deep syrup quality it gets before a really serious thunderstorm.

He turned at a sudden silence behind him, and looked up through tear-reddened eyes at a tall hooded figure in a black robe.

IPSLORE THE RED? it said. The voice was as hollow as a cave, as dense as a neutron star.

Ipslore grinned the terrible grin of the suddenly mad, and held up the child for Death's inspection.

"My son," he said. "I shall call him Coin."

A NAME AS GOOD AS ANY OTHER, said Death politely. His empty sockets stared down at a small round face wrapped in sleep. Despite rumor, Death isn't cruel—merely terribly, terribly good at his job.

"You took his mother," said Ipslore. It was a flat statement, without apparent rancor. In the valley behind the cliffs Ipslore's homestead was a smoking ruin, the rising wind already spreading the fragile ashes across the hissing dunes.

IT WAS A HEART ATTACK AT THE END, said Death. THERE ARE WORSE WAYS TO DIE. TAKE IT FROM ME.

Ipslore looked out to sea. "All my magic could not save her," he said.

THERE ARE PLACES WHERE EVEN MAGIC MAY NOT GO.

"And now you have come for the child?"

NO. THE CHILD HAS HIS OWN DESTINY. I HAVE COME FOR YOU.

"Ah." The wizard stood up, carefully laid the sleeping baby down on the thin grass, and picked up a long staff that had been lying there. It was made of a black metal, with a meshwork of silver and gold carvings that gave it a rich and sinister tastelessness; the metal was octiron, intrinsically magical.

"I made this, you know," he said. "They all said you couldn't make a staff out of metal, they said they should only be of wood, but they were wrong. I put a lot of myself into it. I shall give it to him."

He ran his hands lovingly along the staff, which gave off a faint tone.

He repeated, almost to himself, "I put a lot of myself into it."

IT IS A GOOD STAFF, said Death.

Ipslore held it in the air and looked down at his eighth son, who gave a gurgle.

"She wanted a daughter," he said.

Death shrugged. Ipslore gave him a look compounded of bewilderment and rage.

"What *is* he?"

THE EIGHTH SON OF AN EIGHTH SON OF AN EIGHTH SON, said Death, unhelpfully. The wind whipped at his robe, driving the black clouds overhead.

"What does that make him?"

A SOURCERER, AS YOU ARE WELL AWARE.

Thunder rolled, on cue.

"What is his destiny?" shouted Ipslore, above the rising gale.

Death shrugged again. He was good at it.

SOURCERERS MAKE THEIR OWN DESTINY. THEY TOUCH THE EARTH LIGHTLY.

Ipslore leaned on the staff, drumming on it with his fingers, apparently lost in the maze of his own thoughts. His left eyebrow twitched.

"No," he said, softly, "no. I will make his destiny for him."

I ADVISE AGAINST IT.

"Be quiet! And listen when I tell you that they drove me out, with their books and their rituals and their Lore! They called themselves wizards, and they had less magic in their whole fat bodies than I have in my little finger! Banished! *Me*! For showing that I was human! And what would humans be without love?"

RARE, said Death. NEVERTHELESS—

"Listen! They drove us here, to the ends of the world, and that killed her! They tried to take my staff away!" Ipslore was screaming above the noise of the wind.

"Well, I still have some power left," he snarled. "And I say that my son shall go to Unseen University and wear the Archchancellor's hat and the wizards of the world shall bow to him! And he shall show them what lies in their deepest hearts. Their craven, greedy hearts. He'll show the *world* its true destiny, and there will be no magic greater than his."

No. And the strange thing about the quiet way Death spoke the word was this: it was louder than the roaring of the storm. It jerked Ipslore back to momentary sanity.

Ipslore rocked back and forth uncertainly. "What?" he said.

I SAID NO. NOTHING IS FINAL. NOTHING IS ABSO-
LUTE, EXCEPT ME, OF COURSE. SUCH TINKERING WITH
DESTINY COULD MEAN THE DOWNFALL OF THE WORLD.
THERE MUST BE A CHANCE, HOWEVER SMALL. THE
LAWYERS OF FATE DEMAND A LOOPHOLE IN EVERY
PROPHECY.

Ipslore stared at Death's implacable face.

"I must give them a chance?"

YES.

Tap, tap, tap went Ipslore's fingers on the metal of
the staff.

"Then they shall have their chance," he said,
"when hell freezes over."

NO. I AM NOT ALLOWED TO ENLIGHTEN YOU, EVEN
BY DEFAULT, ABOUT CURRENT TEMPERATURES IN THE
NEXT WORLD.

"Then," Ipslore hesitated, "then they shall have
their chance when my son throws his staff away."

NO WIZARD WOULD EVER THROW HIS STAFF AWAY,
said Death. THE BOND IS TOO GREAT.

"Yet it is possible, you must agree."

Death appeared to consider this. *Must* was not a
word he was accustomed to hearing, but he seemed
to concede the point.

AGREED, he said.

"Is that a small enough chance for you?"

SUFFICIENTLY MOLECULAR.

Ipslore relaxed a little. In a voice that was nearly
normal, he said: "I don't regret it, you know. I would
do it all again. Children are our hope for the future."

THERE IS NO HOPE FOR THE FUTURE, said Death.

"What does it contain, then?"

ME.

"Besides you, I mean!"

Death gave him a puzzled look. I'M SORRY?

The storm reached its howling peak overhead. A seagull went past backwards.

"I meant," said Ipslore, bitterly, "what is there in this world that makes living worthwhile?"

Death thought about it.

CATS, he said eventually, CATS ARE NICE.

"Curse you!"

MANY HAVE, said Death, evenly.

"How much longer do I have?"

Death pulled a large hourglass from the secret recesses of his robe. The two bulbs were enclosed in bars of black and gold, and the sand was nearly all in the bottom one.

OH, ABOUT NINE SECONDS.

Ipslore pulled himself up to his full and still impressive height, and extended the gleaming metal staff toward the child. A hand like a little pink crab reached out from the blanket and grasped it.

"Then let me be the first and last wizard in the history of the world to pass on his staff to his eighth son," he said slowly and sonorously. "And I charge him to use it to—"

I SHOULD HURRY UP, IF I WERE YOU . . .

"—the full," said Ipslore, "becoming the mightiest—"

The lightning screamed from the heart of the cloud, hit Ipslore on the point of his hat, crackled down his arm, flashed along the staff and struck the child.

The wizard vanished in a wisp of smoke. The staff

glowed green, then white, then merely red-hot. The child smiled in his sleep.

When the thunder had died away Death reached down slowly and picked up the boy, who opened his eyes.

They glowed golden, from the inside. For the first time in what, for want of any better word, must be called his life, Death found himself looking at a stare that he found hard to return. The eyes seemed to be focused on a point several inches inside his skull.

I did not mean for that to happen, said the voice of Ipslore, from out of the empty air. *Is he harmed?*

No. Death tore his gaze away from that fresh, knowing smile. HE CONTAINED THE POWER. HE IS A SOURCERER: NO DOUBT HE WILL SURVIVE MUCH WORSE. AND NOW—YOU WILL COME WITH ME.

No.

YES. YOU ARE DEAD, YOU SEE. Death looked around for Ipslore's wavering shade, and failed to find it. WHERE ARE YOU?

In the staff.

Death leaned on his scythe and sighed.

FOOLISH. HOW EASILY COULD I CUT YOU LOOSE.

Not without destroying the staff, said the voice of Ipslore, and it seemed to Death that there was a new, thick, exultant quality to it. *And now the child has accepted the staff you cannot destroy it without destroying him. And that you cannot do without upsetting destiny. My last magic. Rather neat, I feel.*

Death prodded the staff. It crackled, and sparks crawled obscenely along its length.

Strangely enough, he wasn't particularly angry. Anger is an emotion, and for emotion you need glands, and Death didn't have much truck with glands and needed a good run at it to get angry. But he was mildly annoyed. He sighed again. People were always trying this sort of thing. On the other hand, it was quite interesting to watch, and at least this was a bit more original than the usual symbolic chess game, which Death always dreaded because he could never remember how the knight was supposed to move.

YOU'RE ONLY PUTTING OFF THE INEVITABLE, he said.

That's what being alive is all about.

BUT WHAT PRECISELY DO YOU EXPECT TO GAIN?

I shall be by my son's side. I shall teach him, even though he won't know it. I shall guide his understanding. And, when he is ready, I shall guide his steps.

TELL ME, said Death, How DID YOU GUIDE THE STEPS OF YOUR OTHER SONS?

I drove them out. They dared to argue with me, they would not listen to what I could teach them. But this one will.

IS THIS WISE?

The staff was silent. Beside it, the boy chuckled at the sound of a voice only he could hear.

There was no analogy for the way in which Great A'Tuin the world turtle moved against the galactic night. When you are ten thousand miles long, your shell pocked with meteor craters and frosted with comet ice, there is absolutely nothing you can realistically be like except yourself.

So Great A'Tuin swam slowly through the interstellar deeps like the largest turtle there has ever been, carrying on its carapace the four huge elephants that bore on their backs the vast, glittering waterfall-fringed circle of the Discworld, which exists either because of some impossible blip on the curve of probability or because the gods enjoy a joke as much as anyone.

More than most people, in fact.

Near the shores of the Circle Sea, in the ancient, sprawling city of Ankh-Morpork, on a velvet cushion on a ledge high up in the Unseen University, was a hat.

It was a good hat. It was a *magnificent* hat.

It was pointy, of course, with a wide floppy brim, but after disposing of these basic details the designer had really got down to business. There was gold lace on there, and pearls, and bands of purest vermine, and sparkling Ankhstones*, and some incredibly tasteless sequins, and—a dead giveaway, of course—a circle of octarines.

Since they weren't in a strong magical field at the moment they weren't glowing, and looked like rather inferior diamonds.

Spring had come to Ankh-Morpork. It wasn't immediately apparent, but there were signs that were obvious to the cognoscenti. For example, the scum on the river Ankh, that great wide slow waterway that served the double city as reservoir, sewer and frequent morgue, had turned a particularly iridescent green. The city's drunken rooftops sprouted

---

* Like rhinestones, but different river. When it comes to glittering objects, wizards have all the taste and self-control of a deranged magpie.

mattresses and bolsters as the winter bedding was put out to air in the weak sunshine, and in the depths of musty cellars the beams twisted and groaned when their dry sap responded to the ancient call of root and forest. Birds nested among the gutters and eaves of Unseen University, although it was noticeable that however great the pressure on the nesting sites they never, ever, made nests in the invitingly open mouths of the gargoyles that lined the rooftops, much to the gargoyles' disappointment.

A kind of spring had even come to the ancient University itself. Tonight would be the Eve of Small Gods, and a new Archchancellor would be elected.

Well, not exactly *elected*, because wizards didn't have any truck with all this undignified voting business, and it was well known that Archchancellors were selected by the will of the gods, and this year it was a pretty good bet that the gods would see their way clear to selecting old Virrid Wayzygoose, who was a decent old boy and had been patiently waiting his turn for years.

The Archchancellor of Unseen University was the official leader of all the wizards on the Disc. Once upon a time it had meant that he would be the most powerful in the handling of magic, but times were a lot quieter now and, to be honest, senior wizards tended to look upon actual magic as a bit beneath them. They tended to prefer administration, which was safer and nearly as much fun, and also big dinners.

And so the long afternoon wore on. The hat squatted on its faded cushion in Wayzygoose's chambers, while he sat in his tub in front of the fire and soaped his beard. Other wizards dozed in their studies, or took a gentle stroll around the gardens in order to work up an appetite for the evening's feast; about a dozen steps was usually considered quite sufficient.

In the Great Hall, under the carved or painted stares of two hundred earlier Archchancellors, the butler's staff set out the long tables and benches. In the vaulted maze of the kitchens—well, the imagination should need no assistance. It should include lots of grease and heat and shouting, vats of caviar, whole roast oxen, strings of sausages like paperchains strung from wall to wall, the head chef himself at work in one of the cold rooms putting the finishing touches to a model of the University carved for some inexplicable reason out of butter. He kept doing this every time there was a feast—butter swans, butter buildings, whole rancid greasy yellow menageries—and he enjoyed it so much no one had the heart to tell him to stop.

In his own labyrinth of cellars the butler prowled among his casks, decanting and tasting.

The air of expectation had even spread to the ravens who inhabited the Tower of Art, eight hundred feet high and reputedly the oldest building in the world. Its crumbling stones supported thriving miniature forests high above the city's rooftops. Entire species of beetles and small mammals had evolved up there and, since people rarely climbed it these days owing to the tower's distressing tendency to sway in the breeze, the ravens had it all to themselves. Now they were flying around it in a state of some agitation, like gnats before a thunderstorm. If anyone below is going to take any notice of them it might be a good idea.

Something horrible was about to happen.

You can tell, can't you?

You're not the only one.

"What's got into them?" shouted Rincewind above the din.

The Librarian ducked as a leather-bound grimoire shot out from its shelf and jerked to a mid-air halt on the end of its chain. Then he dived, rolled and landed on a copy of *Maleficio's Discouverie of Demonologie* that was industriously bashing at its lectern.

"Oook!" he said.

Rincewind put his shoulder against a trembling bookshelf and forced its rustling volumes back into place with his knees. The noise was terrible.

Books of magic have a sort of life of their own. Some have altogether too much; for example, the first edition of the *Necrotelicomicon* has to be kept between iron plates, the *True Arte of Levitatione* has spent the last one hundred and fifty years up in the rafters, and *Ge Fordge's Compenydyum of Sex Majick* is kept in a vat of ice in a room all by itself and there's a strict rule that it can only be read by wizards who are over eighty and, if possible, dead.

But even the everyday grimoires and incunabula on the main shelves were as restless and nervy as the inmates of a chicken house with something rank scrabbling under the door. From their shut covers came a muffled scratching, like claws.

"What did you say?" screamed Rincewind.

"Oook!"*

"Right!"

Rincewind, as honorary assistant librarian, hadn't progressed much beyond basic indexing and banana-fetching, and he had to admire the way the Librarian ambled among the quivering shelves, here running a black-leather hand over a trembling binding, here comforting a frightened thesaurus with a few soothing simian murmurings.

After a while the Library began to settle down, and Rincewind felt his shoulder muscles relax.

It was a fragile peace, though. Here and there a page rustled. From distant shelves came the ominous creak of a spine. After its initial panic the Library was now as alert and jittery as a long-tailed cat in a rocking-chair factory.

The Librarian ambled back down the aisles. He had a face that only a lorry tire could love and it was permanently locked in a faint smile, but Rincewind could tell by the way the ape crept into his cubby-hole under the desk and hid his head under a blanket that he was deeply worried.

Examine Rincewind, as he peers around the sullen shelves. There are eight levels of wizardry on

---

* A magical accident in the Library, which as has already been indicated is not a place for your average rubber-stamp-and-Dewey-decimal employment, had some time ago turned the Librarian into an orangutan. He had since resisted all efforts to turn him back. He liked the handy long arms, the prehensile toes and the right to scratch himself in public, but most of all he liked the way all the big questions of existence had suddenly resolved themselves into a vague interest in where his next banana was coming from. It wasn't that he was unaware of the despair and nobility of the human condition. It was just that as far as he was concerned you could stuff it.

the Disc; after sixteen years Rincewind has failed to achieve even level one. In fact it is the considered opinion of some of his tutors that he is incapable even of achieving level zero, which most normal people are *born* at; to put it another way, it has been suggested that when Rincewind dies the average occult ability of the human race will actually go up by a fraction.

He is tall and thin and has the scrubby kind of beard that looks like the kind of beard worn by people who weren't cut out by nature to be beard wearers. He is dressed in a dark red robe that has seen better days, possibly better decades. But you can tell he's a wizard, because he's got a pointy hat with a floppy brim. It's got the word "Wizzard" embroidered on it in big silver letters, by someone whose needlework is even worse than their spelling. There's a star on top. It has lost most of its sequins.

Clamping his hat on his head, Rincewind pushed his way through the Library's ancient doors and stepped out into the golden light of the afternoon. It was calm and quiet, broken only by the hysterical croaking of the ravens as they circled the Tower of Art.

Rincewind watched them for a while. The University's ravens were a tough bunch of birds. It took a lot to unsettle them.

On the other hand—

—the sky was pale blue tinted with gold, with a few high wisps of fluffy cloud glowing pinkly in the lengthening light. The ancient chestnut trees in the quadrangle were in full bloom. From an open win-

dow came the sound of a student wizard practicing
the violin, rather badly. It was not what you would
call ominous.

Rincewind leaned against the warm stonework.
And screamed.

The building was shuddering. He could feel it
come up through his hand and along his arms, a
faint rhythmic sensation at just the right frequency
to suggest uncontrollable terror. The stones themselves were frightened.

He looked down in horror at a faint clinking noise.
An ornamental drain cover fell backwards and one
of the University's rats poked its whiskers out. It
gave Rincewind a desperate look as it scrambled up
and fled past him, followed by dozens of its tribe.
Some of them were wearing clothes but that wasn't
unusual for the University, where the high level of
background magic does strange things to genes.

As he stared around him Rincewind could see
other streams of gray bodies leaving the University
by every drainpipe and flowing toward the outside
wall. The ivy by his ear rustled and a group of rats
made a series of death-defying leaps onto his shoulders and slid down his robe. They otherwise ignored him totally but, again, this wasn't particularly
unusual. Most creatures ignored Rincewind.

He turned and fled into the University, skirts
flapping around his knees, until he reached the bursar's study. He hammered on the door, which
creaked open.

"Ah. It's, um, Rincewind, isn't it?" said the bursar,
without much enthusiasm. "What's the matter?"

"We're sinking!"

The bursar stared at him for a few moments. His name was Spelter. He was tall and wiry and looked as though he had been a horse in previous lives and had only just avoided it in this one. He always gave people the impression that he was looking at them with his teeth.

"Sinking?"

"Yes. All the rats are leaving!"

The bursar gave him another stare.

"Come inside, Rincewind," he said, kindly. Rincewind followed him into the low, dark room and across to the window. It looked out over the gardens to the river, oozing peacefully toward the sea.

"You haven't been, um, overdoing it?" said the bursar.

"Overdoing what?" said Rincewind, guiltily.

"This is a building, you see," said the bursar. Like most wizards when faced with a puzzle, he started to roll himself a cigarette. "It's not a ship. There are ways of telling, you know. Absence of porpoises frolicking around the bows, a shortage of bilges, that sort of thing. The chances of foundering are remote. Otherwise, um, we'd have to man the sheds and row for shore. Um?"

"But the rats—"

"Grain ship in harbor, I expect. Some, um, springtime ritual."

"I'm sure I felt the building shaking, too," said Rincewind, a shade uncertainly. Here in this quiet room, with the fire crackling in the grate, it didn't seem quite so real.

"A passing tremor. Great A'Tuin hiccuping, um,

possibly. A grip on yourself, um, is what you should get. You haven't been drinking, have you?"

"No!"

"Um. Would you like to?"

Spelter padded over to a dark oak cabinet and pulled out a couple of glasses, which he filled from the water jug.

"I tend to be best at sherry this time of day," he said, and spread his hands over the glasses. "Say, um, the word—sweet or dry?"

"Um, no," said Rincewind. "Perhaps you're right. I think I'll go and have a bit of rest."

"Good idea."

Rincewind wandered down the chilly stone passages. Occasionally he'd touch the wall and appear to be listening, and then he'd shake his head.

As he crossed the quadrangle again he saw a herd of mice swarm over a balcony and scamper toward the river. The ground they were running over seemed to be moving, too. When Rincewind looked closer he could see that it was because it was covered with ants.

These weren't ordinary ants. Centuries of magical leakage into the walls of the University had done strange things to them. Some of them were pulling very small carts, some of them were riding beetles, but all of them were leaving the University as quickly as possible. The grass on the lawn rippled as they passed.

He looked up as an elderly striped mattress was extruded from an upper window and flopped down onto the flagstones below. After a pause, apparently to catch its breath, it rose a little from the ground. Then it started to float purposefully across the lawn and bore down on Rincewind, who managed to jump out of its way just in time. He heard a high-pitched chittering and caught a glimpse of thousands of determined little legs under the bulging fabric before it hurtled onward. Even the bedbugs were on the move, and in case they didn't find such comfortable quarters elsewhere they were leaving nothing to chance. One of them waved at him and squeaked a greeting.

Rincewind backed away until something touched the back of his legs and froze his spine. It turned out to be a stone seat. He watched it for some time. It didn't seem in any hurry to run away. He sat down gratefully.

There's probably a natural explanation, he thought. Or a perfectly normal unnatural one, anyway.

A gritty noise made him look across the lawn.

There was no natural explanation of *this*. With incredible slowness, easing themselves down parapets and drainpipes in total silence except for the occasional scrape of stone on stone, the gargoyles were leaving the roof.

It's a shame that Rincewind had never seen poor quality stop-motion photography, because then he would have known exactly how to describe what he was seeing. The creatures didn't exactly move, but they managed to progress in a series of high speed tableaux, and lurched past him in a spindly procession of beaks, manes, wings, claws and pigeon droppings.

"What's happening?" he squeaked.

A thing with a goblin's face, harpy's body and hen's legs turned its head in a series of little jerks and spoke in a voice like the peristalsis of mountains (although the deep resonant effect was rather spoiled because, of course, it couldn't close its mouth).

It said: "A Ourcerer is umming! Eee orr ife!"

Rincewind said "Pardon?" But the thing had gone past and was lurching awkwardly across the ancient lawn.*

So Rincewind sat and stared blankly at nothing much for fully ten seconds before giving a little scream and running as fast as he could.

He didn't stop until he'd reached his own room in the Library building. It wasn't much of a room, being mainly used to store old furniture, but it was home.

Against one shadowy wall was a wardrobe. It wasn't one of your modern wardrobes, fit only for nervous adulterers to jump into when the husband returned home early, but an ancient oak affair, dark as night, in whose dusty depths coathangers lurked and bred; herds of flaking shoes roamed its floor. It was quite possible that it was a secret doorway to fabulous worlds, but no one had ever tried to find out because of the distressing smell of mothballs.

And on top of the wardrobe, wrapped in scraps of yellowing paper and old dust sheets, was a large

---

* The furrow left by the fleeing gargoyles caused the University's head gardener to bite through his rake and led to the famous quotation: "How do you get a lawn like this? You mows it and you rolls it for five hundred years and then a bunch of bastards walks across it."

brass-bound chest. It went by the name of the Luggage. Why it consented to be owned by Rincewind was something only the Luggage knew, and it wasn't telling, but probably no other item in the entire chronicle of travel accessories had quite such a history of mystery and grievous bodily harm. It had been described as half suitcase, half homicidal maniac. It had many unusual qualities which may or may not become apparent soon, but currently there was only one that set it apart from any other brass-bound chest. It was snoring, with a sound like someone very slowly sawing a log.

The Luggage might be magical. It might be terrible. But in its enigmatic soul it was kin to every other piece of luggage throughout the multiverse, and preferred to spend its winters hibernating on top of a wardrobe.

Rincewind hit it with a broom until the sawing stopped, filled his pockets with odds and ends from the banana crate he used as a dressing table, and made for the door. He couldn't help noticing that his mattress had gone but that didn't matter because he was pretty clear that he was never going to sleep on a mattress again, ever.

The Luggage landed on the floor with a solid thump. After a few seconds, and with extreme care, it rose up on hundreds of little pink legs. It tilted backwards and forward a bit, stretching every leg, and then it opened its lid and yawned.

"Are you coming or not?"

The lid shut with a snap. The Luggage maneuverd its feet into a complicated shuffle until it was facing the doorway, and headed after its master.

The Library was still in a state of tension, with the occasional clinking* of a chain or muffled crackle of a page. Rincewind reached under the desk and grabbed the Librarian who was still hunched under his blanket.

"Come on, I said!"

"Oook."

"I'll buy you a drink," said Rincewind desperately.

The Librarian unfolded like a four-legged spider. "Oook?"

Rincewind half-dragged the ape from his nest and out through the door. He didn't head for the main gates but for an otherwise undistinguished area of wall where a few loose stones had, for two thousand years, offered students an unobtrusive way in after lights-out. Then he stopped so suddenly that the Librarian cannoned into him and the Luggage ran into both of them.

"Oook!"

"Oh, gods," he said. "Look at that!"

"Oook?"

There was a shiny black tide flowing out of a grating near the kitchens. Early evening starlight glinted off millions of little black backs.

But it wasn't the sight of the cockroaches that was so upsetting. It was the fact that they were marching in step, a hundred abreast. Of course, like all the informal inhabitants of the University the roaches were a little unusual, but there was something

---

* In most old libraries the books are chained to the shelves to prevent them being damaged by people. In the Library of Unseen University, of course, it's more or less the other way about.

particularly unpleasant about the sound of billions of very small feet hitting the stones in perfect time.

Rincewind stepped gingerly over the marching column. The Librarian jumped it.

The Luggage, of course, followed them with a noise like someone tapdancing over a bag of potato chips.

And so, forcing the Luggage to go all the way around to the gates anyway, because otherwise it'd only batter a hole in the wall, Rincewind quit the University with all the other insects and small frightened rodents and decided that if a few quiet beers wouldn't allow him to see things in a different light, then a few more probably would. It was certainly worth a try.

That was why he wasn't present in the Great Hall for dinner. It would turn out to be the most important missed meal of his life.

Further along the University wall there was a faint clink as a grapnel caught the spikes that lined its top. A moment later a slim, black-clad figure dropped lightly into the University grounds and ran soundlessly toward the Great Hall, where it was soon lost in the shadows.

No-one would have noticed it anyway. On the other side of the campus the Sourcerer was walking toward the gates of the University. Where his feet touched the cobbles blue sparks crackled and evaporated the early evening dew.

It was *very* hot. The big fireplace at the turnwise end of the Great Hall was practically incandescent.

Wizards feel the cold easily, so the sheer blast of heat from the roaring logs was melting candles twenty feet away and bubbling the varnish on the long tables. The air over the feast was blue with tobacco smoke, which writhed into curious shapes as it was bent by random drifts of magic. On the center table the complete carcass of a whole roast pig looked extremely annoyed at the fact that someone had killed it without waiting for it to finish its apple, and the model University made of butter was sinking gently into a pool of grease.

There was a lot of beer about. Here and there red-faced wizards were happily singing ancient drinking songs which involved a lot of knee-slapping and cries of "Ho!" The only possible excuse for this sort of thing is that wizards are celibate, and have to find their amusement where they can.

Another reason for the general conviviality was the fact that no one was trying to kill anyone else. This is an unusual state of affairs in magical circles.

The higher levels of wizardry are a perilous place. Every wizard is trying to dislodge the wizards above him while stamping on the fingers of those below; to say that wizards are healthily competitive by nature is like saying that piranhas are naturally a little peckish. However, ever since the great Mage Wars left whole areas of the Disc uninhabitable*, wizards have been forbidden to settle their differences by magical means, because it caused a lot of trouble for the population at large and in any case it was often

---

* At least, by anyone who wanted to wake up the same shape, or even the same species, as they went to bed.

difficult to tell which of the resultant patches of smoking fat had been the winner. So they traditionally resort to knives, subtle poisons, scorpions in shoes and hilarious booby traps involving razorsharp pendulums.

On Small Gods' Eve, however, it was considered extremely bad form to kill a brother wizard, and wizards felt able to let their hair down without fear of being strangled with it.

The Archchancellor's chair was empty. Wayzygoose was dining alone in his study, as befits a man chosen by the gods after their serious discussion with sensible senior wizards earlier in the day. Despite his eighty years, he was feeling a little bit nervous and hardly touched his second chicken.

In a few minutes he would have to make a speech. Wayzygoose had, in his younger days, sought power in strange places; he'd wrestled with demons in blazing octagrams, stared into dimensions that men were not meant to know of, and even outfaced the Unseen University grants committee, but nothing in the eight circles of nothingness was quite so bad as a couple of hundred expectant faces staring up at him through the cigar smoke.

The heralds would soon be coming by to collect him. He sighed and pushed his pudding away untasted, crossed the room, stood in front of the big mirror, and fumbled in the pocket of the robe for his notes.

After a while he managed to get them in some sort of order and cleared his throat.

"My brothers in art," he began, "I cannot tell you how much I—er, how much . . . fine traditions of this ancient university . . . er . . . as I look around me and see the pictures of Archchancellors gone before . . ." He paused, sorted through his notes again, and plunged on rather more certainly. "Standing here tonight I am reminded of the story about the three-legged pedlar and the, er, merchant's daughters. It seems that this merchant . . ."

There was a knock at the door.

"Enter," Wayzygoose barked, and peered at the notes carefully.

"This merchant," he muttered, "this merchant, yes, this merchant had three daughters. I think it was. Yes. It was three. It would appear . . ."

He looked into the mirror, and turned round.

He started to say, "Who are y—"

And found that there are things worse than making speeches, after all.

The small dark figure creeping along the deserted corridors heard the noise, and didn't take too much notice. Unpleasant noises were not uncommon in areas where magic was commonly practiced. The figure was looking for something. It wasn't sure what it was, only that it would know it when it found it.

After some minutes its search led it to Wayzygoose's room. The air was full of greasy coils. Little particles of soot drifted gently on the air currents, and there were several foot-shaped burn marks on the floor.

The figure shrugged. There was no accounting for the sort of things you found in wizard's rooms. It caught sight of its multi-faceted reflection in the shattered mirror, adjusted the set of its hood, and got on with the search.

Moving like one listening to inner directions, it padded noiselessly across the room until it reached the table whereon stood a tall, round and battered leather box. It crept closer and gently raised the lid.

The voice from inside sounded as though it was talking through several layers of carpet when it said, *At last. What kept you?*

"I mean, how did they all get started? I mean, back in the old times, there were real wizards, there was none of this levels business. They just went out and—did it. Pow!"

One or two of the other customers in the darkened bar of the Mended Drum tavern looked around hastily at the noise. They were new in town. Regular customers never took any notice of surprising noises like groans or unpleasantly gristly sounds. It was a lot healthier. In some parts of the city curiosity didn't just kill the cat, it threw it in the river with lead weights tied to its feet.

Rincewind's hands weaved unsteadily over the array of empty glasses on the table in front of him. He'd almost been able to forget about the cockroaches. After another drink he might manage to forget about the mattress, too.

"Whee! A fireball! Fizz! Vanishing like smoke! Whee!—Sorry."

The Librarian carefully pulled what remained of his beer out of the reach of Rincewind's flailing arms.

"Proper magic." Rincewind stifled a belch.

"Oook."

Rincewind stared into the frothy remnants of his last beer, and then, with extreme care in case the top of his head fell off, leaned down and poured some into a saucer for the Luggage. It was lurking under the table, which was a relief. It usually embarrassed him in bars by sidling up to drinkers and terrorizing them into feeding it potato chips.

He wondered fuzzily where his train of thought had been derailed.

"Where was I?"

"Oook," the Librarian hinted.

"Yeah." Rincewind brightened. "*They* didn't have all this levels and grades business, you know. They had sourcerers in those days. They went out in the world and found new spells and had adventures—"

He dipped a finger in a puddle of beer and doodled a design on the stained, scratched timber of the table.

One of Rincewind's tutors had said of him that "to call his understanding of magical theory *abysmal* is to leave no suitable word to describe his grasp of its practice." This had always puzzled him. He objected to the fact that you had to be good at magic to be a wizard. He *knew* he was a wizard, deep in his head. Being good at magic didn't have anything to do with it. That was just an extra, it didn't actually *define* somebody.

"When I was a little boy," he said wistfully, "I saw this picture of a sourcerer in a book. He was standing on a mountain top waving his arms and the waves were coming right up, you know, like they do down in Ankh Bay in a gale, and there were flashes of lightning all around him—"

"Oook?"

"I don't know why they didn't, perhaps he had rubber boots on," Rincewind snapped, and went on dreamily, "And he had this staff and a hat on, just like mine, and his eyes were sort of glowing and there was all this sort of like *glitter* coming out of his fingertips, and I thought one day I'll do that, and—"

"Oook?"

"Just a half, then."

"Oook."

"How do you pay for this stuff? Every time anyone gives you any money you eat it."

"Oook."

"Amazing."

Rincewind completed his sketch in the beer. There was a stick figure on a cliff. It didn't look much like him—drawing in stale beer is not a precise art—but it was meant to.

"That's what I wanted to be," he said. "Pow! Not all this messing around. All this books and stuff, that isn't what it should all be about. What we need is real wizardry."

That last remark would have earned the prize for the day's most erroneous statement if Rincewind hadn't then said:

"It's a pity there aren't any of them around anymore."

*   *   *

Spelter rapped on the table with his spoon.

He was an impressive figure, in his ceremonial robe with the purple-and-vermine* hood of the Venerable Council of Seers and the yellow sash of a fifth level wizard; he'd been fifth level for three years, waiting for one of the sixty-four sixth level wizards to create a vacancy by dropping dead. He was in an amiable mood, however. Not only had he just finished a good dinner, he also had in his quarters a small vial of a guaranteed untastable poison which, used correctly, should guarantee him promotion within a few months. Life looked good.

The big clock at the end of the hall trembled on the verge of nine o'clock.

The tattoo with the spoon hadn't had much effect. Spelter picked up a pewter tankard and brought it down hard.

"Brothers!" he shouted, and nodded as the hubbub died away. "Thank you. Be upstanding, please, for the ceremony of the, um, keys."

There was a ripple of laughter and a general buzz of expectancy as the wizards pushed back their benches and got unsteadily to their feet.

The double doors to the hall were locked and triple barred. An incoming Archchancellor had to request entry three times before they would be unlocked, signifying that he was appointed with the

---

* The vermine is a small black-and-white relative of the lemming, found in the cold Hublandish regions. Its skin is rare and highly valued, especially by the vermine itself; the selfish little bastard will do anything rather than let go of it.

consent of wizardry in general. Or some such thing. The origins were lost in the depths of time, which was as good a reason as any for retaining the custom.

The conversation died away. The assembled wizardry stared at the doors.

There was a soft knocking.

"Go away!" shouted the wizards, some of them collapsing at the sheer subtlety of the humor.

Spelter picked up the great iron ring that contained the keys to the University. They weren't all metal. They weren't all visible. Some of them looked very strange indeed.

"Who is that who knocketh without?" he intoned.

"*I do.*"

What was strange about the voice was this: it seemed to every wizard that the speaker was standing right behind him. Most of them found themselves looking over their shoulders.

In that moment of shocked silence there was the sharp little snick of the lock. They watched in fascinated horror as the iron bolts traveled back of their own accord; the great oak beams of timber, turned by Time into something tougher than rock, slid out of their sockets; the hinges flared from red through yellow to white and then exploded. Slowly, with a terrible inevitability, the doors fell into the hall.

There was an indistinct figure standing in the smoke from the burning hinges.

"Bloody hell, Virrid," said one of the wizards nearby, "that was a good one."

As the figure strode into the light they could all see that it was not, after all, Virrid Wayzygoose.

He was at least a head shorter than any other wizard, and wore a simple white robe. He was also several decades younger; he looked about ten years old, and in one hand he held a staff considerably taller than he was.

"Here, he's no wizard—"

"Where's his hood, then?"

"Where's his *hat*?"

The stranger walked up the line of astonished wizards until he was standing in front of the top table. Spelter looked down at a thin young face framed by a mass of blond hair, and most of all he looked into two golden eyes that glowed from within. But he felt they weren't looking at him. They seemed to be looking at a point six inches beyond the back of his head. Spelter got the impression that he was in the way, and considerably surplus to immediate requirements.

He rallied his dignity and pulled himself up to his full height.

"What is the meaning of, um, this?" he said. It was pretty weak, he had to admit, but the steadiness of that incandescent glare appeared to be stripping all the words out of his memory.

"I have come," said the stranger.

"Come? Come for what?"

"To take my place. Where is the seat for me?"

"Are you a student?" demanded Spelter, white with anger. "What is your name, young man?"

The boy ignored him and looked around at the assembled wizards.

"Who is the most powerful wizard here?" he said. "I wish to meet him."

Spelter nodded his head. Two of the college porters, who had been sidling toward the newcomer for the last few minutes, appeared at either elbow.

"Take him out and throw him in the street," said Spelter. The porters, big solid serious men, nodded. They gripped the boy's pipestem arms with hands like banana bunches.

"Your father will hear of this," said Spelter severely.

"He already has," said the boy. He glanced up at the two men and shrugged.

"What's going on here?"

Spelter turned to see Skarmer Billias, head of the Order of the Silver Star. Whereas Spelter tended toward the wiry, Billias was expansive, looking rather like a small captive balloon that had for some reason been draped in blue velvet and vermine; between them, the wizards averaged out as two normalsized men.

Unfortunately, Billias was the type of person who prided himself on being good with children. He bent down as far as his dinner would allow and thrust a whiskery red face toward the boy.

"What's the matter, lad?" he said.

"This *child* had forced his way into here because, he says, he wants to meet a powerful wizard," said Spelter, disapprovingly. Spelter disliked children intensely, which was perhaps why they found him so fascinating. At the moment he was successfully preventing himself from wondering about the door.

"Nothing wrong with that," said Billias. "Any lad worth his salt wants to be a wizard. I wanted to be a wizard when I was a lad. Isn't that right lad?"

"Are you puissant?" said the boy.

"Hmm?"

"I said, are you puissant? How powerful are you?"

"Powerful?" said Billias. He stood up, fingered his eighth-level sash, and winked at Spelter. "Oh, pretty powerful. Quite powerful as wizards go."

"Good. I challenge you. Show me your strongest magic. And when I have beaten you, why, then I shall be Archchancellor."

"Why, you impudent—" began Spelter, but his protest was lost in the roar of laughter from the rest of the wizards. Billias slapped his knees, or as near to them as he could reach.

"A duel, eh?" he said. "Pretty good, eh?"

"Duelling is forbidden, as well you know," said Spelter. "Anyway, it's totally ridiculous! I don't know who did the doors for him, but I will not stand here and see you waste all our time—"

"Now, now," said Billias. "What's your name, lad?"

"Coin."

"Coin *sir*," snapped Spelter.

"Well, now, Coin," said Billias. "You want to see the best I can do, eh?"

"Yes."

"Yes *sir*," snapped Spelter. Coin gave him an unblinking stare, a stare as old as time, the kind of stare that basks on rocks on volcanic islands and never gets tired. Spelter felt his mouth go dry.

Billias held out his hands for silence. Then, with a theatrical flourish, he rolled up the sleeve of his left arm and extended his hand.

The assembled wizards watched with interest. Eighth-levels were above magic, as a rule, spending most of their time in contemplation—normally of the next menu—and, of course, avoiding the attentions of ambitious wizards of the seventh-level. This should be worth seeing.

Billias grinned at the boy, who returned it with a stare that focused on a point a few inches beyond the back of the old wizard's head.

Somewhat disconcerted, Billias flexed his fingers. Suddenly this wasn't quite the game he had intended, and he felt an overpowering urge to impress. It was swiftly overtaken by a surge of annoyance at his own stupidity in being unnerved.

"I shall show you," he said, and took a deep breath, "Maligree's Wonderful Garden."

There was a susurration from the diners. Only four wizards in the entire history of the University had ever succeeded in achieving the complete Garden. Most wizards could create the trees and flowers, and a few had managed the birds. It wasn't the most powerful spell, it couldn't move mountains, but achieving the fine detail built into Maligree's complex syllables took a finely tuned skill.

"You will observe," Billias added, "nothing up my sleeve."

His lips began to move. His hands flickered through the air. A pool of golden sparks sizzled in the palm of his hand, curved up, formed a faint sphere, began to fill in the detail . . .

Legend had it that Maligree, one of the last of the true sourcerers, created the Garden as a small, timeless, private self-locking universe where he could have a quiet smoke and a bit of a think while avoiding the cares of the world. Which was itself a puzzle, because no wizard could possibly understand how any being as powerful as a sourcerer could have a care in the world. Whatever the reason, Maligree retreated further and further into a world of his own and then, one day, closed the entrance after him.

The garden was a glittering ball in Billias's hands. The nearest wizards craned admiringly over his shoulders, and looked down into a two-foot sphere that showed a delicate, flower-strewn landscape; there was a lake in the middle distance, complete in every ripple, and purple mountains behind an interesting-looking forest. Tiny birds the size of bees flew from tree to tree, and a couple of deer no larger than mice glanced up from their grazing and stared out at Coin.

Who said critically: "It's quite good. Give it to me."

He took the intangible globe out of the wizard's hands and held it up.

"Why isn't it bigger?" he said.

Billias mopped his brow with a lace-edged handkerchief.

"Well," he said weakly, so stunned by Coin's tone that he was quite unable to be affronted, "since the old days, the efficacity of the spell has rather—"

Coin stood with his head on one side for a moment, as though listening to something. Then he whispered a few syllables and stroked the surface of the sphere.

It expanded. One moment it was a toy in the boy's hands, and the next . . .

. . . the wizards were standing on cool grass, in a shady meadow rolling down to the lake. There was a gentle breeze blowing from the mountains; it was scented with thyme and hay. The sky was deep blue shading to purple at the zenith.

The deer watched the newcomers suspiciously from their grazing ground under the trees.

Spelter looked down in shock. A peacock was pecking at his bootlaces.

"—" he began, and stopped. Coin was still holding a sphere, a sphere of air. Inside it, distorted as though seen through a fish-eye lens or the bottom of a bottle, was the Great Hall of Unseen University.

The boy looked around at the trees, squinted thoughtfully at the distant, snow-capped mountains, and nodded at the astonished men.

"It's not bad," he said. "I should like to come here again." He moved his hands in a complicated motion that seemed, in some unexplained way, to turn them *inside out*.

Now the wizards were back in the hall, and the boy was holding the shrinking Garden in his palm. In the heavy, shocked silence he put it back into Billias's hands, and said: "That was quite interesting. Now I will do some magic."

He raised his hands, stared at Billias, and vanished him.

Pandemonium broke out, as it tends to on these occasions. In the center of it stood Coin, totally composed, in a spreading cloud of greasy smoke.

Ignoring the tumult, Spelter bent down slowly and, with extreme care, picked a peacock feather off the floor. He rubbed it thoughtfully back and forth across his lips as he looked from the doorway to the boy to the vacant Archchancellor's chair, and his thin mouth narrowed, and he began to smile.

An hour later, as thunder began to roll in the clear skies above the city, and Rincewind was beginning to sing gently and forget all about cockroaches, and a lone mattress was wandering the streets, Spelter shut the door of the Archchancellor's study and turned to face his fellow mages.

There were six of them, and they were very worried.

They were so worried, Spelter noted, that they were listening to him, a mere fifth level wizard.

"He's gone to bed," he said, "with a hot milk drink."

"Milk?" said one of the wizards, with tired horror in his voice.

"He's too young for alcohol," explained the bursar.

"Oh, yes. Silly of me."

The hollow-eyed wizard opposite said: "Did you see what he did to the door?"

"I know what he did to Billias!"

"*What* did he do?"

"I don't want to know!"

"Brothers, brothers," said Spelter soothingly. He looked down at their worried faces and thought: too many dinners. Too many afternoons waiting for the servants to bring in the tea. Too much time spent in stuffy rooms reading old books written by dead men. Too much gold brocade and ridiculous ceremony. Too much fat. The whole University is ripe for one good push . . .

Or one good pull . . .

"I wonder if we really have, um, a problem here," he said.

Gravie Derment of the Sages of the Unknown Shadow hit the table with his fist.

"Good grief, man!" he snapped. "Some child wanders in out of the night, beats two of the University's finest, sits down in the Archchancellor's chair and you wonder if we have a problem? The boy's a natural! From what we've seen tonight, there isn't a wizard on the Disc who could stand against him!"

"Why should we stand against him?" said Spelter, in a reasonable tone of voice.

"Because he's more powerful than we are!"

"Yes?" Spelter's voice would have made a sheet of glass look like a plowed field, it made honey look like gravel.

"It stands to reason—"

Gravie hesitated. Spelter gave him an encouraging smile.

"Ahem."

The ahemmer was Marmaric Carding, head of the Hoodwinkers. He steepled his beringed fingers and peered sharply at Spelter over the top of them. The bursar disliked him intensely. He had considerable doubt about the man's intelligence. He suspected it might be quite high, and that behind those vein-crazed jowls was a mind full of brightly polished little wheels, spinning like mad.

"He does not seem overly inclined to use that power," said Carding.

"What about Billias and Virrid?"

"Childish pique," said Carding.

The other wizards stared from him to the bursar. They were aware of something going on, and couldn't quite put their finger on it.

The reason that wizards didn't rule the Disc was quite simple. Hand any two wizards a piece of rope and they would instinctively pull in opposite directions. Something about their genetics or their training left them with an attitude toward mutual co-operation that made an old bull elephant with terminal toothache look like a worker ant.

Spelter spread his hands. "Brothers," he said again, "do you not see what has happened? Here is a gifted youth, perhaps raised in isolation out in the untutored, um, countryside, who, feeling the ancient call of the magic in his bones, has journeyed far across tortuous terrain, through who knows what perils, and at last has reached his journey's end, alone and afraid, seeking only the steadying influence of us, his tutors, to shape and *guide* his talents? Who are we to turn him away, into the, um, wintry blast, shunning his—"

The oration was interrupted by Gravie blowing his nose.

"It's not winter," said one of the other wizards flatly, "and it's quite a warm night."

"Out into the *treacherously changeable spring weather*," snarled Spelter, "and cursed indeed would be the man who failed, um, at this time—"

"It's nearly summer."

Carding rubbed the side of his nose thoughtfully.

"The boy has a staff," he said. "Who gave it to him? Did you ask?"

"No," said Spelter, still glowering at the almanackical interjector.

Carding started to look at his fingernails in what Spelter considered to be a meaningful way.

"Well, whatever the problem, I feel sure it can wait until morning," he said in what Spelter felt was an ostentatiously bored voice.

"Ye gods, he blew Billias away!" said Gravie. "And they say there's nothing in Virrid's room but soot!"

"They were perhaps rather foolish," said Carding smoothly. "I am sure, my good brother, that you would not be defeated in affairs of the Art by a mere stripling?"

Gravie hesitated. "Well, er," he said, "no. Of course not." He looked at Carding's innocent smile and coughed loudly. "Certainly not, of course. Billias was very foolish. However, some prudent caution is surely—"

"Then let us all be cautious in the morning," said Carding cheerfully. "Brothers, let us adjourn this meeting. The boy sleeps, and in that at least he is showing us the way. This will look better in the light."

"I have seen things that didn't," said Gravie darkly, who didn't trust Youth. He held that no good ever came of it.

The senior wizards filed out and back to the Great Hall, where the dinner had got to the ninth course and was just getting into its stride. It takes more than a bit of magic and someone being blown to smoke in front of him to put a wizard off his food.

For some unexplained reason Spelter and Carding

were the last to leave. They sat at either end of the long table, watching each other like cats. Cats can sit at either end of a lane and watch each other for hours, performing the kind of mental maneuvering that would make a grand master appear impulsive by comparison, but cats have got nothing on wizards. Neither was prepared to make a move until he had run the entire forthcoming conversation through his mind to see if it left him a move ahead.

Spelter weakened first.

"All wizards are brothers," he said. "We should trust one another. I have information."

"I know," said Carding. "You know who the boy is."

Spelter's lips moved soundlessly as he tried to foresee the next bit of the exchange. "You can't be certain of that," he said, after a while.

"My dear Spelter, you blush when you inadvertently tell the truth."

"I didn't blush!"

"Precisely," said Carding, "my point."

"All right," Spelter conceded. "But you think you know something else."

The fat wizard shrugged. "A mere suspicion of a hunch," he said. "But why should I *ally*," he rolled the unfamiliar word around his tongue, "with you, a mere fifth level? I could more certainly obtain the information by rendering down your living brain. I mean no offense, you understand, I ask only for knowledge."

The events of the next few seconds happened far too fast to be understood by non-wizards, but went approximately like this:

Spelter had been drawing the signs of Megrim's Accelerator in the air under cover of the table. Now he muttered a syllable under his breath and fired the spell along the tabletop, where it left a smoking path in the varnish and met, about halfway, the silver snakes of Brother Hushmaster's Potent Asp-Spray as they spewed from Carding's fingertips.

The two spells cannoned into one another, turned into a ball of green fire and exploded, filling the room with fine yellow crystals.

The wizards exchanged the kind of long, slow glare you could roast chestnuts on.

Bluntly, Carding was surprised. He shouldn't have been. Eighth-level wizards are seldom faced with challenging tests of magical skill. In theory there are only seven other wizards of equal power and every lesser wizard is, by definition—well, lesser. This makes them complacent. But Spelter, on the other hand, was at the fifth level.

It may be quite tough at the top, and it is probably even tougher at the bottom, but halfway up it's so tough you could use it for horseshoes. By then all the no-hopers, the lazy, the silly and the downright unlucky have been weeded out, the field's cleared, and every wizard stands alone and surrounded by mortal enemies on every side. There's the pushy fours below, waiting to trip him up. There's the arrogant sixes above, anxious to stamp out all ambition. And, of course, all around are his fellow fives, ready for any opportunity to reduce the competition a little. And there's no standing still. Wizards of the fifth level are mean and tough and have reflexes of steel and their eyes are thin and narrow from staring down the length of that metaphorical last furlong at the end of which rests the prize of prizes, the Archchancellor's hat.

The novelty of cooperation began to appeal to Carding. There was worthwhile power here, which could be bribed into usefulness for as long as it was necessary. Of course, *afterwards* it might have to be—discouraged . . .

Spelter thought: patronage. He'd heard the term used, though never within the University, and he knew it meant getting those above you to give you a leg up. Of course, no wizard would normally dream of giving a colleague a leg up unless it was in order to catch them on the hop. The mere thought of actually encouraging a competitor . . . But on the other hand, this old fool might be of assistance for a while, and *afterwards*, well . . .

They looked at one another with mutual, grudging admiration and unlimited mistrust, but at least it was a mistrust each one felt he could rely on. Until afterwards.

"His name is Coin," said Spelter. "He says his father's name is Ipslore."

"I wonder how many brothers has he got?" said Carding.

"I'm sorry?"

"There hasn't been magic like that in this university in centuries," said Carding, "maybe for thousands of years. I've only ever read about it."

"We banished an Ipslore thirty years ago," said Spelter. "According to the records, he'd got married. I can see that if he had sons, um, they'd be wizards, but I don't understand how—"

"That wasn't wizardry. That was sourcery," said Carding, leaning back in his chair.

Spelter stared at him across the bubbling varnish. "Sourcery?"

"The eighth son of a wizard would be a sourcerer."

"I didn't know that!"

"It is not widely advertised."

"Yes, but—sourcerers were a long time ago, I mean, the magic was a lot stronger then, um, men were different . . . it didn't have anything to do with, well, *breeding*." Spelter was thinking, eight sons, that means he did it eight times. At least. Gosh.

"Sourcerers could do everything," he went on. "They were nearly as powerful as the gods. Um. There was no end of trouble. The gods simply wouldn't allow that sort of thing anymore, depend upon it."

"Well, there was trouble because the sourcerers fought among themselves," said Carding, "But one sourcerer wouldn't be any trouble. One sourcerer correctly advised, that is. By older and wiser minds."

"But he wants the Archchancellor's hat!"

"Why can't he have it?"

Spelter's mouth dropped open. This was too much, even for him.

Carding smiled at him amiably.

"But the hat—"

"It's just a symbol," said Carding. "It's nothing special. If he wants it, he can have it. It's a small enough thing. Just a symbol, nothing more. A figurehat."

"Figurehat?"

"Worn by a figurehead."

"But the gods choose the Archchancellor!"

Carding raised an eyebrow. "Do they?" he said, and coughed.

"Well, yes, I suppose they do. In a manner of speaking."

"In a manner of speaking?"

Carding got up and gathered his skirts around him. "I think," he said, "that you have a great deal to learn. By the way, where is that hat?"

"I don't know," said Spelter, who was still quite shaken. "Somewhere in, um, Virrid's apartments, I suppose."

"We'd better fetch it," said Carding.

He paused in the doorway and stroked his beard reflectively. "I remember Ipslore," he said. "We were students together. Wild fellow. Odd habits. Superb wizard, of course, before he went to the bad. Had a funny way of twitching his eyebrow, I remember, when he was excited." Carding looked blankly across forty years of memory, and shivered.

"The hat," he reminded himself. "Let's find it. It would be a shame if anything happened to it."

In fact the hat had no intention of letting anything happen to it, and was currently hurrying toward the Mended Drum under the arm of a rather puzzled, black-clad thief.

The thief, as will become apparent, was a special type of thief. This thief was an artist of theft. Other thieves merely stole everything that was not nailed down, but this thief stole the nails as well. This thief had scandalised Ankh by taking a particular interest in stealing, with astonishing success, things that were in fact not only nailed down but also guarded by keen-eyed guards in inaccessible strong rooms. There are artists that will paint an entire chapel ceiling; this was the kind of thief that could steal it.

This particular thief was credited with stealing the jewelled disembowelling knife from the Temple of Offler the Crocodile God during the middle of Evensong, and the silver shoes from the Patrician's finest racehorse while it was in the process of winning a race. When Gritoller Mimpsey, vice-president of the Thieves' Guild, was jostled in the marketplace and then found on returning home that a freshly-stolen handful of diamonds had vanished from their place of concealment, he knew who to blame.* This was the type of thief that could steal the initiative, the moment and the words right out of your mouth.

However, it was the first time it had stolen something that not only asked it to, in a low but authoritative voice, but gave precise and somehow unarguable instructions about how it was to be disposed of.

It was that cusp of the night that marks the turning point of Ankh-Morpork's busy day, when those who make their living under the sun are resting after their labors and those who turn an honest dollar by the cold light of the moon are just getting

---

* This was because Gritoller had swallowed the jewels for safe keeping.

up the energy to go to work. The day had, in fact, reached that gentle point when it was too late for housebreaking and too early for burglary.

Rincewind sat alone the crowded, smoky room, and didn't take much notice when a shadow passed over the table and a sinister figure sat down opposite him. There was nothing very remarkable about sinister figures in this place. The Drum jealousy guarded its reputation as the most stylishly disreputable tavern in Ankh-Morpork and the big troll that now guarded the door carefully vetted customers for suitability in the way of black cloaks, glowing eyes, magic swords and so forth. Rincewind never found out what he did to the failures. Perhaps he ate them.

When the figure spoke, its husky voice came from the depths of a black velvet hood, lined with fur.

"Psst," it said.

"Not very," said Rincewind, who was in a state of mind where he couldn't resist it, "but I'm working on it."

"I'm looking for a wizard," said the voice. It sounded hoarse with the effort of disguising itself but, again, this was nothing unusual in the Drum.

"Any wizard in particular?" Rincewind said guardedly. People could get into trouble this way.

"One with a keen sense of tradition who would not mind taking risks for high reward," said another voice. It appeared to be coming from a round black leather box under the stranger's arm.

"Ah," said Rincewind, "that narrows it down a bit, then. Does this involve a perilous journey into unknown and probably dangerous lands?"

"It does, as a matter of fact."

"Encounters with exotic creatures?" Rincewind smiled.

"Could be."

"Almost certain death?"

"Almost certainly."

Rincewind nodded, and picked up his hat.

"Well, I wish you every success in your search," he said, "I'd help you myself, only I'm not going to."

"What?"

"Sorry. I don't know why, but the prospect of certain death in unknown lands at the claws of exotic monsters isn't for me. I've tried it, and I couldn't get the hang of it. Each to their own, that's what I say, and I was cut out for boredom." He rammed his hat on his head and stood up a little unsteadily.

He'd reached the foot of the steps leading up into the street when a voice behind him said: "A *real* wizard would have accepted."

He could have kept going. He could have walked up the stairs, out into the street, got a pizza at the Klatchian takeaway in Sniggs Alley, and gone to bed. History would have been totally changed, and in fact would also have been considerably shorter, but he would have got a good night's sleep although, of course, it would have been on the floor.

The future held its breath, waiting for Rincewind to walk away.

He didn't do this for three reasons. One was alcohol. One was the tiny flame of pride that flickers in the heart of even the most careful coward. But the third was the voice.

It was beautiful. It sounded like wild silk looks.

The subject of wizards and sex is a complicated one, but as has already been indicated it does, in essence, boil down to this: when it comes to wine, women and song, wizards are allowed to get drunk and croon as much as they like.

The reason given to young wizards was that the practice of magic is hard and demanding and incompatible with sticky and furtive activities. It was a lot more sensible, they were told, to stop worrying about that sort of thing and really get to grips with Woddeley's *Occult Primer* instead. Funnily enough this didn't seem to satisfy, and young wizards suspected that the real reason was that the rules were made by old wizards. With poor memories. They were quite wrong, although the real reason had long been forgotten: if wizards were allowed to go around breeding all the time, there was a risk of sourcery.

Of course, Rincewind had been around a bit and had seen a thing or two, and had thrown off his early training to such an extent that he was quite capable of spending hours at a time in a woman's company without having to go off for a cold shower and a lie-down. But that voice would have made even a statue get down off its pedestal for a few brisk laps of the playing field and fifty press-ups. It was a voice that could make "Good morning" sound like an invitation to bed.

The stranger threw back her hood and shook out her long hair. It was almost pure white. Since her skin was tanned golden the general effect was calculated to hit the male libido like a lead pipe.

Rincewind hesitated, and lost a splendid opportunity to keep quiet. From the top of the stairs came a thick trollish voice:

"Ere, I *thed* you can't go freu dere—"

She sprang forward and shoved a round leather box into Rincewind's arms.

"Quick, you must come with me," she said. "You're in great danger!"

"Why?"

"Because I will kill you if you don't."

"Yes, but hang on a moment, in that case—" Rincewind protested feebly.

Three members of the Patrician's personal guard appeared at the top of the stairs. Their leader beamed down at the room. The smile suggested that he intended to be the only one to enjoy the joke.

"Don't nobody move," he suggested.

Rincewind heard a clatter behind him as more guards appeared at the back door.

The Drum's other customers paused with their hands on assorted hilts. These weren't the normal city watch, cautious and genially corrupt. These were walking slabs of muscle and they were absolutely unbribable, if only because the Patrician could outbid anyone else. Anyway, they didn't seem to be looking for anyone except the woman. The rest of the clientele relaxed and prepared to enjoy the show. Eventually it might be worth joining it, once it was certain which was the winning side.

Rincewind felt the pressure tighten on his wrist.

"Are you mad?" he hissed. "This is messing with the Man!"

There was a swish and the sergeant's shoulder suddenly sprouted a knife hilt. Then the girl spun around and with surgical precision planted a small foot in the groin of the first guard through the door. Twenty pairs of eyes watered in sympathy.

Rincewind grabbed his hat and tried to dive under the nearest table, but that grip was steel. The next guard to approach got another knife in the thigh. Then she drew a sword like a very long needle and raised it threateningly.

"Anyone else?" she said.

One of the guards raised a crossbow. The Librarian, sitting hunched over his drink, reached out a lazy arm like two broom handles strung with elastic and slapped him backwards. The bolt rebounded from the star on Rincewind's hat and hit the wall by a respected procurer who was sitting two tables away. His bodyguards threw another knife which just missed a thief across the room, who picked up a bench and hit two guards, who struck out at the nearest drinkers. After that one thing sort of led to another and pretty soon everyone was fighting to get something—either away, out or even.

Rincewind found himself pulled relentlessly behind the bar. The landlord was sitting on his moneybags under the counter with two machetes crossed on his knees, enjoying a quiet drink. Occasionally the sound of breaking furniture would make him wince.

The last thing Rincewind saw before he was dragged away was the Librarian. Despite looking like a hairy rubber sack full of water, the orangutan had the weight and reach of any man in the room and was currently sitting on a guard's shoulders and trying, with reasonable success, to unscrew his head.

Of more concern to Rincewind was the fact that he was being dragged upstairs.

"My dear lady," he said desperately. "What do you have in mind?"

"Is there a way onto the roof?"

"Yes. What's in this box?"

"Shhh!"

She halted at a bend in the dingy corridor, reached into a belt pouch and scattered a handful of small metal objects on the floor behind them. Each one was made of four nails welded together so that, however the things fell, one was always pointing upwards.

She looked critically at the nearest doorway.

"You haven't got about four feet of cheesewire on you, have you?" she said wistfully. She'd drawn another throwing knife and was throwing it up and catching it again.

"I don't think so," said Rincewind weakly.

"Pity. I've run out. Okay, come on."

"Why? I haven't done anything!"

She went to the nearest window, pushed open the shutters and paused with one leg over the sill.

"Fine," she said, over her shoulder. "Stay here and explain it to the guards."

"Why are they chasing you?"

"I don't know."

"Oh, come on! There must be a reason!"

"Oh, there's plenty of reasons. I just don't know which one. Are you coming?"

Rincewind hesitated. The Patrician's personal guard was not known for its responsive approach to community policing, preferring to cut bits off instead. Among the things they took a dim view of was, well, basically, people being in the same universe. Running away from them was likely to be a capital offense.

"I think maybe I'll come along with you," he said gallantly. "A girl can come to harm all alone in this city."

Freezing fog filled the streets of Ankh-Morpork. The flares of street traders made little yellow haloes in the smothering billows.

The girl peered around a corner.

"We've lost them," she said. "Stop shaking. You're safe now."

"What, you mean I'm all alone with a female homicidal maniac?" said Rincewind. "Fine."

She relaxed and laughed at him.

"I was watching you," she said. "An hour ago you were afraid that your future was going to be dull and uninteresting."

"I *want* it to be dull and uninteresting," said Rincewind bitterly. "I'm *afraid* it's going to be short."

"Turn your back," she commanded, stepping into an alley.

"Not on your life," he said.

"I'm going to take my clothes off."

Rincewind spun around, his face red. There was a rustling behind him, and a waft of scent. After a while she said, "You can look around now."

He didn't.

"You needn't worry. I've put some more on."

He opened his eyes. The girl was wearing a demure white lace dress with fetchingly puffed sleeves. He opened his mouth. He realized with absolute clarity that up to now the trouble he had been in was simple, modest and nothing he couldn't talk his way out of given a decent chance or, failing that, a running start. His brain started to send urgent messages to his sprinting muscles, but before they could get through she'd grabbed his arm again.

"You really shouldn't be so nervous," she said sweetly. "Now, let's have a look at this thing."

She pulled the lid off the round box in Rincewind's un-protesting hands, and lifted out the Archchancellor's hat.

The octarines around its crown blazed in all eight colors of the spectrum, creating the kind of effects in the foggy alley that it would take a very clever special effects director and a whole battery of star filters to achieve by any non-magical means. As she raised it high in the air it created its own nebula of colors that very few people ever see in legal circumstances.

Rincewind sank gently to his knees.

She looked down at him, puzzled.

"Legs given out?"

"It's—it's the hat. The *Archchancellor's* hat," said Rincewind, hoarsely. His eyes narrowed. "You've stolen it!" he shouted, struggling back to his feet and grabbing for the sparkling brim.

"It's just a hat."

"Give it to me this minute! Women mustn't touch it! It belongs to wizards!"

"Why are you getting so worked up?" she said.

Rincewind opened his mouth. Rincewind closed his mouth.

He wanted to say: It's the Archchancellor's hat, don't you understand? It's worn by the head of all wizards, well, on the head of the head of all wizards, no, metaphorically it's worn by all wizards, potentially, anyway, and it's what every wizard aspires to, it's the symbol of organized magic, it's the pointy tip of the profession, it's a symbol, it's what it means to all wizards . . .

And so on. Rincewind had been told about the hat on his first day at University, and it had sunk into his impressionable mind like a lead weight into a jelly. He wasn't sure of much in the world, but he was certain that the Archchancellor's hat was important. Maybe even wizards need a little magic in their lives.

Rincewind, said the hat.

He stared at the girl. "It spoke to me!"

"Like a voice in your head?"

"Yes!"

"It did that to me, too."

"But it knew my name!"

Of course we do, stupid fellow. We are supposed to be a magic *hat after all.*

The hat's voice wasn't only clothy. It also had a strange choral effect, as if an awful lot of voices were talking at the same time, in almost perfect unison.

Rincewind pulled himself together.

"O great and wonderful hat," he said pompously, "strike down this impudent girl who has had the audacity, nay, the—"

Oh, do shut up. She stole us because we ordered her to. It was a near thing, too.

"But she's a—" Rincewind hesitated. "She's of the female persuasion . . ." he muttered.

So was your mother.

"Yes, well, but she ran away before I was born," Rincewind mumbled.

Of all the disreputable taverns in all the city you could have walked into, you walked into his, complained the hat.

"He was the only wizard I could find," said the girl. "He looked the part. He had 'Wizard' written on his hat and everything."

Don't believe everything you read. Too late now, anyway. We haven't got much time.

"Hold on, hold on," said Rincewind urgently, "What's going on? You *wanted* her to steal you? *Why* haven't we got much time?" He pointed an accusing finger at the hat. "Anyway, you can't go around letting yourself be stolen, you're supposed to be on—on the Archchancellor's head! The ceremony was tonight, I should have been there—"

Something terrible is happening at the University. It is vital that we are not taken back, do you understand? You must take us to Klatch, where there is someone fit to wear me.

"Why?" There was something very strange about the voice, Rincewind decided. It sounded impossible to disobey, as though it was solid destiny. If it told him to walk over a cliff, he thought, he'd be halfway down before it could occur to him to disobey.

The death of all wizardry is at hand.

Rincewind looked around guiltily.

"Why?" he said.

The world is going to end.

"What, again?"

I mean it, said the hat sulkily. *The triumph of the Ice Giants, the Apocralypse, the Teatime of the Gods, the whole thing.*

"Can we stop it?"

The future is uncertain on that point.

Rincewind's expression of determined terror faded slowly.

"Is this a riddle?" he said.

Perhaps it would be simpler if you just did what you're told and didn't try to understand things, said the hat. *Young woman, you will put us back in our box. A great many people will shortly be looking for us.*

"Hey, hold on," said Rincewind. "I've seen you around here for years and you never talked before."

I didn't have anything that needed to be said.

Rincewind nodded. That seemed reasonable.

"Look, just shove it in its box, and let's get going," said the girl.

"A bit more respect if you please, young lady," said Rincewind haughtily. "That is the symbol of ancient wizardry you happen to be addressing."

"You carry it, then," she said.

"Hey, look," said Rincewind, scrambling along after her as she swept down the alleys, crossed a narrow street and entered another alley between a couple of houses that leaned together so drunkenly that their upper storys actually touched. She stopped.

"Well?" she snapped.

"You're the mystery thief, aren't you?" he said,

"Everyone's been talking about you, how you've taken things even from locked rooms and everything. You're different than I imagined . . ."

"Oh?" she said coldly. "How?"

"Well, you're . . . shorter."

"Oh, come *on*."

The street cressets, not particularly common in this part of the city in any case, gave out altogether here. There was nothing but watchful darkness ahead.

"I said come on," she repeated. "What are you afraid of?"

Rincewind took a deep breath. "Murderers, muggers, thieves, assassins, pickpockets, cutpurses, reevers, snigsmen, rapists and robbers," he said. "That's the *Shades* you're going into!"*

"Yes, but people won't come looking for us in here," she said.

"Oh, they'll come in all right, they just won't come out," said Rincewind. "Nor will we. I mean, a beautiful young woman like you . . . it doesn't bear thinking about . . . I mean, some of the people in there . . ."

"But I'll have you to protect me," she said.

Rincewind thought he heard the sound of marching feet several streets away.

---

* The Ankh-Morpork Merchants' Guild publication *Wellcome to Ankh-Morporke, Citie of One Thousand Surprises* describes the area of Old Morpork known as The Shades as "a folklorique network of old alleys and picturesque streets, wherre exitment and romans lurkes arounde everry corner and much may be heard the traditinal street cries of old time also the laughing visages of the denuizens as they goe about their business private." In other words, you have been warned.

"You know," he sighed, "I knew you'd say that."

Down these mean streets a man must walk, he thought. And along some of them he will break into a run.

It is so black in the Shades on this foggy spring night that it would be too dark to read about Rincewind's progress through the eerie streets, so the descriptive passage will lift up above the level of the ornate rooftops, the forest of twisty chimneys, and admire the few twinkling stars that manage to pierce the swirling billows. It will try to ignore the sounds drifting up from below—the patter of feet, the rushes, the gristly noises, the groans, the muffled screams. It could be that some wild animal is pacing through the Shades after two weeks on a starvation diet.

Somewhere near the center of the Shades—the district has never been adequately mapped—is a small courtyard. Here at least there are torches on the walls, but the light they throw is the light of the Shades themselves: mean, reddened, dark at the core.

Rincewind staggered into the yard and hung onto the wall for support. The girl stepped into the ruddy light behind him, humming to herself.

"Are you all right?" she said.

"Nurrgh," said Rincewind.

"Sorry?"

"Those men," he bubbled, "I mean, the way you kicked his . . . when you grabbed them by the . . . when you stabbed that one right in . . . who *are* you?"

"My name is Conina."

Rincewind looked at her blankly for some time.

"Sorry," he said, "doesn't ring a bell."

"I haven't been here long," she said.

"Yes, I didn't think you were from around these parts," he said. "I would have heard."

"I've taken lodgings here. Shall we go in?"

Rincewind glanced up at the dingy pole just visible in the smoky light of the spitting torches. It indicated that the hostelry behind the small dark door was the Troll's Head.

It might be thought that the Mended Drum, scene of unseemly scuffles only an hour ago, was a seedy disreputable tavern. In fact it was a *reputable* disreputable tavern. Its customers had a certain rough-hewn respectability—they might murder each other in an easygoing way, as between equals, but they didn't do it vindictively. A child could go in for a glass of lemonade and be certain of getting nothing worse than a clip around the ear when his mother heard his expanded vocabulary. On quiet nights, and when he was certain the Librarian wasn't going to come in, the landlord was even known to put bowls of peanuts on the bar.

The Troll's Head was a cesspit of a different odor. Its customers, if they reformed, tidied themselves up and generally improved their image out of all recognition might, just might, aspire to be considered the utter dregs of humanity. And in the Shades, a dreg is a dreg.

By the way, the thing on the pole isn't a sign. When they decided to call the place the Troll's Head, they didn't mess about.

Feeling sick, and clutching the grumbling hatbox to his chest, Rincewind stepped inside.

Silence. It wrapped itself around them, nearly as thickly as the smoke of a dozen substances guaranteed to turn any normal brain to cheese. Suspicious eyes peered through the smog.

A couple of dice clattered to a halt on a tabletop. They sounded very loud, and probably weren't showing Rincewind's lucky number.

He was aware of the stares of several score of customers as he followed the demure and surprisingly small figure of Conina into the room. He looked sideways into the leering faces of men who would kill him sooner than think, and in fact would find it a great deal easier.

Where a respectable tavern would have had a bar there was just a row of squat black bottles and a couple of big barrels on trestles against the wall.

The silence tightened like a tourniquet. Any minute now, Rincewind thought.

A big fat man wearing nothing but a fur vest and a leather loincloth pushed back his stool and lurched to his feet and winked evilly at his colleagues. When his mouth opened, it was like a hole with a hem.

"Looking for a man, little lady?" he said.

She looked up at him.

"Please keep away."

A snake of laughter writhed around the room. Conina's mouth snapped shut like a letterbox.

"Ah," the big man gurgled, "that's right, I likes a girl with spirit—"

Conina's hand moved. It was a pale blur, stopping *here* and *here*: after a few seconds of disbelief the man gave a little grunt and folded up, very slowly.

Rincewind shrank back as every other man in the room leaned forward. His instinct was to run, and he knew it was an instinct that would get him instantly killed. It was the Shades out there. Whatever was going to happen to him next was going to happen to him here. It was not a reassuring thought.

A hand closed around his mouth. Two more grabbed the hatbox from his arms.

Conina spun past him, lifting her skirt to place a neat foot on a target beside Rincewind's waist. Someone whimpered in his ear and collapsed. As the girl pirouetted gracefully around she picked up two bottles, knocked out their bottoms on the shelf and landed with their jagged ends held out in front of her. Morpork daggers, they were called in the patois of the streets.

In the face of them, the Troll's Head's clientele lost interest.

"Someone got the hat," Rincewind muttered through dry lips, "They slipped out of the back way."

She glared at him and made for the door. The Head's crowd of customers parted automatically, like sharks recognizing another shark, and Rincewind darted anxiously after her before they came to any conclusion about him.

They ran out into another alley and pounded down it. Rincewind tried to keep up with the girl; people following her tended to tread on sharp things, and he wasn't sure she'd remember he was on her side, whatever side that was.

A thin, half-hearted drizzle was falling. And at the end of the alley was a faint blue glow.

"Wait!"

The terror in Rincewind's voice was enough to slow her down.

"What's wrong?"

"Why's he stopped?"

"I'll ask him," said Conina, firmly.

"Why's he covered in snow?"

She stopped and turned around, arms thrust into her sides, one foot tapping impatiently on the damp cobbles.

"Rincewind, I've known you for an hour and I'm astonished you've lived even that long!"

"Yes, but I have, haven't I? I've got a sort of talent for it. Ask anyone. I'm an addict."

"Addicted to what?"

"Life. I got hooked on it at an early age and I don't want to give it up and take it from me, this doesn't look right!"

Conina looked back at the figure surrounded by the glowing blue aura. It seemed to be looking at something in its hands.

Snow was settling on its shoulder like really bad dandruff. *Terminal* dandruff. Rincewind had an instinct for these things, and he had a deep suspicion that the man had gone where shampoo would be no help at all.

They sidled along a glistening wall.

"There's something very strange about him," she conceded.

"You mean the way he's got his own private blizzard?"

"Doesn't seem to upset him. He's smiling."

"A frozen grin, I'd call it."

The man's icicle-hung hands had been taking the lid off the box, and the glow from the hat's octarines shone up into a pair of greedy eyes that were already heavily rimed with frost.

"Know him?" said Conina.

Rincewind shrugged. "I've seen him around," he said. "He's called Larry the Fox or Fezzy the Stoat or something. Some sort of rodent, anyway. He just steals things. He's harmless."

"He looks incredibly cold." Conina shivered.

"I expect he's gone to a warmer place. Don't you think we should shut the box?"

It's perfectly safe now, said the hat's voice from inside the glow. *And so perish all enemies of wizardry.*

Rincewind wasn't about to trust what a hat said.

"We need something to shut the lid," he muttered. "A knife or something. You wouldn't have one, would you?"

"Look the other way," Conina warned.

There was a rustle and another gust of perfume.

"You can look back now."

Rincewind was handed a twelve-inch throwing knife. He took it gingerly. Little particles of metal glinted on its edge.

"Thanks." He turned back. "Not leaving you short, am I?"

"I have others."

"I'll bet."

Rincewind reached out gingerly with the knife. As it neared the leather box its blade went white and started to steam. He whimpered a little as the cold struck his hand—a burning, stabbing cold, a cold that crept up his arm and made a determined assault on his mind. He forced his numb fingers into action and, with great effort, nudged the edge of the lid with the tip of the blade.

The glow faded. The snow became sleet, then melted into drizzle.

Conina nudged him aside and pulled the box out of the frozen arms.

"I wish there was something we could do for him. It seems wrong just to leave him here."

"He won't mind," said Rincewind, with conviction.

"Yes, but we could at least lean him against the wall. Or something."

Rincewind nodded, and grabbed the frozen thief by his icicle arm. The man slipped out of his grasp and hit the cobbles.

Where he shattered.

Conina looked at the pieces.

"Urg," she said.

There was a disturbance further up the alley, coming from the back door of the Troll's Head. Rincewind felt the knife snatched from his hand and then go past his ear in a flat trajectory that ended in the doorpost twenty yards away. A head that had been sticking out withdrew hurriedly.

"We'd better go," said Conina, hurrying along the alley. "Is there somewhere we can hide? Your place?"

"I generally sleep at the University," said Rincewind, hopping along behind her.

You must not return to the University, growled the hat from the depths of its box. Rincewind nodded distractedly. The idea certainly didn't seem attractive.

"Anyway, they don't allow women inside after dark," he said.

"And before dark?"

"Not then, either."

Conina sighed. "That's silly. What have you wizards got against women, then?"

Rincewind's brow wrinkled. "We're not supposed to put anything against women," he said. "That's the whole point."

Sinister gray mists rolled through the docks of Morpork, dripping from the rigging, coiling around the drunken rooftops, lurking in alleys. The docks at night were thought by some to be even more dangerous than the Shades. Two muggers, a sneak thief and someone who had merely tapped Conina on the shoulder to ask her the time had already found this out.

"Do you mind if I ask you a question?" said Rincewind, stepping over the luckless pedestrian who lay coiled around his private pain.

"Well?"

"I mean, I wouldn't like to cause offense."

"Well?"

"It's just that I can't help noticing—"

"Hmmm?"

"You have this certain way with strangers." Rincewind ducked, but nothing happened.

"What are you doing down there?" said Conina, testily.

"Sorry."

"I know what you're thinking. I can't help it, I take after my father."

"Who was he, then? Cohen the Barbarian?" Rincewind grinned to show it was a joke. At least, his lips moved in a desperate crescent.

"No need to laugh about it, wizard."

"What?"

"It's not my fault."

Rincewind's lips moved soundlessly. "Sorry," he said. "Have I got this right? Your father really is *Cohen the Barbarian*?"

"Yes." The girl scowled at Rincewind. "Everyone has to have a father," she added. "Even you, I imagine."

She peered around a corner.

"All clear. Come on," she said, and then when they were striding along the damp cobbles she continued: "I expect your father was a wizard, probably."

"I shouldn't think so," said Rincewind. "Wizardry isn't allowed to run in families." He paused. He knew Cohen, he'd even been a guest at one of his weddings when he married a girl of Conina's age; you could say this about Cohen, he crammed every hour full of minutes. "A lot of people would like to take after Cohen, I mean, he was the best fighter, the greatest thief, he—"

"A lot of *men* would," Conina snapped. She leaned against a wall and glared at him.

"Listen," she said, "There's this long word, see, an old witch told me about it . . . can't remember it . . . you wizards know about long words."

Rincewind thought about long words. "Marmalade?" he volunteered.

She shook her head irritably. "It means you take after your parents."

Rincewind frowned. He wasn't too good on the subject of parents.

"Kleptomania? Recidivist?" he hazarded.

"Begins with an H."

"Hedonism?" said Rincewind desperately.

"Herrydeterry," said Conina. "This witch explained it to me. My mother was a temple dancer for some mad god or other, and father rescued her, and—they stayed together for a while. They say I get my looks and figure from her."

"And very good they are, too," said Rincewind, with hopeless gallantry.

She blushed. "Yes, well, but from *him* I got sinews you could moor a boat with, reflexes like a snake on a hot tin, a terrible urge to steal things and this dreadful sensation every time I meet someone that I should be throwing a knife through his eye at ninety feet. I can, too," she added with a trace of pride.

"Gosh."

"It tends to put men off."

"Well, it would," said Rincewind weakly.

"I mean, when they find out, it's very hard to hang onto a boyfriend."

"Except by the throat, I imagine," said Rincewind.

"Not what you really need to build up a proper relationship."

"No. I can see," said Rincewind. "Still, pretty good if you want to be a famous barbarian thief."

"But not," said Conina, "if you want to be a hairdresser."

"Ah."

They stared into the mist.

"*Really* a hairdresser?" said Rincewind.

Conina sighed.

"Not much call for a barbarian hairdresser, I expect," said Rincewind. "I mean, no one wants a shampoo-and-beheading."

"It's just that every time I see a manicure set I get this terrible urge to lay about me with a double-handed cuticle knife. I mean sword," said Conina.

Rincewind sighed. "I know how it is," he said. "I wanted to be a wizard."

"But you *are* a wizard."

"Ah. Well, of course, but—"

"Quiet!"

Rincewind found himself rammed against the wall, where a trickle of condensed mist inexplicably began to drip down his neck. A broad throwing knife had mysteriously appeared in Conina's hand, and she was crouched like a jungle animal or, even worse, a jungle human.

"What—" Rincewind began.

"Shut up!" she hissed. "Something's coming!"

She stood up in one fluid movement, spun on one leg and let the knife go.

There was a single, hollow, wooden thud.

Conina stood and stared. For once, the heroic blood that pounded through her veins, drowning out all chances of a lifetime in a pink pinny, was totally at a loss.

"I've just killed a wooden box," she said.

Rincewind looked around the corner.

The Luggage stood in the dripping street, the

knife still quivering in its lid, and stared at her. Then it changed its position slightly, its little legs moving in a complicated tango pattern, and stared at Rincewind. The Luggage didn't have any features at all, apart from a lock and a couple of hinges, but it could stare better than a rockful of iguanas. It could outstare a glass-eyed statue. When it came to a look of betrayed pathos, the Luggage could leave the average kicked spaniel moping back in its kennel. It had several arrowheads and broken swords sticking in it.

"What is it?" hissed Conina.

"It's just the Luggage," said Rincewind wearily.

"Does it belong to you?"

"Not really. Sort of."

"Is it dangerous?"

The Luggage shuffled around to stare at her again.

"There's two schools of thought about that," said Rincewind. "There's some people who say it's dangerous, and others who say it's very dangerous. What do you think?"

The Luggage raised its lid a fraction.

The Luggage was made from the wood of the sapient peartree, a plant so magical that it had nearly died out on the Disc and survived only in one or two places; it was a sort of rosebay willowherb, only instead of bomb sites it sprouted in areas that had seen vast expenditures of magic. Wizards' staves were traditionally made of it; so was the Luggage.

Among the Luggage's magical qualities was a fairly simple and direct one: it would follow its adopted owner anywhere. Not anywhere in any particular set of dimensions, or country, or universe, or lifetime. *Anywhere.* It was about as easy to shake off as a head cold and considerably more unpleasant.

The Luggage was also extremely protective of its owner. It would be hard to describe its attitude to the rest of creation, but one could start with the phrase "bloody-minded malevolence" and work up from there.

Conina stared at that lid. It looked very much like a mouth.

"I think I'd vote for 'terminally dangerous,'" she said.

"It likes potato chips," volunteered Rincewind, and then added, "Well, that's a bit strong. It *eats* potato chips."

"What about people?"

"Oh, and people. About fifteen so far, I think."

"Were they good or bad?"

"Just dead, I think. It also does your laundry for you, you put your clothes in and they come out washed and ironed."

"And covered in blood?"

"You know, that's the funny thing," said Rince-wind.

"The funny thing?" repeated Conina, her eyes not leaving the Luggage.

"Yes, because, you see, the inside isn't always the same, it's sort of multidimensional, and—"

"How does it feel about women?"

"Oh, it's not choosy. It ate a book of spells last year. Sulked for three days and then spat it out."

"It's horrible," said Conina, and backed away.

"Oh, yes," said Rincewind, "absolutely."

"I mean the way it stares!"

"It's very good at it, isn't it?"

We must leave for Klatch, said a voice from the hatbox. *One of these boats will be adequate. Commandeer it.*

Rincewind looked at the dim, mist-wreathed shapes that loomed in the mist under a forest of rigging. Here and there a riding light made a little fuzzy ball of light in the gloom.

"Hard to disobey, isn't it?" said Conina.

"I'm trying," said Rincewind. Sweat prickled on his forehead.

Go aboard now, said the hat. Rincewind's feet began to shuffle of their own accord.

"Why are you doing this to me?" he moaned.

Because I have no alternative. Believe me, if I could have found an eighth level mage I would have done so. I must not be worn!

"Why not? You are the Archchancellor's hat."

And through me speak all the Archchancellors who ever lived. I am the University. I am the Lore. I am the symbol of magic under the control of men—and I will not be worn by a sorcerer! There must be no more sorcerers! The world is too worn out for sourcery!

Conina coughed.

"Did you understand any of that?" she said, cautiously.

"I understood some of it, but I didn't believe it," said Rincewind. His feet remained firmly rooted to the cobbles.

They called me a figurehat! The voice was heavy with sarcasm. *Fat wizards who betray everything the University ever stood for, and they called me a figurehat! Rincewind, I command you. And you, madam. Serve me well and I will grant you your deepest desire.*

"How can you grant my deepest desire if the world's going to end?"

The hat appeared to think about it. *Well, have you got a deepest desire that need only take a couple of minutes?*

"Look, how can you do magic? You're just a—" Rincewind's voice trailed off.

I AM magic. Proper magic. Besides, you don't get worn by some of the world's greatest wizards for two thousand years without learning a few things. Now. We must flee.

But with dignity of course.

Rincewind looked pathetically at Conina, who shrugged again.

"Don't ask me," she said. "This looks like an adventure. I'm doomed to have them, I'm afraid. That's genetics* for you."

"But I'm no good at them! Believe me, I've been through dozens!" Rincewind wailed.

Ah. Experience, said the hat.

"No, really, I'm a terrible coward, I always run away." Rincewind's chest heaved. "Danger has stared me in the back of the head, oh, hundreds of times!"

I don't want you to go into danger.

"Good!"

I want you to stay OUT of danger.

Rincewind sagged. "Why me?" he moaned.

---

* The study of genetics on the Disc had failed at an early stage, when wizards tried the experimental crossing of such well known subjects as fruit flies and sweet peas. Unfortunately they didn't quite grasp the fundamentals, and the resultant offspring—a sort of green bean thing that buzzed—led a short sad life before being eaten by a passing spider.

For the good of the University. For the honor of wizardry. For the sake of the world. For your heart's desire. And I'll freeze you alive if you don't.

Rincewind breathed a sigh almost of relief. He wasn't good on bribes, or cajolery, or appeals to his better nature. But threats, now, threats were familiar. He knew where he was with threats.

The sun dawned on Small Gods' Day like a badly poached egg. The mists had closed in over Ankh-Morpork in streamers of silver and gold—damp, warm, silent. There was the distant grumbling of springtime thunder, out on the plains. It seemed warmer than it ought to be.

Wizards normally slept late. On this morning, however, many of them had got up early and were wandering the corridors aimlessly. They could feel the change in the air.

The University was filling up with magic.

Of course, it was usually full of magic anyway, but it was an old, comfortable magic, as exciting and dangerous as a bedroom slipper. But seeping through the ancient fabric was a new magic, saw-edged and vibrant, bright and cold as comet fire. It sleeted through the stones and crackled off sharp edges like static electricity on the nylon carpet of Creation. It buzzed and sizzled. It curled wizardly beards, poured in wisps of octarine smoke from fingers that had done nothing more mystical for three decades than a little light illusion. How can the effect be described with delicacy and taste? For most of the wizards, it was like being an elderly man who, suddenly faced with a beautiful young woman, finds to his horror and delight and astonishment that the flesh is suddenly as willing as the spirit.

And in the halls and corridors of the University the word was being whispered: *Sourcery!*

A few wizards surreptitiously tried spells that they hadn't been able to master for years, and watched in amazement as they unrolled perfectly. Sheepishly at first, and then with confidence, and then with shouts and whoops, they threw fireballs to one another or produced live doves out of their hats or made multi-colored sequins fall out of the air.

Sourcery! One or two wizards, stately men who had hitherto done nothing more blameworthy that eat a live oyster, turned themselves invisible and chased the maids and bedders through the corridors.

Sourcery! Some of the bolder spirits had tried out ancient flying spells and were bobbing a little uncertainly among the rafters. Sourcery!

Only the Librarian didn't share in the manic breakfast. He watched the antics for some time, pursing his prehensile lips, and then knuckled stiffly off toward his Library. If anyone had bothered to notice, they'd have heard him bolting the door.

It was deathly quiet in the Library. The books were no longer frantic. They'd passed through their fear and out into the calm waters of abject terror, and they crouched on their shelves like so many mesmerized rabbits.

A long hairy arm reached up and grabbed *Casplock's Compleet Lexicon of Majik with Precepts for the Wise* before it could back away, soothed its terror

with a long-fingered hand, and opened it under
"S." The Librarian smoothed the trembling page
gently and ran a horny nail down the entries until
he came to:

> **Sourcerer,** *n. (mythical). A proto-wizard, a
> doorway through which new majik may enterr the
> world, a wizard not limited by the physical capa-
> bilities of hys own bodie, not by Destinie, nor by
> Deathe. It is written that there once werre sourcer-
> ers in the youth of the world but not may there by
> nowe and blessed be, for sourcery is not for menne
> and the return of sourcery would mean the Ende of
> the Worlde . . . If the Creator hadd meant menne
> to bee as goddes, he ould have given them wings.
> SEE ALSO: thee Apocralypse, the legende of thee
> Ice Giants, and thee Teatime of the Goddes.*

The Librarian read the cross-references, turned
back to the first entry, and stared at it through deep
dark eyes for a long time. Then he put the book
back carefully, crept under his desk, and pulled the
blanket over his head.

But in the minstrel gallery over the Great Hall
Carding and Spelter watched the scene with entirely different emotions.

Standing side by side they looked almost exactly
like the number 10.

"What is happening?" said Spelter. He'd had a
sleepless night, and wasn't thinking very straight.

"Magic is flowing into the University," said Carding. "That's what sourcerer means. A channel for
magic. Real magic, my boy. Not the tired old stuff

we've made do with these past centuries. This is the dawning of a . . . a—"

"New, um, dawn?"

"Exactly. A time of miracles, a . . . a—"

"Anus mirabilis?"

Carding frowned. "Yes," he said, eventually, "something like that, I expect. You have quite a way with words, you know."

"Thank you, brother."

The senior wizard appeared to ignore the familiarity. Instead he turned and leaned on the carved rail, watching the magical displays below them. His hands automatically went to his pockets for his tobacco pouch, and then paused. He grinned, and snapped his fingers. A lighted cigar appeared in his mouth.

"Haven't been able to do that in years," he mused. "Big changes, my boy. They haven't realized it yet, but it's the end of Orders and Levels. That was just a—rationing system. We don't need them anymore. Where is the boy?"

"Still asleep—" Spelter began.

"I am here," said Coin.

He stood in the archway leading to the senior wizard's quarters, holding the octiron staff that was half again as tall as he was. Little veins of yellow fire coruscated across its matt black surface, which was so dark that it looked like a slit in the world.

Spelter felt the golden eyes bore through him, as if his innermost thoughts were being scrolled across the back of his skull.

"Ah," he said, in a voice that he believed was jolly and avuncular but in fact sounded like a strangled death rattle. After a start like that his contribution could only get worse, and it did. "I see you're, um, up," he said.

"My dear boy," said Carding.

Coin gave him a long, freezing stare.

"I saw you last night," he said. "Are you puissant?"

"Only mildly," said Carding, hurriedly recalling the boy's tendency to treat wizardry as a terminal game of conkers. "But not so puissant as you, I'm sure."

"I am to be made Archchancellor, as is my destiny?"

"Oh, absolutely," said Carding. "No doubt about it. May I have a look at your staff? Such an interesting design—"

He reached out a pudgy hand.

It was a shocking breach of etiquette in any case; no wizard should even think of touching another's staff without his express permission. But there are people who can't quite believe that children are fully human, and think that the operation of normal good manners doesn't apply to them.

Carding's fingers curled around the black staff.

There was a noise that Spelter felt rather than heard, and Carding bounced across the gallery and struck the opposite wall with a sound like a sack of lard hitting a pavement.

"Don't do that," said Coin. He turned and looked through Spelter, who had gone pale, and added: "Help him up. He is probably not badly hurt."

The bursar scuttled hurriedly across the floor and bent over Carding, who was breathing heavily and had gone an odd color. He patted the wizard's hand until Carding opened one eye.

"Did you see what happened?" he whispered.

"I'm not sure. Um. What did happen?" hissed Spelter.

"It bit me."

"The next time you touch the staff," said Coin, matter-of-factly, "you will die. Do you understand?"

Carding raised his head gently, in case bits of it fell off.

"Absolutely," he said.

"And now I would like to see the University," the boy continued. "I have heard a great deal about it . . ."

Spelter helped Carding to his unsteady feet and supported him as they trotted obediently after the boy.

"Don't touch his staff," muttered Carding.

"I'll remember, um, not to," said Spelter firmly. "What did it feel like?"

"Have you ever been bitten by a viper?"

"No."

"In that case you'll understand exactly what it felt like."

"Hmmm?"

"It wasn't like a snake bite at all."

They hurried after the determined figure as Coin marched down the stairs and through the ravished doorway of the Great Hall.

Spelter dodged in front, anxious to make a good impression.

"This is the Great Hall," he said. Coin turned his

golden gaze toward him, and the wizard felt his mouth dry up. "It's called that because it's a hall, d'you see. And big."

He swallowed. "It's a big hall," he said, fighting to stop the last of his coherence being burned away by the searchlight of that stare. "A great big hall, which is why it's called—"

"Who are those people?" said Coin. He pointed with his staff. The assembled wizards, who had turned to watch him enter, backed out of the way as though the staff was a flamethrower.

Spelter followed the sourcerer's stare. Coin was pointing to the portraits and statues of former Archchancellors, which decorated the walls. Full-bearded and point-hatted, clutching ornamental scrolls or holding mysterious symbolic bits of astrological equipment, they stared down with ferocious self-importance or, possibly, chronic constipation.

"From these walls," said Carding, "two hundred supreme mages look down upon you."

"I don't care for them," said Coin, and the staff streamed octarine fire. The Archchancellors vanished.

"And the windows are too small—"

"The ceiling is too high—"

"Everything is too *old*—"

The wizards threw themselves flat as the staff flared and spat. Spelter pulled his hat over his eyes and rolled under a table when the very fabric of the University flowed around him. Wood creaked, stone groaned.

Something tapped him on the head. He screamed.

"Stop that!" shouted Carding above the din. "And pull your hat up! Show a little dignity!"

"Why are you under the table, then?" said Spelter sourly.

"We must seize our opportunity!"

"What, like the staff?"

"Follow me!"

Spelter emerged into a bright, a horrible bright new world.

Gone were the rough stone walls. Gone were the dark, owl-haunted rafters. Gone was the tiled floor, with its eye-boggling pattern of black and white tiles.

Gone, too, were the high small windows, with their gentle patina of antique grease. Raw sunlight streamed into the hall for the first time.

The wizards stared at one another, mouths open, and what they saw was not what they had always thought they'd seen. The unforgiving rays transmuted rich gold embroidery into dusty gilt, exposed opulent fabric as rather stained and threadbare velvet, turned fine flowing beards into nicotine-stained tangles, betrayed splendid diamonds as rather inferior Ankh-stones. The fresh light probed and prodded, stripping away the comfortable shadows.

And, Spelter had to admit, what was left didn't inspire confidence. He was suddenly acutely aware that under his robes—his tattered, badly-faded robes, he realized with an added spasm of guilt; the robes with the perforated area where the mice had got at them—he was still wearing his bedroom slippers.

The hall was now almost all glass. What wasn't

glass was marble. It was all so splendid that Spelter felt quite unworthy.

He turned to Carding, and saw that his fellow wizard was staring at Coin with his eyes gleaming.

Most of the other wizards had the same expression. If wizards weren't attracted to power they wouldn't be wizards, and this was real power. The staff had them charmed like so many cobras.

Carding reached out to touch the boy on the shoulder, and then thought better of it.

"Magnificent," he said, instead.

He turned to the assembled wizardry and raised his arms. "My brothers," he intoned, "we have in our midst a wizard of great power!"

Spelter tugged at his robe.

"He nearly killed you," he hissed. Carding ignored him.

"And I propose—" Carding swallowed—"I propose him for Archchancellor!"

There was a moment's silence, and then a burst of cheering and shouts of dissent. Several quarrels broke out at the back of the crowd. The wizards nearer the front weren't quite so ready to argue. They could see the smile on Coin's face. It was bright and cold, like the smile on the face of the moon.

There was a commotion, and an elderly wizard fought his way to the front of the throng.

Spelter recognized Ovin Hakardly, a seventh-level wizard and a lecturer in Lore. He was red with anger, except where he was white with rage. When he spoke, his words seared through the air like so many knives, clipped as topiary, crisp as biscuits.

"Are you mad?" he said. "No one but a wizard of

the eighth level may become Archchancellor! And he must be elected by the other most senior wizards in solemn convocation! (Duly guided by the gods, of course.) It is the Lore! (The very idea!)"

Hakardly had studied the Lore of magic for years and, because magic always tends to be a two-way process, it had made its mark on him; he gave the impression of being as fragile as a cheese straw, and in some unaccountable way the dryness of his endeavours had left him with the ability to pronounce punctuation.

He stood vibrating with indignation and, he became aware, he was rapidly standing alone. In fact he was the center of an expanding circle of empty floor fringed with wizards who were suddenly ready to swear that they'd never clapped eyes on him in their life.

Coin had raised his staff.

Hakardly raised an admonitory finger.

"You do not frighten me, young man," he snapped. "Talented you may be, but magical talent alone is not enough. There are many other qualities required of a great wizard. Administrative ability, for example, and wisdom, and the—"

Coin lowered his staff.

"The Lore applies to all wizards, does it not?" he said.

"Absolutely! It was drawn up—"

"But I am not a wizard, Lord Hakardly."

The wizard hesitated. "Ah," he said, and hesitated again. "Good point," he said.

"But I am well aware of the need for wisdom, foresight and good advice, and I would be honored if you could see your way clear to providing those much-valued commodities. For example—why is it that wizards do not rule the world?"

"What?"

"It is a simple question. There are in this room—" Coin's lips moved for a fraction of a second—"four hundred and seventy-two wizards, skilled in the most subtle of arts. Yet all you rule are these few acres of rather inferior architecture. Why is this?"

The most senior wizards exchanged knowing glances.

"Such it may appear," said Hakardly eventually, "but, my child, we have domains beyond the ken of the temporal power." His eyes gleamed. "Magic can surely take the mind to inner landscape of arcane—"

"Yes, yes," said Coin. "Yet there are extremely solid walls outside your University. Why is this?"

Carding ran his tongue over his lips. It was extraordinary. The child was speaking his thoughts.

"You squabble for power," said Coin, sweetly, "and yet, beyond these walls, to the man who carts nightsoil or the average merchant, is there really so much difference between a high-level mage and a mere conjuror?"

Hakardly stared at him in complete and untrammeled astonishment.

"Child, it's obvious to the meanest citizen," he said. "The robes and trimmings themselves—"

"Ah," said Coin, "the robes and trimmings. Of course."

A short, heavy and thoughtful silence filled the hall.

"It seems to me," said Coin eventually, "that wizards rule only wizards. Who rules in the reality outside?"

"As far as the city is concerned, that would be the Patrician, Lord Vetinari," said Carding with some caution.

"And is he a fair and just ruler?"

Carding thought about it. The Patrician's spy network was said to be superb. "I would say," he said carefully, "that he is unfair and unjust, but scrupulously evenhanded. He is unfair and unjust to everyone, without fear or favor."

"And you are content with this?" said Coin.

Carding tried not to catch Hakardly's eye.

"It's not a case of being content with it," he said. "I suppose we've not given it much thought. A wizard's true vocation, you see—"

"Is it really true that the wise suffer themselves to be ruled in this way?"

Carding growled. "Of course not! Don't be silly! We merely tolerate it. That's what wisdom is all about, you'll find that out when you grow up, it's a case of biding one's time—"

"Where is this Patrician? I would like to see him."

"That can be arranged, of course," said Carding. "The Patrician is always graciously pleased to grant wizards an interview, and—"

"Now *I* will grant *him* an interview," said Coin. "He must learn that wizards have bided their time long enough. Stand back, please."

He pointed the staff.

* * *

The temporal ruler of the sprawling city of Ankh-Morpork was sitting in his chair at the foot of the steps leading up to the throne, looking for any signs of intelligence in intelligence reports. The throne had been empty for more than two thousand years, since the death of the last of the line of the kings of Ankh. Legend said that one day the city would have a king again, and went on with various comments about magic swords, strawberry birthmarks and all the other things that legends gabble on about in these circumstances.

In fact the only real qualification now was the ability to stay alive for more than about five minutes after revealing the existence of any magic swords or birthmarks, because the great merchant families of Ankh had been ruling the city for the last twenty centuries and were about to relinquish power as the average limpet is to let go of its rock.

The current Patrician, head of the extremely rich and powerful Vetinari family, was thin, tall and apparently as coldblooded as a dead penguin. Just by looking at him you could tell he was the sort of man you'd expect to keep a white cat, and caress it idly while sentencing people to death in a piranha tank; and you'd hazard for good measure that he probably collected rare thin porcelain, turning it over and over in his blue-white fingers while distant screams echoed from the depths of the dungeons. You wouldn't put it past him to use the word "exquisite" and have thin lips. He looked the kind of person who, when they blink, you mark it off on the calendar.

Practically none of this was in fact the case, although he did have a small and exceedingly elderly wire-haired terrier called Wuffles that smelled badly and wheezed at people. It was said to be the only thing in the entire world he truly cared about. He did of course sometimes have people horribly tortured to death, but this was considered to be perfectly acceptable behavior for a civic ruler and generally approved of by the overwhelming majority of citizens.* The people of Ankh are of a practical persuasion, and felt that the Patrician's edict forbidding all street theater and mime artists made up for a lot of things. He didn't administer a reign of terror, just the occasional light shower.

The Patrician sighed, and laid the latest report on top of the large heap beside the chair.

When he had been a little boy he had seen a showman who could keep a dozen plates spinning in the air. If the man had been capable of working the same trick with a hundred of them, Lord Vetinari considered, he would just about begin to be ready for training in the art of ruling Ankh-Morpork, a city once described as resembling an overturned termite heap without the charm.

He glanced out of the window at the distant pillar of the Tower of Art, the center of Unseen University, and wondered vaguely whether any of those tiresome old fools could come up with a better way of collating all this paperwork. They wouldn't, of course—you couldn't expect a wizard to understand anything as basic as elementary civic espionage.

---

* The overwhelming majority of citizens being defined in this case as everyone not currently hanging upside down over a scorpion pit.

He sighed again, and picked up the transcript of what the president of the Thieves' Guild had said to his deputy at midnight in the soundproof room hidden behind the office in the Guild headquarters, and . . .

Was in the Great Ha . . .

Was *not* in the Great Hall of Unseen University, where he had spent some interminable dinners, but there were a lot of wizards around him and they were . . .

. . . *different.*

Like Death, which some of the city's less fortunate citizens considered he intimately resembled, the Patrician never got angry until he had time to think about it. But sometimes he thought very quickly.

He stared around at the assembled wizards, but there was something about them that choked the words of outrage in his throat. They looked like sheep who had suddenly found a trapped wolf at exactly the same time as they heard about the idea of unity being strength.

There was something about their eyes.

"What is the meaning of this outr—" he hesitated, and concluded, "this? A merry Small Gods' Day prank, is it?"

His eyes swivelled to meet those of a small boy holding a long metal staff. The child was smiling the oldest smile the Patrician had ever seen.

Carding coughed.

"My lord," he began.

"Out with it, man," snapped Lord Vetinari.

Carding had been diffident, but the Patrician's tone was just that tiny bit too peremptory. The wizard's knuckles went white.

"I am a wizard of the eighth level," he said quietly, "and you will not use that tone to me."

"Well said," said Coin.

"Take him to the dungeons," said Carding.

"We haven't got any dungeons," said Spelter. "This is a university."

"Then take him to the wine cellars," snapped Carding. "And while you're down there, build some dungeons."

"Have you the faintest inkling of what you are doing?" said the Patrician. "I demand to know the meaning of this—"

"You demand nothing at all," said Carding. "And the meaning is that from now on the wizards will rule, as it was ordained. Now take—"

"*You*? Rule Ankh-Morpork? Wizards who can barely govern themselves?"

"Yes!" Carding was aware that this wasn't the last word in repartee, and was even more alive to the fact that the dog Wuffles, who had been teleported along with his master, had waddled painfully across the floor and was peering shortsightedly at the wizard's boots.

"Then all truly wise men would prefer the safety of a nice deep dungeon," said the Patrician. "And now you will cease this foolery and replace me in my palace, and it is just possible that we will say no more about this. Or at least that you won't have the chance to."

Wuffles gave up investigating Carding's boots and trotted toward Coin, shedding a few hairs on the way.

"This *pantomime* has gone on long enough," said the Patrician. "Now I am getting—"

Wuffles growled. It was a deep, primeval noise, which struck a chord in the racial memory of all those present and filled them with an urgent desire to climb a tree. It suggested long gray shapes hunting in the dawn of time. It was astonishing that such a small animal could contain so much menace, and all of it was aimed at the staff in Coin's hand.

The Patrician strode forward to snatch the animal, and Carding raised his hand and sent a blaze of orange and blue fire searing across the room.

The Patrician vanished. On the spot where he had been standing a small yellow lizard blinked and glared with malevolent reptilian stupidity.

Carding looked in astonishment at his fingers, as if for the first time.

"All right," he whispered hoarsely.

The wizards stared down at the panting lizard, and then out at the city sparkling in the early morning light. Out there was the council of aldermen, the city watch, the Guild of Thieves, the Guild of Merchants, the priesthoods . . . and none of them knew what was about to hit them.

It has begun, said the hat, from its box on the deck.

"What has?" said Rincewind.

The rule of sourcery.

Rincewind looked blank. "Is that good?"

Do you ever understand anything anyone says to you?

Rincewind felt on firmer ground here. "No," he said. "Not always. Not lately. Not often."

"Are you sure you *are* a wizard?" said Conina.

"It's the only thing I've ever been sure of," he said, with conviction.

"How strange."

Rincewind sat on the Luggage in the sun on the foredeck of the *Ocean Waltzer* as it lurched peacefully across the green waters of the Circle Sea. Around them men did what he was sure were important nautical things, and he hoped they were doing them correctly, because next to heights he hated depths most of all.

"You look worried," said Conina, who was cutting his hair. Rincewind tried to make his head as small as possible as the blades flashed by.

"That's because I am."

"What exactly is the Apocralypse?"

Rincewind hesitated. "Well," he said, "it's the end of the world. Sort of."

"Sort of? *Sort of* the end of the world? You mean we won't be certain? We'll look around and say 'Pardon me, did you hear something?'?"

"It's just that no two seers have ever agreed about it. There have been all kinds of vague predictions. Quite mad, some of them. So it was called the Apocralypse." He looked embarrassed. "It's a sort of apocryphal Apocalypse. A kind of pun, you see."

"Not very good."

"No. I suppose not."*

---

* Wizards' tastes in the matter of puns are about the same as their taste in glittery objects.

Conina's scissors snipped busily.

"I must say the captain seemed quite happy to have us aboard," she observed.

"That's because they think it's lucky to have a wizard on the boat," said Rincewind. "It isn't, of course."

"Lots of people believe it," she said.

"Oh, it's lucky for other people, just not for me. I can't swim."

"What, not a stroke?"

Rincewind hesitated, and twiddled the star on his hat cautiously.

"About how deep is the sea here, would you say? Approximately?" he said.

"About a dozen fathoms, I believe."

"Then I could probably swim about a dozen fathoms, whatever they are."

"Stop trembling like that, I nearly had your ear off," Conina snapped. She glared at a passing seaman and waved her scissors. "What's the matter, you never saw a man have a haircut before?"

Someone up in the rigging made a remark which caused a ripple of ribald laughter in the topgallants, unless they were forecastles.

"I shall pretend I didn't hear that," said Conina, and gave the comb a savage yank, dislodging numerous inoffensive small creatures.

"Ow!"

"Well, you should keep still!"

"It's a little difficult to keep still knowing who it is that's waving a couple of steel blades around my head!"

And so the morning passed, with scudding wavelets, the creaking of the rigging, and a rather complex layer cut. Rincewind had to admit, looking at himself in a shard of mirror, that there was a definite improvement.

The captain had said that they were bound for the city of Al Khali, on the hubward coast of Klatch.

"Like Ankh, only with sand instead of mud," said Rincewind, leaning over the rail. "But quite a good slave market."

"Slavery is immoral," said Conina firmly.

"Is it? Gosh," said Rincewind.

"Would you like me to trim your beard?" said Conina, hopefully.

She stopped, scissors drawn, and stared out to sea.

"Is there a kind of sailor that uses a canoe with sort of extra bits on the side and a sort of red eye painted on the front and a small sail?" she said.

"I've heard of Klatchian slave pirates," said Rincewind, "but this is a big boat. I shouldn't think one of them would dare attack it."

"One of them wouldn't," said Conina, still staring at the fuzzy area where the sea became the sky, "but these five might."

Rincewind peered at the distant haze, and then looked up at the man on watch, who shook his head.

"Come on," he chuckled, with all the humor of a blocked drain. "You can't really see anything out there. Can you?"

"Ten men in each canoe," said Conina grimly.

"Look, a joke's a joke—"

"With long curvy swords."

"Well, I can't see a—"

"—their long and rather dirty hair blowing in the wind—"

"With split ends, I expect?" said Rincewind sourly.

"Are you trying to be funny?"

"Me?"

"And here's me without a weapon," said Conina, sweeping back across the deck. "I bet there isn't a decent sword anywhere on this boat."

"Never mind. Perhaps they've just come for a quick shampoo."

While Conina rummaged frantically in her pack Rincewind sidled over to the Archchancellor's hat-box and cautiously raised the lid.

"There's nothing out there, is there?" he asked.

How should I know? Put me on.

"What? On my head?"

Good grief.

"But I'm not an Archchancellor!" said Rincewind. "I mean, I've heard of cool-headed, but—"

I need to use your eyes. Now put me on. On your head.

"Um."

Trust me.

Rincewind couldn't disobey. He gingerly removed his battered gray hat, looked longingly at its disheveled star, and lifted the Archchancellor's hat out of its box. It felt rather heavier than he'd expected. The octarines around the crown were glowing faintly.

He lowered it carefully onto his new hairstyle, clutching the brim tightly in case he felt the first icy chill.

In fact he simply felt incredibly light. And there was a feeling of great knowledge and power—not actually present, but just, mentally speaking, on the tip of his metaphorical tongue.

Odd scraps of memory flickered across his mind, and they weren't any memories he remembered remembering before. He probed gently, as one touches a hollow tooth with the tongue, and there they were—

Two hundred dead Archchancellors, dwindling into the leaden, freezing past, one behind the other, watched him with blank gray eyes.

That's why it's so cold, he told himself, the warmth seeps into the dead world. Oh, no . . .

When the hat spoke, he saw two hundred pairs of pale lips move.

Who are you?

Rincewind, thought Rincewind. And in the inner recesses of his head he tried to think privately to himself . . . help.

He felt his knees begin to buckle under the weight of centuries.

What's it like, being dead? he thought.

Death is but a sleep, said the dead mages.

But what does it *feel* like? Rincewind thought.

You will have an unrivalled chance to find out when those war canoes get here, Rincewind.

With a yelp of terror he thrust upwards and forced the hat off his head. Real life and sound flooded back in, but since someone was frantically banging a gong very close to his ear this was not much of an improvement. The canoes were visible to everyone now, cutting through the water with an eerie silence. Those black-clad figures manning the paddles should have been whooping and screaming; it wouldn't have made it any better, but it would have seemed more appropriate. The silence bespoke an unpleasant air of purpose.

"Gods, that was awful," he said. "Mind you, so is this."

Crew members scurried across the deck, cutlasses in hand. Conina tapped Rincewind on the shoulder.

"They'll try to take us alive," she said.

"Oh," said Rincewind weakly. "Good."

Then he remembered something else about Klatchian slavers, and his throat went dry.

"You'll—you'll be the one they'll be after," he said. "I've heard about what they do—"

"Should I know?" said Conina. To Rincewind's horror she didn't appear to have found a weapon.

"They'll throw you in a seraglio!"

She shrugged. "Could be worse."

"But it's got all these spikes and when they shut the door—" hazarded Rincewind. The canoes were close enough now to see the determined expressions of the rowers.

"That's not a seraglio. That's an Iron Maiden. Don't you know what a seraglio is?"

"Um . . ."

She told him. He went crimson.

"Anyway, they'll have to capture me first," said Conina primly. "It's you who should be worrying."

"Why me?"

"You're the only other one who's wearing a dress."

Rincewind bridled. "It's a robe—"

"Robe, dress. You better hope they know the difference."

A hand like a bunch of bananas with rings on grabbed Rincewind's shoulder and spun him around. The captain, a Hublander built on generous bear-like lines, beamed at him through a mass of facial hair.

"Hah!" he said. "They know not that we aboard a wizard have! To create in their bellies the burning green fire! Hah?"

The dark forests of his eyebrows wrinkled as it became apparent that Rincewind wasn't immediately ready to hurl vengeful magic at the invaders.

"Hah?" he insisted, making a mere single syllable do the work of a whole string of blood-congealing threats.

"Yes, well, I'm just—I'm just girding my loins," said Rincewind. "That's what I'm doing. Girding them. Green fire, you want?"

"Also to make hot lead run in their bones," said the captain. "Also their skins to blister and living scorpions without mercy to eat their brains from inside, and—"

The leading canoe came alongside and a couple of grapnels thudded into the rail. As the first of the slavers appeared the captain hurried away, drawing his sword. He stopped for a moment and turned to Rincewind.

"You gird quickly," he said. "Or no loins. Hah?"

Rincewind turned to Conina, who was leaning on the rail examining her fingernails.

"You'd better get on with it," she said. "That's fifty green fires and hot leads to go, with a side order for blisters and scorpions. Hold the mercy."

"This sort of thing is always happening to me," he moaned.

He peered over the rail to what he thought of as the main floor of the boat. The invaders were winning by sheer weight of numbers, using nets and ropes to tangle the struggling crew. They worked in absolute silence, clubbing and dodging, avoiding the use of swords wherever possible.

"Musn't damage the merchandise," said Conina. Rincewind watched in horror as the captain went down under a press of dark shapes, screaming, "Green fire! Green fire!"

Rincewind backed away. He wasn't any good at magic, but he'd had a hundred percent success at staying alive up to now and didn't want to spoil the record. All he needed to do was to learn how to swim in the time it took to dive into the sea. It was worth a try.

"What are you waiting for? Let's go while they're occupied," he said to Conina.

"I need a sword," she said.

"You'll be spoiled for choice in a minute."

"One will be enough."

Rincewind kicked the Luggage.

"Come on," he snarled. "You've got a lot of floating to do."

The Luggage extended its little legs with exaggerated nonchalance, turned slowly, and settled down beside the girl.

"Traitor," said Rincewind to its hinges.

The battle already seemed to be over. Five of the raiders stalked up the ladder to the afterdeck, leaving most of their colleagues to round up the defeated crew below. The leader pulled down his mask and leered briefly and swarthily at Conina; and then he turned and leered for a slightly longer period at Rincewind.

"This is a robe," said Rincewind quickly. "And you'd better watch out, because I'm a wizard." He took a deep breath. "Lay a finger on me, and you'll make me wish you hadn't. I warn you."

"A wizard? Wizards don't make good strong slaves," mused the leader.

"Absolutely right," said Rincewind. "So if you'll just see your way clear to letting me go—"

The leader turned back to Conina and signaled to one of his companions. He jerked a tattooed thumb toward Rincewind.

"Do not kill him too quickly. In fact—" He paused, and treated Rincewind to a smile full of teeth. "Maybe . . . yes. And why not? Can you sing, wizard?"

"I might be able to," said Rincewind, cautiously. "Why?"

"You could be just the man the Seriph needs for a job in the harem." A couple of slavers sniggered.

"It could be a *unique* opportunity," the leader went on, encouraged by this audience appreciation. There was more broadminded approval from behind him.

Rincewind backed away. "I don't think so," he said, "thanks all the same. I'm not cut out for that kind of thing."

"Oh, but you could be," said the leader, his eyes bright. "You could be."

"Oh, for goodness sake," muttered Conina. She glanced at the men on either side of her, and then her hands moved. The one stabbed with the scissors was possibly better off than the one she raked with the comb, given the kind of mess a steel comb can make of a face. Then she reached down, snatched up a sword dropped by one of the stricken men, and lunged at the other two.

The leader turned at the screams, and saw the Luggage behind him with its lid open. And then Rincewind cannoned into the back of him, pitching him forward into whatever oblivion lay in the multidimensional depths of the chest.

There was the start of a bellow, abruptly cut off.

Then there was a click like the shooting of the bolt on the gates of Hell.

Rincewind backed away, trembling. "A unique opportunity," he muttered under his breath, having just got the reference.

At least he had a unique opportunity to watch Conina fight. Not many men ever got to see it twice.

Her opponents started off grinning at the temerity of a slight young girl in attacking them, and then rapidly passed through various stages of puzzlement, doubt, concern and abject gibbeting terror as they apparently became the center of a flashing, tightening circle of steel.

She disposed of the last of the leader's bodyguard with a couple of thrusts that made Rincewind's eyes water and, with a sigh, vaulted the rail on the main deck. To Rincewind's annoyance the Luggage barrelled after her, cushioning its fall by dropping heavily onto a slaver, and adding to the sudden panic of the invaders because, while it was bad enough to be attacked with deadly and ferocious accuracy by a rather pretty girl in a white dress with flowers on it, it was even worse for the male ego to be tripped up and bitten by a travel accessory; it was pretty bad for all the rest of the male, too.

Rincewind peered over the railing.

"Showoff," he muttered.

A throwing knife clipped the wood near his chin and ricocheted past his ear. He raised his hand to the sudden stinging pain, and stared at it in horror before gently passing out. It wasn't blood in general he couldn't stand the sight of, it was just his blood in particular that was so upsetting.

The market in Sator Square, the wide expanse of cobbles outside the black gates of the University, was in full cry.

It was said that everything in Ankh-Morpork was for sale except for the beer and the women, both of which one merely hired. And most of the merchandise was available in Sator market, which over the years had grown, stall by stall, until the newcomers were up against the ancient stones of the University itself; in fact they made a handy display area for bolts of cloth and racks of charms.

No one noticed the gates swing back. But a silence rolled out of the University, spreading out across the noisy, crowded square like the first fresh wavelets of the tide trickling over a brackish swamp. In fact it wasn't true silence at all, but a great roar of anti-noise.

Silence isn't the opposite of sound, it is merely its absence. But this was the sound that lies on the far side of silence, anti-noise, its shadowy decibels throttling the market cries like a fall of velvet.

The crowds stared around wildly, mouthing like goldfish and with about as much effect. All heads turned toward the gates.

Something else was flowing out besides that cacophony of hush. The stalls nearest the empty gateway began to grind across the cobbles, shedding merchandise. Their owners dived out of the way as the stalls hit the row behind them and scraped relentlessly onward, piling up until a wide avenue of clean, empty stones stretched the whole width of the square.

Ardrothy Longstaff, Purveyor of Pies Full of Personality, peered over the top of the wreckage of his stall in time to see the wizards emerge.

He knew wizards, or up until now he'd always thought he did. They were vague old boys, harmless enough in their way, dressed like ancient sofas, always ready customers for any of his merchandise that happened to be marked down on account of age and rather more personality than a prudent housewife would be prepared to put up with.

But these wizards were something new to Ardrothy. They walked out into Sator Square as if they owned it. Little blue sparks flashed around their feet. They seemed a little taller, somehow.

Or perhaps it was just the way they carried themselves.

Yes, that was it . . .

Ardrothy had a touch of magic in his genetic makeup, and as he watched the wizards sweep across the square it told him that the very best thing he could do for his health would be to pack his knives, and mincers in his little pack and have it away out of the city at any time in the next ten minutes.

The last wizard in the group lagged behind his colleagues and looked around the square with disdain.

"There used to be fountains out here," he said. "You people—be off."

The traders stared at one another. Wizards normally spoke imperiously, that was to be expected. But there was an edge to the voice that no one had heard before. It had knuckles in it.

Ardrothy's eyes swivelled sideways. Arising out of the ruins of his jellied starfish and clam stall like an avenging angel, dislodging various molluscs from his beard and spitting vinegar, was Miskin Koble, who was said to be able to open oysters with one hand. Years of pulling limpets off rocks and wrestling the giant cockles in Ankh Bay had given him the kind of physical development normally associated with tectonic plates. He didn't so much stand up as unfold.

Then he thudded his way toward the wizard and pointed a trembling finger at the ruins of his stall, from which half a dozen enterprising lobsters were making a determined bid for freedom. Muscles moved around the edges of his mouth like angry eels.

"Did you do that?" he demanded.

"Stand aside, oaf," said the wizard, three words which in the opinion of Ardrothy gave him the ongoing life expectancy of a glass cymbal.

"I hates wizards," said Koble. "I really hates wizards. So I am going to hit you, all right?"

He brought his fist back and let fly.

The wizard raised an eyebrow, yellow fire sprang up around the shellfish salesman, there was a noise like tearing silk, and Koble had vanished. All that was left was his boots, standing forlornly on the cobbles with little wisps of smoke coming out of them.

No one knows why smoking boots always remain, no matter how big the explosion. It seems to be just one of those things.

It seemed to the watchful eyes of Ardrothy that the wizard himself was nearly as shocked as the crowd, but he rallied magnificently and gave his staff a flourish.

"You people had better jolly well learn from this," he said. "No one raises their hand to a wizard, do you understand? There are going to be a lot of changes around here. Yes, what do you want?"

This last comment was to Ardrothy, who was trying to sneak past unnoticed. He scrabbled quickly in his pie tray.

"I was just wondering if your honorship would care to purchase one of these finest pies," he said hurriedly. "Full of nourish—"

"Watch closely, pie-selling person," said the wizard. He stretched out his hand, made a strange gesture with his fingers, and produced a pie out of the air.

It was fat, golden-brown and beautifully glazed. Just by looking at it Ardrothy knew it was packed edge to edge with prime lean pork, with none of those spacious areas of good fresh air under the lid that represented his own profit margin. It was the kind of pie piglets hope to be when they grew up.

His heart sank. His ruin was floating in front of him with short-crust pastry on it.

"Want a taste?" said the wizard. "There's plenty more where that came from."

"Wherever it came from," said Ardrothy.

He looked past the shiny pastry to the face of the wizard, and in the manic gleam of those eyes he saw the world turning upside down.

He turned away, a broken man, and set out for the nearest city gate.

As if it wasn't bad enough that wizards were killing people, he thought bitterly, they were taking away their livelihood as well.

A bucket of water splashed into Rincewind's face, jerking him out of a dreadful dream in which a hundred masked women were attempting to trim his hair with broadswords and cutting it very fine indeed. Some people, having a nightmare like that, would dismiss it as castration anxiety, but Rincewind's subconscious knew being-cut-to-tiny-bits-mortal-dread when it saw it. It saw it most of the time.

He sat up.

"Are you all right?" said Conina, anxiously.

Rincewind swivelled his eyes around the cluttered deck.

"Not necessarily," he said cautiously. There didn't seem to be any black-clad slavers around, at least vertically. There were a good many crew members, all of them maintaining a respectful distance from Conina. Only the captain stood reasonably close, an inane grin on his face.

"They left," said Conina. "Took what they could and left."

"They bastards," said the captain, "but they paddle pretty fast!" Conina winced as he gave her a ringing slap on the back. "She fight real good for a lady," he added. "Yes!"

Rincewind got unsteadily to his feet. The boat was scudding along cheerfully toward a distant smear on the horizon that had to be hubward Klatch. He was totally unharmed. He began to cheer up a bit.

The captain gave them both a hearty nod and hurried off to shout orders connected with sails and ropes and things. Conina sat down on the Luggage, which didn't seem to object.

"He said he's so grateful he'll take us all the way to Al Khali," she said.

"I thought that's what we arranged anyway," said Rincewind. "I saw you give him money, and everything."

"Yes, but he *was* planning to overpower us and sell me as a slave when he got there."

"What, not sell me?" said Rincewind, and then snorted, "Of course, it's the wizard's robes, he wouldn't dare—"

"Um. Actually, he said he'd have to give you away," said Conina, picking intently at an imaginary splinter on the Luggage's lid.

"*Give* me away?"

"Yes. Um. Sort of like, one free wizard with every concubine sold? Um."

"I don't see what vegetables have got to do with it."

Conina gave him a long, hard stare, and when he didn't break into a smile she sighed and said, "Why are you wizards always nervous around women?"

Rincewind bridled at this slur. "I like that!" he said, "I'll have you know that—look, anyway, the point is, I get along very well with women in general, it's just women with swords that upset me." He considered this for a while, and added, "Everyone with swords upset me, if it comes to that."

Conina picked industriously at the splinter. The Luggage gave a contented creak.

"I know something else that'll upset you," she muttered.

"Hmmm?"

"The hat's gone."

"What?"

"I couldn't help it, they just grabbed whatever they could—"

"The slavers have made off with the hat?"

"Don't you take that tone with me! *I* wasn't having a quiet sleep at the time—"

Rincewind waved his hands frantically. "Nonono, don't get excited, I wasn't taking any tone—I want to think about this . . ."

"The captain says they'll probably go back to Al Khali," he heard Conina say. "There's a place where the criminal element hang out, and we can soon—"

"I don't see why we have to do anything," said Rincewind. "The hat wanted to keep out the way of the University, and I shouldn't think those slavers ever drop in there for a quick sherry."

"You'll let them run off with it?" said Conina, in genuine astonishment.

"Well, someone's got to do it. The way I see it, why me?"

"But you said it's the symbol of wizardry! What wizards all aspire to! You can't just let it go like that!"

"You watch me." Rincewind sat back. He felt oddly surprised. He was making a decision. It was his. It belonged to him. No-one was forcing him to make it. Sometimes it seemed that his entire life consisted of getting into trouble because of what other people wanted, but this time he'd made a decision and that was that. He'd get off the boat at Al Khali and find some way of going home. Someone else could save the world, and he wished them luck. He'd made a decision.

His brow furrowed. Why didn't he feel happy about it?

Because it's the wrong bloody decision, you idiot.

Right, he thought, I've had enough voices in my head. Out.

But I belong here.

You mean you're me?

Your conscience.

Oh.

You can't let the hat be destroyed. It's the symbol . . .

. . . all right, I know . . .

. . . the symbol of magic under the Lore. Magic

under the control of mankind. You don't want to go back to those dark Ians . . .

. . . What? . . .

Ians . . .

Do I mean aeons?

Right. Aeons. Go back aeons to the time when raw magic ruled. The whole framework of reality trembled daily. It was pretty terrible, I can tell me.

How do I know?

Racial memory.

Gosh. Have I got one of those?

Well. A part of one.

Yes, all right, but why me?

In your soul you know you are a true wizard. The word "Wizard" is engraved on your heart.

"Yes, but the trouble is I keep meeting people who might try to find out," said Rincewind miserably.

"What did you say?" said Conina.

Rincewind stared at the smudge on the horizon and sighed.

"Just talking to myself," he said.

Carding surveyed the hat critically. He walked around the table and stared at it from a new angle. At last he said: "It's pretty good. Where did you get the octarines?"

"They're just very good Ankhstones," said Spelter. "They fooled you, did they?"

It was a *magnificent* hat. In fact, Spelter had to admit, it looked a lot better than the real thing. The old Archchancellor's hat had looked rather battered, its gold thread tarnished and unravelling.

The replica was a considerable improvement. It had style.

"I especially like the lace," said Carding.

"It took ages."

"Why didn't you try magic?" Carding waggled his fingers, and grasped the tall cool glass that appeared in mid-air. Under its paper umbrella and fruit salad it contained some sticky and expensive alcohol.

"Didn't work," said Spelter. "Just couldn't seem, um, to get it right. I had to sew every sequin on by hand." He picked up the hatbox.

Carding coughed into his drink. "Don't put it away just yet," he said, and took it out of the bursar's hands. "I've always wanted to try this—"

He turned to the big mirror on the bursar's wall and reverently lowered the hat on his rather grubby locks.

It was the ending of the first day of the sourcery, and the wizards had managed to change everything except themselves.

They had all tried, on the quiet and when they thought no one else was looking. Even Spelter had a go, in the privacy of his study. He had managed to become twenty years younger with a torso you could crack rocks on, but as soon as he stopped concentrating he sagged, very unpleasantly, back into his old familiar shape and age. There was something elastic about the way you were. The harder you threw it, the faster it came back. The worse it was when it hit, too. Spiked iron balls, broadswords and large heavy sticks with nails in were generally considered pretty fearsome weapons, but they were nothing at all compared to twenty years suddenly applied with considerable force to the back of the head.

This was because sourcery didn't seem to work on things that were instrinsically magical. Nevertheless, the wizards had made a few important improvements. Carding's robe, for example, had become a silk and lace confection of overpoweringly expensive tastelessness, and gave him the appearance of a big red jelly draped with antimacassars.

"It suits me, don't you think?" said Carding. He adjusted the hat brim, giving it an inappropriately rakish air.

Spelter said nothing. He was looking out of the window.

There had been a few improvements all right. It had been a busy day.

The old stone walls had vanished. There were some rather nice railings now. Beyond them, the city fairly sparkled, a poem in white marble and red tiles. The river Ankh was no longer the silt-laden sewer he'd grown up knowing, but a glittering glass-clear ribbon in which—a nice touch—fat carp mouthed and swam in water pure as snowmelt.*

From the air Ankh-Morpork must have been blinding. It gleamed. The detritus of millennia had been swept away.

It made Spelter strangely uneasy. He felt out of place, as though he was wearing new clothes that itched. Of course, he was wearing new clothes and

---

* Of course, Ankh-Morpork's citizens had always claimed that the river water was incredibly pure in any case. Any water that had passed through so many kidneys, they reasoned, had to be very pure indeed.

they did itch, but that wasn't the problem. The new world was all very nice, it was exactly how it should be, and yet, and yet—had he wanted to change, he thought, or had he only wanted things rearranged more suitably?

"I said, don't you think it was made for me?" said Carding.

Spelter turned back, his face blank.

"Um?"

"The hat, man."

"Oh. Um. Very—suitable."

With a sigh Carding removed the baroque head-piece and carefully replaced it in its box. "We'd better take it to him," he said. "He's starting to ask about it."

"I'm still bothered about where the real hat is," said Spelter.

"It's in here," said Carding firmly, tapping the lid.

"I mean the, um, real one."

"This *is* the real one."

"I meant—"

"This is the Archchancellor's Hat," said Carding carefully. "You should know, you made it."

"Yes, but—" began the bursar wretchedly.

"After all, you wouldn't make a *forgery*, would you?"

"Not as, um, such—"

"It's just a hat. It's whatever people think it is. People see the Archchancellor wearing it, they think it's the original hat. In a certain sense, it *is*. Things are defined by what they do. And people, of course. Fundamental basis of wizardry, is that." Carding paused dramatically, and plonked the hatbox into Spelter's arms. "*Cogitum ergot hatto*, you might say."

Spelter had made a special study of old languages, and did his best.

"'I think, therefore I am a hat?'" he hazarded.

"What?" said Carding, as they set off down the stairs to the new incarnation of the Great Hall.

"'I considered I'm a mad hat?'" Spelter suggested.

"Just shut up, all right?"

The haze still hung over the city, its curtains of silver and gold turned to blood by the light of the setting sun which streamed in through the windows of the hall.

Coin was sitting on a stool with his staff across his knees. It occurred to Spelter that he had never seen the boy without it, which was odd. Most wizards kept their staves under the bed, or hooked up over the fireplace.

He didn't like this staff. It was black, but not because that was its color, more because it seemed to be a moveable hole into some other, more unpleasant set of dimensions. It didn't have eyes but, nevertheless, it seemed to stare at Spelter as if it knew his innermost thoughts, which at the moment was more than *he* did.

His skin prickled as the two wizards crossed the floor and felt the blast of a raw magic flowing outward from the seated figure.

Several dozen of the most senior wizards were clustered around the stool, staring in awe at the floor.

Spelter craned to see, and saw—

The world.

It floated in a puddle of black night somehow set into the floor itself, and Spelter knew with a terrible certainty that it *was* the world, not some image or simple projection. There were cloud patterns and everything. There were the frosty wastes of the Hublands, the Counterweight Continent, the Circle Sea, the Rimfall, all tiny and pastel-colored but nevertheless real . . .

Someone was speaking to him.

"Um?" he said, and the sudden drop in metaphorical temperature jerked him back into reality. He realized with horror that Coin had just directed a remark at him.

"I'm sorry?" he corrected himself. "It was just that the world . . . so beautiful . . ."

"Our Spelter is an aesthete," said Coin, and there was a brief chuckle from one or two wizards who knew what the word meant, "but as to the world, it could be improved. I had said, Spelter, that everywhere we look we can see cruelty and inhumanity and greed, which tell us that the world is indeed governed badly, does it not?"

Spelter was aware of two dozen pairs of eyes turning to him.

"Um," he said. "Well, you can't change human nature."

There was dead silence.

Spelter hesitated. "Can you?" he said.

"That remains to be seen," said Carding. "But if we change the world, then human nature also will change. Is that not so, brothers?"

"We have the city," said one of the wizards. "I myself have created a castle—"

"We rule the city, but who rules the world?" said Carding. "There must be a thousand petty kings and emperors and chieftains down there."

"Not one of whom can read without moving his lips," said a wizard.

"The Patrician could read," said Spelter.

"Not if you cut off his index finger," said Carding. "What happened to the lizard, anyway? Never mind. The point is, the world should surely be run by men of wisdom and philosophy. It must be guided. We've spent centuries fighting amongst ourselves, but together . . . who knows what we could do?"

"Today the city, tomorrow the world," said someone at the back of the crowd.

Carding nodded.

"Tomorrow the world, and—" he calculated quickly—"on Friday the universe!"

That leaves the weekend free, thought Spelter. He recalled the box in his arms, and held it out toward Coin. But Carding floated in front of him, seized the box in one fluid movement and offered it to the boy with a flourish.

"The Archchancellor's hat," he said. "Rightfully yours, we think."

Coin took it. For the first time Spelter saw uncertainty cross his face.

"Isn't there some sort of formal ceremony?" he said.

Carding coughed.

"I—er, no," he said. "No, I don't think so." He

glanced up at the other senior mages, who shook their heads. "No. We've never had one. Apart from the feast, of course. Er. You see, it's not like a coronation, the Archchancellor, you see, he leads the fraternity of wizards, he's," Carding's voice ran down slowly in the light of that golden gaze, "he's you see . . . he's the . . . first . . . among . . . equals . . ."

He stepped back hurriedly as the staff moved eerily until it pointed toward him. Once again Coin seemed to be listening to an inner voice.

"No," he said eventually, and when he spoke next his voice had that wide, echoing quality that, if you are not a wizard, you can only achieve with a lot of very expensive audio equipment. "There will be a ceremony. There must be a ceremony, people must understand that wizards are ruling, but it will not be here. I will select a place. And all the wizards who have passed through these gates will attend, is that understood?"

"Some of them live far off," said Carding, carefully. "It will take them some time to travel, so when were you thinking of—"

"They are wizards!" shouted Coin. "They can be here in the twinkling of an eye! I have given them the power! Besides," his voice dropped back to something like normal pitch, "the University is finished. It was never the true home of magic, only its prison. I will build us a new place."

He lifted the new hat out of its box, and smiled at it. Spelter and Carding held their breath.

"But—"

They looked around. Hakardly the Lore master

had spoken, and now stood with his mouth opening and shutting.

Coin turned to him, one eyebrow raised.

"You surely don't mean to close the University?" said the old wizard, his voice trembling.

"It is no longer necessary," said Coin. "It's a place of dust and old books. It is behind us. Is that not so . . . brothers?"

There was a chorus of uncertain mumbling. The wizards found it hard to imagine life without the old stones of UU. Although, come to think of it, there was a lot of dust, of course, and the books were pretty old . . .

"After all . . . brothers . . . who among you has been into your dark library these past few days? The magic is inside you now, not imprisoned between covers. Is that not a joyous thing? Is there not one among you who has done more magic, *real* magic, in the past twenty-four hours than he has done in the whole of his life before? Is there one among you who does not, in his heart of hearts, truly agree with me?"

Spelter shuddered. In his heart of hearts an inner Spelter had woken, and was struggling to make himself heard. It was a Spelter who suddenly longed for those quiet days, only hours ago, when magic was gentle and shuffled around the place in old slippers and always had time for a sherry and wasn't like a hot sword in the brain and, above all, didn't kill people.

Terror seized him as he felt his vocal chords twang to attention and prepare, despite all his efforts, to disagree.

The staff was trying to find him. He could feel it searching for him. It would vanish him, just like poor old Billias. He clamped his jaws together, but it wouldn't work. He felt his chest heave. His jaw creaked.

Carding, shifting uneasily, stood on his foot. Spelter yelped.

"Sorry," said Carding.

"Is something the matter, Spelter?" said Coin.

Spelter hopped on one leg, suddenly released, his body flooding with relief as his toes flooded with agony, more grateful than anyone in the entire history of the world that seventeen stones of wizardry had chosen his instep to come down heavily on.

His scream seemed to have broken the spell. Coin sighed, and stood up.

"It has been a good day," he said.

It was two o'clock in the morning. River mists coiled like snakes through the streets of Ankh-Morpork, but they coiled alone. Wizards did not hold with other people staying up after midnight, and so no one did. They slept the troubled sleep of the enchanted, instead.

In the Plaza of Broken Moons, once the boutique of mysterious pleasures from whose flare-lit and curtain-hung stalls the late-night reveller could obtain anything from a plate of jellied eels to the venereal disease of his choice, the mists coiled and dripped into chilly emptiness.

The stalls had gone, replaced by gleaming marble and a statue depicting the spirit of something or other, surrounded by illuminated fountains. Their dull splashing was the only sound that broke the cholesterol of silence that had the heart of the city in its grip.

Silence reigned too in the dark bulk of Unseen University. Except—

Spelter crept along the shadowy corridors like a two-legged spider, darting—or at least limping quickly—from pillar to archway, until he reached the forbidding doors of the Library. He peered nervously at the darkness around him and, after some hesitation, tapped very, very lightly.

Silence poured from the heavy woodwork. But, unlike the silence that had the rest of the city under its thrall, this was a watchful, alert silence; it was the silence of a sleeping cat that had just opened one eye.

When he could bear it no longer Spelter dropped to his hands and knees and tried to peer under the doors. Finally he put his mouth as close as he could to the drafty, dusty gap under the bottommost hinge and whispered: "I say! Um. Can you hear me?"

He felt sure that something moved, far back in the darkness.

He tried again, his mood swinging between terror and hope with every erratic thump of his heart.

"I say? It's me, um, Spelter. You know? Could you speak to me, please?"

Perhaps large leathery feet were creeping gently across the floor in there, or maybe it was only the creaking of Spelter's nerves. He tried to swallow away the dryness in his throat, and had another go.

"Look, all right, but, look, they're talking about shutting the Library!"

The silence grew louder. The sleeping cat had cocked an ear.

"What is happening is all wrong!" the bursar confided, and clapped his hand over his mouth at the enormity of what he had said.

"Oook?"

It was the faintest of noises, like the eructation of cockroaches.

Suddenly emboldened, Spelter pressed his lips closer to the crack.

"Have you got the, um, Patrician in there?"

"Oook."

"What about the little doggie?"

"Oook."

"Oh. Good."

Spelter lay full length in the comfort of the night, and drummed his fingers on the chilly floor.

"You wouldn't care to, um, let me in too?" he ventured.

"Oook!"

Spelter made a face in the gloom.

"Well, would you, um, let me come in for a few minutes? We need to discuss something urgently, man to man."

"Eeek."

"I meant ape."

"Oook."

"Look, won't you come out, then?"

"Oook."

Spelter sighed. "This show of loyalty is all very well, but you'll starve in there."

"Oook oook."

"*What* other way in?"

"Oook."

"Oh, have it your way," Spelter sighed. But, somehow, he felt better for the conversation. Everyone else in the University seemed to be living in a dream, whereas the Librarian wanted nothing more in the whole world than soft fruit, a regular supply of index cards and the opportunity, every month or so, to hop over the wall of the Patrician's private menagerie.* It was strangely reassuring.

"So you're all right for bananas and so forth?" he inquired, after another pause.

"Oook."

"Don't let anyone in, will you? Um. I think that's frightfully important."

"Oook."

"Good." Spelter stood up and dusted off his knees. Then he put his mouth to the keyhole and added, "Don't trust anyone."

"Oook."

It was not completely dark in the Library, because the serried rows of magical books gave off a faint octarine glow, caused by thaumaturgical leakage into a strong occult field. It was just bright enough to illuminate the pile of shelves wedged against the door.

The former Patrician had been carefully decanted into a jar on the Librarian's desk. The Librarian himself sat under it, wrapped in his blanket and holding Wuffles on his lap.

Occasionally he would eat a banana.

---

* No one ever had the courage to ask him what he did there.

Spelter, meanwhile, limped back along the echoing passages of the University, heading for the security of his bedroom. It was because his ears were nervously straining the tiniest of sounds out of the air that he heard, right on the cusp of audibility, the sobbing.

It wasn't a normal noise up here. In the carpeted corridors of the senior wizards' quarters there were a number of sounds you might hear late at night, such as snoring, the gentle clinking of glasses, tuneless singing and, once in a while, the zip and sizzle of a spell gone wrong. But the sound of someone quietly crying was such a novelty that Spelter found himself edging down the passage that led to the Archchancellor's suite.

The door was ajar. Telling himself that he really shouldn't, tensing himself for a hurried dash, Spelter peered inside.

Rincewind stared.

"What *is* it?" he whispered.

"I think it's a temple of some sort," said Conina.

Rincewind stood and gazed upwards, the crowds of Al Khali bouncing off and around him in a kind of human Brownian motion. A temple, he thought. Well, it was big, and it was impressive, and the architect had used every trick in the book to make it look even bigger and even more impressive than it was, and to impress upon everyone looking at it that they, on the other hand, were very small and ordinary and didn't have as many domes. It was the kind of place that looked exactly as you were always going to remember it.

But Rincewind felt he knew holy architecture when he saw it, and the frescoes on the big and, of course, impressive walls above him didn't look at all religious. For one thing, the participants were enjoying themselves. Almost certainly, they were enjoying themselves. Yes, they must be. It would be pretty astonishing if they weren't.

"They're not dancing, are they?" he said, in a desperate attempt not to believe the evidence of his own eyes. "Or maybe it's some sort of acrobatics?"

Conina squinted upwards in the hard, white sunlight.

"I shouldn't think so," she said, thoughtfully.

Rincewind remembered himself. "I don't think a young woman like you should be looking at this sort of thing," he said sternly.

Conina gave him a smile. "I think wizards are expressly forbidden to," she said sweetly. "It's supposed to turn you blind."

Rincewind turned his face upwards again, prepared to risk maybe one eye. This sort of thing is only to be expected, he told himself. They don't know any better. Foreign countries are, well, foreign countries. They do things differently there.

Although some things, he decided, were done in very much the same way, only with rather more inventiveness and, by the look of it, far more often.

"The temple frescoes of Al Khali are famous far and wide," said Conina, as they walked through crowds of children who kept trying to sell Rincewind things and introduce him to nice relatives.

"Well, I can see they would be," Rincewind agreed. "Look, push off, will you? No, I don't want to buy whatever it is. No, I don't want to meet her. Or him, either. *Or* it, you nasty little boy. Get *off*, will you?"

The last scream was to the group of children riding sedately on the Luggage, which was plodding along patiently behind Rincewind and making no attempt to shake them off. Perhaps it was sickening for something, he thought, and brightened up a bit.

"How many people are there on this continent, do you think?" he said.

"I don't know," said Conina, without turning round. "Millions, I expect?"

"If I were wise, I wouldn't be here," said Rincewind, with feeling.

They had been in Al Khali, gateway to the whole mysterious continent of Klatch, for several hours. He was beginning to suffer.

A decent city should have a bit of fog about it, he considered, and people should live indoors, not spend all their time out on the streets. There shouldn't be all this sand and heat. As for the wind . . .

Ankh-Morpork had its famous smell, so full of personality that it could reduce a strong man to tears. But Al Khali had its wind, blowing from the vastness of the deserts and continents nearer the rim. It was a gentle breeze, but it didn't stop and eventually it had the same effect on visitors that a cheese-grater achieves on a tomato. After a while it seemed to have worn away your skin and was rasping directly across the nerves.

To Conina's sensitive nostrils it carried aromatic messages from the heart of the continent, compounded of the chill of deserts, the stink of lions, the compost of jungles and the flatulence of wildebeest.

Rincewind, of course, couldn't smell any of this. Adaptation is a wonderful thing, and most Morporkians would be hard put to smell a burning feather mattress at five feet.

"Where to next?" he said. "Somewhere out of the wind?"

"My father spent some time in Khali when he was hunting for the Lost City of Ee," said Conina. "And I seem to remember he spoke very highly of the *soak*. It's a kind of bazaar."

"I suppose we just go and look for the second-hand hat stalls," said Rincewind. "Because the whole idea is totally—"

"What I was hoping was that maybe we could be attacked. That seems the most sensible idea. My father said that very few strangers who entered the *soak* ever came out again. Some very murderous types hang out there, he said."

Rincewind gave this due consideration.

"Just run that by me again, will you?" he said. "After you said we should be attacked I seemed to hear a ringing in my ears."

"Well, we want to meet the criminal element, don't we?"

"Not exactly *want*," said Rincewind. "That wasn't the phrase I would have chosen."

"How would you put it, then?"

"Er. I think the phrase 'not want' sums it up pretty well."

"But you agreed that we should get the hat!"

"But not die in the process," said Rincewind, wretchedly. "That won't do anyone any good. Not me, anyway."

"My father always said that death is but a sleep," said Conina.

"Yes, the hat told me that," said Rincewind, as they turned down a narrow, crowded street between white adobe walls. "But the way I see it, it's a lot harder to get up in the morning."

"Look," said Conina, "there's not much risk. You're with me."

"Yes, and you're looking forward to it, aren't you," said Rincewind accusingly, as Conina piloted them along a shady alley, with their retinue of pubescent entrepreneurs at their heels. "It's the old herrydeterry at work."

"Just shut up and try to look like a victim, will you?"

"I can do that all right," said Rincewind, beating off a particularly stubborn member of the Junior Chamber of Commerce, "I've had a lot of practice. For the last time, I don't want to buy *anyone*, you wretched child!"

He looked gloomily at the walls around them. At least there weren't any of those disturbing pictures here, but the hot breeze still blew the dust around him and he was sick and tired of looking at sand. What he wanted was a couple of cool beers, a cold bath and a change of clothing; it probably wouldn't make him feel better, but it would at least make feeling awful more enjoyable. Not that there was any beer here, probably. It was a funny thing, but in chilly cities like Ankh-Morpork the big drink was beer, which cooled you down, but in places like this, where the whole sky was an oven with the door left open, people drank tiny little sticky drinks which set fire to the back of your throat. And the architecture was all wrong. And they had statues in their temples that, well, just weren't suitable. This wasn't the right kind of place for wizards. Of course, they had some local grown alternative, enchanters or some such, but not what you'd call *decent* magic . . .

Conina strolled ahead of him, humming to herself.

You rather like her, don't you? I can tell, said a voice in his head.

Oh blast, thought Rincewind, you're not my conscience again, are you?

Your libido. It's a bit stuffy in here, isn't it? You haven't had it done up since the last time I was around.

Look, go away, will you? I'm a wizard! Wizards are ruled by their heads, not by their hearts!

And I'm getting votes from your glands, and they're telling me that as far as your body is concerned your brain is in a minority of one.

Yes? But it's got the casting vote, then.

Hah! That's what you think. Your heart has got nothing to do with this, by the way, it's merely a muscular organ which powers the circulation of the blood. But look at it like this—you quite like her, don't you?

Well . . . Rincewind hesitated. Yes, he thought, er . . .

She's pretty good company, eh? Nice voice?

Well, of course . . .

You'd like to see more of her?

Well . . . Rincewind realized with some surprise that, yes, he would. It wasn't that he was entirely unused to the company of women, but it always seemed to cause trouble and, of course, it was a well known fact that it was bad for the magical abilities, although he had to admit that his particular magical abilities, being approximately those of a rubber hammer, were shaky enough to start with.

Then you've got nothing to lose, have you? his libido put in, in an oily tone of thought.

It was at this point Rincewind realized that something important was missing. It took him a little while to realize what it was.

No one had tried to sell him anything for several minutes. In Al Khali, that probably meant you were dead.

He, Conina and the Luggage were alone in a long, shady alley. He could hear the bustle of the city some way away, but immediately around them there was nothing except a rather expectant silence.

"They've run off," said Conina.

"Are we going to be attacked?"

"Could be. There's been three men following us on the rooftops."

Rincewind squinted upwards at almost the same time as three men, dressed in flowing black robes, dropped lightly into the alleyway in front of them. When he looked around two more appeared from around a corner. All five were holding long curved swords and, although the lower halves of their faces were masked, it was almost certain that they were grinning evilly.

Rincewind rapped sharply on the Luggage's lid.

"Kill," he suggested. The Luggage stood stock still for a moment, and then plodded over and stood next to Conina. It looked slightly smug and, Rincewind realized with jealous horror, rather embarrassed.

"Why, you—" he growled, and gave it a kick— "you *handbag*."

He sidled closer to the girl, who was standing there with a thoughtful smile on her face.

"What now?" he said. "Are you going to offer them all a quick perm?"

The men edged a little closer. They were, he noticed, only interested in Conina.

"I'm not armed," she said.

"What happened to your legendary comb?"

"Left it on the boat."

"You've got nothing?"

Conina shifted slightly to keep as many of the men as possible in her field of vision.

"I've got a couple of hairclips," she said out of the corner of her mouth.

"Any good?"

"Don't know. Never tried."

"You got us into this!"

"Relax. I think they'll just take us prisoner."

"Oh, that's fine for you to say. You're not marked down as this week's special offer."

The Luggage snapped its lid once or twice, a little uncertain about things. One of the men gingerly extended his sword and prodded Rincewind in the small of the back.

"They want to take us somewhere, see?" said Conina. She gritted her teeth. "Oh, no," she muttered.

"What's the matter now?"

"I can't do it!"

"What?"

Conina put her head in her hands. "I can't let myself be taken prisoner without a fight! I can feel a thousand barbarian ancestors accusing me of betrayal!" she hissed urgently.

"Pull the other one."

"No, really. This won't take a minute."

There was a sudden blur and the nearest man collapsed in a small gurgling heap. Then Conina's elbows went back and into the stomachs of the men behind her. Her left hand rebounded past Rincewind's ear with a noise like tearing silk and felled the man behind him. The fifth made a run for it and was brought down by a flying tackle, hitting his head heavily on the wall.

Conina rolled off him and sat up, panting, her eyes bright.

"I don't like to say this, but I feel better for that," she said. "It's terrible to know that I betrayed a fine hairdressing tradition, of course. Oh."

"Yes," said Rincewind somberly, "I wondered if you'd noticed them."

Conina's eyes scanned the line of bowmen who had appeared along the opposite wall. They had that stolid, impassive look of people who have been paid to do a job, and don't much mind if the job involves killing people.

"Time for those hairclips," said Rincewind.

Conina didn't move.

"My father always said that it was pointless to undertake a direct attack against an enemy extensively armed with efficient projectile weapons," she said.

Rincewind, who knew Cohen's normal method of speech, gave her a look of disbelief.

"Well, what he *actually* said," she added, "was never enter an arse-kicking contest with a porcupine."

Spelter couldn't face breakfast.

He wondered whether he ought to talk to Carding, but he had a chilly feeling that the old wizard wouldn't listen and wouldn't believe him anyway. In fact he wasn't quite sure he believed it himself . . .

Yes he was. He'd never forget it, although he intended to make every effort.

One of the problems about living in the University these days was that the building you went to sleep in probably wasn't the same building when you woke up. Rooms had a habit of changing and moving around, a consequence of all this random magic. It built up in the carpets, charging up the wizards to such an extent that shaking hands with somebody was a sure-fire way of turning them into something. The build up of magic, in fact, was overflowing the capacity of the area to hold it. If something wasn't done about it soon, then even the common people would be able to use it—a chilling thought but, since Spelter's mind was already so full of chilling thoughts you could use it as an ice tray, not one he was going to spend much time worrying about.

Mere household geography wasn't the only difficulty, though. Sheer pressure of thaumaturgical inflow was even affecting the food. What was a forkful of kedgeree when you lifted it off the plate might well have turned into something else by the time it entered your mouth. If you were lucky, it was inedible. If you were *unlucky*, it was edible but probably not something you liked to think you were about to eat or, worse, had already eaten half of.

Spelter found Coin in what had been, late last night, a broom cupboard. It was a lot bigger now. It was only because Spelter had never heard of aircraft hangars that he didn't know what to compare it with, although, to be fair, very few aircraft hangars have marble floors and a lot of statuary around the place. A couple of brooms and a small battered bucket in one corner looked distinctly out of place, but not as out of place as the crushed tables in the former Great Hall which, owing to the surging tides of magic now flowing through the place, had shrunk to the approximate size of what Spelter, if he had ever seen one, would have called a small telephone booth.

He sidled into the room with extreme caution and took his place among the council of wizards. The air was greasy with the feel of power.

Spelter created a chair beside Carding and leaned across to him.

"You'll never believe—" he began.

"Quiet!" hissed Carding. "This is amazing!"

Coin was sitting on his stool in the middle of the circle, one hand on his staff, the other extended and holding something small, white and egg-like. It was strangely fuzzy. In fact, Spelter thought, it wasn't something small seen close to. It was something *huge*, but a long way off. And the boy was holding it in his hand.

"What's he doing?" Spelter whispered.

"I'm not exactly sure," murmured Carding. "As far as we can understand it, he's creating a new home for wizardry."

Streamers of colored light flashed about the indistinct ovoid, like a distant thunderstorm. The glow lit Coin's preoccupied face from below, giving it the semblance of a mask.

"I don't see how we will all fit in," the bursar said. "Carding, last night I saw—"

"It is finished," said Coin. He held up the egg, which flashed occasionally from some inner light and gave off tiny white prominences. Not only was it a long way off, Spelter thought, it was also extremely heavy; it went right through heaviness and out the other side, into that strange negative realism where lead would be a vacuum. He grabbed Carding's sleeve again.

"Carding, listen, it's important, listen, when I looked in—"

"I really wish you'd stop doing that."

"But the staff, his staff, it's not—"

Coin stood up and pointed the staff at the wall, where a doorway instantly appeared. He marched out through it, leaving the wizards to follow him.

He went through the Archchancellor's garden, followed by a gaggle of wizards in the same way that a comet is followed by its tail, and didn't stop until he reached the banks of the Ankh. There were some hoary old willows here, and the river flowed, or at any rate moved, in a horseshoe bend around a small newthaunted meadow known rather optimistically as Wizards Pleasaunce. On summer evenings, if the wind was blowing toward the river, it was a nice area for an afternoon stroll.

The warm silver haze still hung over the city as Coin padded through the damp grass until he reached the center. He tossed the egg, which drifted in a gentle arc and landed with a squelch.

He turned to the wizards as they hurried up.

"Stand well back," he commanded. "And be prepared to run."

He pointed the octiron staff at the half-sunken thing. A bolt of octarine light shot from its tip and struck the egg, exploding into a shower of sparks that left blue and purple afterimages.

There was a pause. A dozen wizards watched the egg expectantly.

A breeze shook the willow trees in a totally unmysterious way.

Nothing else happened.

"Er—" Spelter began.

And then came the first tremor. A few leaves fell out of the trees and some distant water bird took off in fright.

The sound started as a low groaning, experienced rather than heard, as though everyone's feet had suddenly become their ears. The trees trembled, and so did one or two wizards.

The mud around the egg began to bubble.

And exploded.

The ground peeled back like lemon rind. Gouts of

steaming mud spattered the wizards as they dived for the cover of the trees. Only Coin, Spelter and Carding were left to watch the sparkling white building arise from the meadow, grass and dirt pouring off it. Other towers erupted from the ground behind them; buttresses *grew* through the air, linking tower with tower.

Spelter whimpered when the soil flowed away from around his feet, and was replaced by flagstones flecked with silver. He lurched as the floor rose inexorably, carrying the three high above the treetops.

The rooftops of the University went past and fell away below them. Ankh-Morpork spread out like a map, the river a trapped snake, the plains a misty blur. Spelter's ears popped, but the climb went on, into the clouds.

They emerged drenched and cold into blistering sunlight with the cloud cover spreading away in every direction. Other towers were rising around them, glinting painfully in the sharpness of the day.

Carding knelt down awkwardly and felt the floor gingerly. He signalled to Spelter to do the same.

Spelter touched a surface that was smoother than stone. It felt like ice would feel if ice was slightly warm, and looked like ivory. While it wasn't exactly transparent, it gave the impression that it would like to be.

He got the distinct feeling that, if he closed his eyes, he wouldn't be able to feel it at all.

He met Carding's gaze.

"Don't look at, um, me," he said. "I don't know what it is either."

They looked up at Coin, who said: "It's magic."

"Yes, lord, but what is it made of?" said Carding.

"It is *made* of magic. Raw magic. Solidified. Curdled. Renewed from second to second. Could you imagine a better substance to build the new home of sourcery?"

The staff flared for a moment, melting the clouds. The Discworld appeared below them, and from up here you could see that it was indeed a disc, pinned to the sky by the central mountain of Cori Celesti, where the gods lived. There was the Circle Sea, so close that it might even be possible to dive into it from here; there was the vast continent of Klatch, squashed by perspective. The Rimfall around the edge of the world was a sparkling curve.

"It's too big," said Spelter under his breath. The world he had lived in hadn't stretched much further than the gates of the University, and he'd preferred it that way. A man could be comfortable in a world that size. He certainly couldn't be comfortable about being half a mile in the air standing on something that wasn't, in some fundamental way, there.

The thought shocked him. He was a wizard, and he was worrying about magic.

He sidled cautiously back toward Carding, who said: "It isn't exactly what I expected."

"Um?"

"It looks a lot smaller up here, doesn't it."

"Well, I don't know. Listen, I must tell you—"

"Look at the Ramtops, now. You could almost reach out and touch them."

They stared out across two hundred leagues toward the towering mountain range, glittering and white and cold. It was said that if you travelled hubwards through the secret valleys of the Ramtops, you would find, in the frozen lands under Cori Celesti itself, the secret realm of the Ice Giants, imprisoned after their last great battle with the gods. In those days the mountains had been mere islands in a great sea of ice, and ice lived on them still.

Coin smiled his golden smile.

"What did you say, Carding?" he said.

"It's the clear air, lord. And they look so close and small. I only said I could almost touch them—"

Coin waved him into silence. He extended one thin arm, rolling back his sleeve in the traditional sign that magic was about to be performed without trickery. He reached out, and then turned back with his fingers closed around what was, without any shadow of a doubt, a handful of snow.

The two wizards observed it in stunned silence as it melted and dripped onto the floor.

Coin laughed.

"You find it so hard to believe?" he said. "Shall I pick pearls from rim-most Krull, or sand from the Great Nef? Could your old wizardry do half as much?"

It seemed to Spelter that his voice took on a metallic edge. He stared intently at their faces.

Finally Carding sighed and said rather quietly, "No. All my life I have sought magic, and all I found was colored lights and little tricks and old, dry books. Wizardry has done nothing for the world."

"And if I tell you that I intend to dissolve the Orders and close the University? Although, of course, my senior *advisors* will be accorded all due status."

Carding's knuckles whitened, but he shrugged.

"There is little to say," he said. "What good is a candle at noonday?"

Coin turned to Spelter. So did the staff. The filigree carvings were regarding him coldly. One of them, near the top of the staff, looked unpleasantly like an eyebrow.

"You're very quiet, Spelter. Do you not agree?"

No. The world had sourcery once, and gave it up for wizardry. Wizardry is magic for men, not gods. It's not for us. There was something wrong with it, and we have forgotten what it was. I liked wizardry. It didn't upset the world. It fitted. It was right. A wizard was all I wanted to be.

He looked down at his feet.

"Yes," he whispered.

"Good," said Coin, in a satisfied tone of voice. He strolled to the edge of the tower and looked down at the street map of Ankh-Morpork far below. The Tower of Art came barely a tenth of the way toward them.

"I believe," he said, "I believe that we will hold the ceremony next week, at full moon."

"Er. It won't be full moon for three weeks," said Carding.

"Next week," Coin repeated. "If I say the moon will be full, there will be no argument." He continued to stare down at the model buildings of the University, and then pointed.

"What's that?"

Carding craned.

"Er. The Library. Yes. It's the Library. Er."

The silence was so oppressive that Carding felt

something more was expected of him. Anything would be better than that silence.

"It's where we keep the books, you know. Ninety thousand volumes, isn't it, Spelter?"

"Um? Oh. Yes. About ninety thousand, I suppose."

Coin leaned on the staff and stared.

"Burn them," he said. "All of them."

Midnight strutted its black stuff along the corridors of Unseen University as Spelter, with rather less confidence, crept cautiously toward the impassive doors of the Library. He knocked, and the sound echoed so loudly in the empty building that he had to lean against the wall and wait for his heart to slow down a bit.

After a while he heard a sound like heavy furniture being moved about.

"Oook?"

"It's me."

"Oook?"

"Spelter."

"Oook."

"Look, you've got to get out! He's going to burn the Library!"

There was no reply.

Spelter let himself sag to his knees.

"He'll do it, too," he whispered. "He'll probably make *me* do it, it's that staff, um, it knows everything that's going on, it knows that I know about it . . . please help me . . ."

"Oook?"

"The other night, I looked into his room . . . the

staff, the staff was *glowing*, it was standing there in the middle of the room like a beacon and the boy was on the bed sobbing, I could feel it reaching out, teaching him, whispering terrible things, and then it noticed me, you've got to help me, you're the only one who isn't under the—"

Spelter stopped. His face froze. He turned around very slowly, without willing it, because something was gently spinning him.

He knew the University was empty. The wizards had all moved into the New Tower, where the lowliest student had a suite more splendid than any senior mage had before.

The staff hung in the air a few feet away. It was surrounded by a faint octarine glow.

He stood up very carefully and, keeping his back to the stonework and his eyes firmly fixed on the thing, slithered gingerly along the wall until he reached the end of the corridor. At the corner he noted that the staff, while not moving had revolved on its axis to follow him.

He gave a little cry, grasped the skirts of his robe, and ran.

The staff was in front of him. He slid to a halt and stood there, catching his breath.

"You don't frighten me," he lied, and turned on his heel and marched off in a different direction, snapping his fingers to produce a torch that burned with a fine white flame (only its penumbra of octarine proclaimed it to be of magical origin).

Once again, the staff was in front of him. The light of his torch was sucked into a thin, singing steam of white fire that flared and vanished with a "pop."

He waited, his eyes watering with blue after-images, but if the staff was still there it didn't seem to be inclined to take advantage of him. When vision returned he felt he could make out an even darker shadow on his left. The stairway down to the kitchens.

He darted for it, leaping down the unseen steps and landing heavily and unexpectedly on uneven flags. A little moonlight filtered through a grating in the distance and somewhere up there, he knew, was a doorway into the outside world.

Staggering a little, his ankles aching, the noise of his own breath booming in his ears as though he'd stuck his entire head in a seashell, Spelter set off across the endless dark desert of the floor.

Things clanked underfoot. There were no rats here now, of course, but the kitchen had fallen into disuse lately—the University's cooks had been the best in the world, but now any wizard could conjure up meals beyond mere culinary skill. The big copper pans hung neglected on the wall, their sheen already tarnishing, and the kitchen ranges under the giant chimney arch were filled with nothing but chilly ash . . .

The staff lay across the back door like a bar. It spun up as Spelter tottered toward it and hung, radiating quiet malevolence, a few feet away. Then, quite smoothly, it began to glide toward him.

He backed away, his feet slipping on the greasy stones. A thump across the back of his thighs made him yelp, but as he reached behind him he found it was only one of the chopping blocks.

His hand groped desperately across its scarred surface and, against all hope, found a cleaver buried in the wood. In an instinctive gesture as ancient as mankind, Spelter's fingers closed around its handle.

He was out of breath and out of patience and out of space and time and also scared, very nearly, out of his mind.

So when the staff hovered in front of him he wrenched the chopper up and around with all the strength he could muster. . . .

And hesitated. All that was wizardly in him cried out against the destruction of so much power, power that perhaps even now could be used, used by him . . .

And the staff swung around so that its axis was pointing directly at him.

And several corridors away, the Librarian stood braced with his back against the Library door, watching the blue and white flashes that flickered across the floor. He heard the distant snap of raw energy, and a sound that started low and ended up in zones of pitch that even Wuffles, lying with his paws over his head, could not hear.

And then there was a faint, ordinary tinkling noise, such as might be made by a fused and twisted metal cleaver dropping onto flagstones.

It was the sort of noise that makes the silence that comes after it roll forward like a warm avalanche.

The Librarian wrapped the silence around him like a cloak and stood staring up at the rank on rank of books, each one pulsing faintly in the glow of its own magic. Shelf after shelf looked down* at him. They had heard. He could feel the fear.

The orangutan stood statue-still for several minutes, and then appeared to reach a decision. He knuckled his way across to his desk and, after much rummaging, produced a heavy key-ring bristling with keys. Then he went back and stood in the middle of the floor and said, very deliberately, "Oook."

The books craned forward on their shelves. Now he had their full attention.

"What is this place?" said Conina.

Rincewind looked around him, and made a guess.

They were still in the heart of Al Khali. He could hear the hum of it beyond the walls. But in the middle of the teeming city someone had cleared a vast space, walled it off, and planted a garden so romantically natural that it looked as real as a sugar pig.

"It looks like someone has taken twice five miles of inner city, and girdled them around with walls and towers," he hazarded.

"What a strange idea," said Conina.

"Well, some of the religions here—well, when you die, you see, they think you go to this sort of garden, where there's all this sort of music and, and," he continued, wretchedly, "sherbet and, and— young women."

---

* Or up, or obliquely. The layout of the Library of Unseen University was a topographical nightmare, the sheer presence of so much stored magic twisting dimensions and gravity into the kind of spaghetti that would make M. C. Escher go for a good lie down, or possibly sideways.

Conina took in the green splendor of the walled garden, with its peacocks, intricate arches and slightly wheezy fountains. A dozen reclining women stared back at her, impassively. A hidden string orchestra was playing the complicated Klatchian *bhong* music.

"I'm not dead," she said. "I'm sure I would have remembered. Besides, this isn't *my* idea of paradise." She looked critically at the reclining figures, and added, "I wonder who does their hair?"

A sword point prodded her in the small of the back, and the two of them set out along the ornate path toward a small domed pavilion surrounded by olive trees. She scowled.

"Anyway, I don't like sherbet."

Rincewind didn't comment. He was busily examining the state of his own mind, and wasn't happy at the sight of it. He had a horrible feeling that he was falling in love.

He was sure he had all the symptoms. There were the sweaty palms, the hot sensation in the stomach, the general feeling that the skin of his chest was made of tight elastic. There was the feeling every time Conina spoke, that someone was running hot steel into his spine.

He glanced down at the Luggage, tramping stoically alongside him, and recognized the symptoms.

"Not you, too?" he said.

Possibly it was only the play of sunlight on the Luggage's battered lid, but it was just possible that for an instant it looked redder than usual.

Of course, sapient pearwood has this sort of weird mental link with its owner . . . Rincewind shook his head. Still, it'd explain why the thing wasn't its normal malignant self.

"It'd never work," he said. "I mean, she's a female and you're a, well, you're a—" He paused. "Well, whatever you are, you're of the wooden persuasion. It'd never work. People would talk."

He turned and glared at the black-robed guards behind him.

"I don't know what you're looking at," he said severely.

The Luggage sidled over to Conina, following her so closely that she banged an ankle on it.

"Push off," she snapped, and kicked it again, this time on purpose.

Insofar as the Luggage ever had an expression, it looked at her in shocked betrayal.

The pavilion ahead of them was an ornate onion-shaped dome, studded with precious stones and supported on four pillars. Its interior was a mass of cushions on which lay a rather fat, middle-aged man surrounded by three young women. He wore a purple robe interwoven with gold thread; they, as far as Rincewind could see, demonstrated that you could make six small saucepan lids and a few yards of curtain netting go a long way although—he shivered— not really far enough.

The man appeared to be writing. He glanced up at them.

"I suppose you don't know a good rhyme for 'thou'?" he said peevishly.

Rincewind and Conina exchanged glances.

"Plough?" said Rincewind. "Bough?"

"Cow?" suggested Conina, with forced brightness.

The man hesitated. "Cow I quite like," he said, "Cow has got possibilities. Cow might, in fact, do. Do pull up a cushion, by the way. Have some sherbet. Why are you standing there like that?"

"It's these ropes," said Conina.

"I have this allergy to cold steel," Rincewind added.

"Really, how tiresome," said the fat man, and clapped a pair of hands so heavy with rings that the sound was more of a clang. Two guards stepped forward smartly and cut the bonds, and then the whole battalion melted away, although Rincewind was acutely conscious of dozens of dark eyes watching them from the surrounding foliage. Animal instinct told him that, while he now appeared to be alone with the man and Conina, any aggressive moves on his part would suddenly make the world a sharp and painful place. He tried to radiate tranquillity and total friendliness. He tried to think of something to say.

"Well," he ventured, looking around at the brocaded hangings, the ruby-studded pillars and the gold filigree cushions, "you've done this place up nicely. It's—" he sought for something suitably descriptive—"well, pretty much of a miracle of rare device."

"One aims for simplicity," sighed the man, still scribbling busily. "Why are you here? Not that it isn't always a pleasure to meet fellow students of the poetic muse."

"We were brought here," said Conina.

"Men with swords," added Rincewind.

"Dear fellows, they do so like to keep in practice. Would you like one of these?"

He snapped his fingers at one of the girls.

"Not, er, right now," Rincewind began, but she'd picked up a plate of golden-brown sticks and demurely passed it toward him. He tried one. It was delicious, a sort of sweet crunchy flavor with a hint of honey. He took two more.

"Excuse me," said Conina, "but who are you? And where is this?"

"My name is Creosote, Seriph of Al Khali," said the fat man, "and this is my Wilderness. One does one's best."

Rincewind coughed on his honey stick.

"Not Creosote as in 'As rich as Creosote'?" he said.

"That was my dear father. I am, in fact, rather richer. When one has a great deal of money, I am afraid, it is hard to achieve simplicity. One does one's best." He sighed.

"You could try giving it away," said Conina.

He sighed again. "That isn't easy, you know. No, one just has to try to do a little with a lot."

"No, no, but look," said Rincewind spluttering bits of stick, "they say, I mean, everything you touch turns into *gold*, for goodness sake."

"That could make going to the lavatory a bit tricky," said Conina brightly. "Sorry."

"One hears such stories about oneself," said Creosote, affecting not to have heard. "So tiresome. As if wealth mattered. True riches lie in the treasure houses of literature."

"The Creosote *I* heard of," said Conina slowly,

"was head of this band of, well, mad killers. The original Assassins, feared throughout hubward Klatch. No offense meant."

"Ah yes, dear father," said Creosote junior. "The *hashishim*. Such a novel ideal.* But not really very efficient. So we hired Thugs instead."

"Ah. Named after a religious sect," said Conina knowingly.

Creosote gave her a long look. "No," he said slowly, "I don't think so. I think we named them after the way they push people's faces through the back of their heads. Dreadful, really."

He picked up the parchment he had been writing on, and continued, "I seek a more cerebral life, which is why I had the city center converted into a Wilderness. So much better for the mental flow. One does one's best. May I read you my latest oeuvre?"

"Egg?" said Rincewind, who wasn't following this.

Creosote thrust out one pudgy hand and declaimed as follows:

> *"A summer palace underneath the bough,*
> *A flask of wine, a loaf of bread, some lamb couscous*
> *with courgettes, roast peacock tongues, kebabs, iced*
> *sherbet, selection of sweets from the trolley and*
> *choice of Thou,*
> *Singing beside me in the Wilderness,*
> *And Wilderness is—"*

---

* The Hashishim, who derived their name from the vast quantities of *hashish* they consumed, were unique among vicious killers in being both deadly and, at the same time, inclined to giggle, groove to interesting patterns of light and shade on their terrible knife blades and, in extreme cases, fall over.

He paused, and picked up his pen thoughtfully.

"Maybe cow isn't such a good idea," he said. "Now that I come to look at it—"

Rincewind glanced at the manicured greenery, carefully arranged rocks and high surrounding walls. One of the Thous winked at him.

"This is a Wilderness?" he said.

"My landscape gardeners incorporated all the essential features, I believe. They spent simply ages getting the rills sufficiently sinuous. I am reliably informed that they contain prospects of rugged grandeur and astonishing natural beauty."

"And scorpions," said Rincewind, helping himself to another honey stick.

"I don't know about that," said the poet. "Scorpions sound *unpoetic* to me. Wild honey and locusts seem more appropriate, according to the standard poetic instructions, although I've never really developed the taste for insects."

"I always understood that the kind of locust people ate in wildernesses was the fruit of a kind of tree," said Conina. "Father always said it was quite tasty."

"Not insects?" said Creosote.

"I don't think so."

The Seriph nodded at Rincewind. "You might as well finish them up, then," he said. "Nasty crunchy things, I couldn't see the point."

"I don't wish to sound ungrateful," said Conina, over the sound of Rincewind's frantic coughing. "But why did you have us brought here?"

"Good question." Creosote looked at her blankly for a few seconds, as if trying to remember why they were there.

"You really are a most attractive young woman," he said. "You can't play a dulcimer, by any chance?"

"How many blades has it got?" said Conina.

"Pity," said the Seriph, "I had one specially imported."

"My father taught me to play the harmonica," she volunteered.

Creosote's lips moved soundlessly as he tried out the idea.

"No good," he said. "Doesn't scan. Thanks all the same, though." He gave her another thoughtful look. "You know, you really are most becoming. Has anyone ever told you your neck is as a tower of ivory?"

"Never," said Conina.

"Pity," said Creosote again. He rummaged among his cushions and produced a small bell, which he rang.

After a while a tall, saturnine figure appeared from behind the pavilion. He had the look of someone who could think his way through a corkscrew without bending, and a certain something about the eyes which would have made the average rabid rodent tiptoe away, discouraged.

That man, you would have said, has got Grand Vizier written all over him. No one can tell him anything about defrauding widows and imprisoning impressionable young men in alleged jewel caves. When it comes to dirty work he probably wrote the book or, more probably, stole it from someone else.

He wore a turban with a pointy hat sticking out of it. He had a long thin mustache, of course.

"Ah, Abrim," said Creosote.

"Highness?"

"My Grand Vizier," said the Seriph.

—thought so—, said Rincewind to himself.

"These people, why did we have them brought here?"

The vizier twirled his mustache, probably foreclosing another dozen mortgages.

"The hat, highness," he said. "The hat, if you remember."

"Ah, yes. Fascinating. Where did we put it?"

"Hold on," said Rincewind urgently. "This hat . . . it wouldn't be a sort of battered pointy one, with lots of stuff on it? Sort of lace and stuff, and, and—" he hesitated—"no one's tried to put it on, have they?"

"It specifically warned us not to," said Creosote, "so Abrim got a slave to try it on, of course. He said it gave him a headache."

"It also told us that you would shortly be arriving," said the vizier, bowing slightly at Rincewind, "and therefore I—that is to say, the Seriph felt that you might be able to tell us more about this wonderful artifact?"

There is a tone of voice known as interrogative, and the vizier was using it; a slight edge to his words suggested that, if he didn't learn more about the hat very quickly, he had various activities in mind in which further words like "red hot" and "knives" would appear. Of course, all Grand Viziers talk like that all the time. There's probably a school somewhere.

"Gosh, I'm glad you've found it," said Rincewind, "That hat is gngngnh—"

"I beg your pardon?" said Abrim, signalling a

couple of lurking guards to step forward. "I missed the bit after the young lady—" he bowed at Conina—"elbowed you in the ear."

"I think," said Conina, politely but firmly, "you better take us to see it."

Five minutes later, from its resting place on a table in the Seriph's treasury, the hat said, *At last. What kept you?*

It is at a time like this, with Rincewind and Conina probably about to be the victims of a murderous attack, and Coin about to address the assembled cowering wizards on the subject of treachery, and the Disc about to fall under a magical dictatorship, that it is worth mentioning the subject of poetry and inspiration.

For example, the Seriph, in his bijou wildernessette, has just riffled back through his pages of verse to revise the lines which begin:

> *"Get up! For morning in the cup of day,*
> *Has dropped the spoon that scares the stars away."*

—and he has sighed, because the white-hot lines searing across his imagination never seem to come out exactly as he wants them.

It is, in fact, impossible that they ever will.

Sadly, this sort of thing happens all the time.

It is a well-known established fact throughout the many-dimensional worlds of the multiverse that most really great discoveries are owed to one brief moment of inspiration. There's a lot of spadework first, of course, but what clinches the whole thing is the sight of, say, a falling apple or a boiling kettle or the water slopping over the edge of the bath. Something goes click inside the observer's head and then everything falls into place. The shape of DNA, it is popularly said, owes its discovery to the chance sight of a spiral staircase when the scientist's mind was just at the right receptive temperature. Had he used the elevator, the whole science of genetics might have been a good deal different.*

This is thought of as somehow wonderful. It isn't. It is tragic. Little particles of inspiration sleet through the universe all the time traveling through the densest matter in the same way that a neutrino passes through a candyfloss haystack, and most of them miss.

Even worse, most of the ones that hit the exact cerebral target hit the *wrong* one.

For example, the weird dream about a lead doughnut on a mile-high gantry, which in the right mind would have been the catalyst for the invention of repressed-gravitational electricity generation (a cheap and inexhaustible and totally non-polluting form of power which the world in question had been seeking for centuries, and for the lack of which it was plunged into a terrible and pointless war) was in fact had by a small and bewildered duck.

By another stroke of bad luck, the sight of a herd of white horses galloping through a field of wild hyacinths would have led a struggling composer to write the famous *Flying God Suite*, bringing succour

---

* Although, possibly, quicker. And only licensed to carry fourteen people.

and balm to the souls of millions, had he not been at home in bed with shingles. The inspiration therefore fell to a nearby frog, who was not in much of a position to make a startling contribution to the field of tone poetry.

Many civilizations have recognized this shocking waste and tried various methods to prevent it, most of them involving enjoyable but illegal attempts to tune the mind into the right wavelength by the use of exotic herbage or yeast products. It never works properly.

And so Creosote, who had dreamt the inspiration for a rather fine poem about life and philosophy and how they both look much better through the bottom of a wine glass, was totally unable to do anything about it because he had as much poetic ability as a hyena.

Why the gods allow this sort of thing to continue is a mystery.

Actually, the flash of inspiration needed to explain it clearly and precisely has taken place, but the creature who received it—a small female bluetit—has never been able to make the position clear, even after some really strenuous coded messages on the tops of milk bottles. By a strange coincidence, a philosopher who had been devoting some sleepless nights to the same mystery woke up that morning with a wonderful new idea for getting peanuts out of bird tables.

Which brings us rather neatly onto the subject of magic.

A long way out in the dark gulfs of interstellar space, one single inspiration particle is clipping along unaware of its destiny, which is just as well, because its destiny is to strike, in a matter of hours, a tiny area of Rincewind's mind.

It would be a tough destiny even if Rincewind's creative node was a reasonable size, but the particle's karma had handed it the problem of hitting a moving target the size of a small raisin over a distance of several hundred lightyears. Life can be very difficult for a little subatomic particle in a great big universe.

If it pulls it off, however, Rincewind will have a serious philosophic idea. If it doesn't, a nearby brick will have an important insight which it will be totally unequipped to deal with.

The Seriph's palace, known to legend as the Rhoxie, occupied most of the center of Al Khali that wasn't occupied by the wilderness. Most things connected with Creosote were famed in mythology and the arched, domed, many-pillared palace was said to have more rooms than any man had been able to count. Rincewind didn't know which number he was in.

"It's magic, isn't it?" said Abrim the vizier.

He prodded Rincewind in the ribs.

"You're a wizard," he said. "Tell me what it does."

"How do you know I'm a wizard?" said Rincewind desperately.

"It's written on your hat," said the vizier.

"Ah."

"And you were on the boat with it. My men saw you."

"The Seriph employs slavers?" snapped Conina. "That doesn't sound very *simple*!"

"Oh, I employ the slavers. I am the vizier, after all," said Abrim. "It is rather expected of me."

He gazed thoughtfully at the girl, and then nodded at a couple of the guards.

"The current Seriph is rather *literary* in his views," he said. "I, on the other hand, am not. Take her to the seraglio, although," he rolled his eyes and gave an irritable sigh, "I'm sure the only fate that awaits her there is boredom, and possibly a sore throat."

He turned to Rincewind.

"Don't say anything," he said. "Don't move your hands. Don't try any sudden feats of magic. I am protected by strange and powerful amulets."

"Now just hold on a minute—" Rincewind began, and Conina said, "All right. I've always wondered what a harem looked like."

Rincewind's mouth went on opening and shutting, but no sounds came out. Finally he managed, "Have you?"

She waggled an eyebrow at him. It was probably a signal of some sort. Rincewind felt he ought to have understood it, but peculiar passions were stirring in the depths of his being. They weren't actually going to make him brave, but they were making him angry. Speeded up, the dialogue behind his eyes was going something like this:

Ugh.

Who's that?

Your conscience. I feel terrible. Look, they're marching her off to the harem.

Rather her than me, thought Rincewind, but without much conviction.

Do something!

There's too many guards! They'll kill me!

So they'll kill you, it's not the end of the world.

It will be for me, thought Rincewind grimly.

But just think how good you'll feel in your next life—

Look, just shut up, will I? I've had just about enough of me.

Abrim stepped across to Rincewind and looked at him curiously.

"Who are you talking to?" he said.

"I warn you," said Rincewind, between clenched teeth, "I have this magical box on legs which is absolutely merciless with attackers, one word from me and—"

"I'm impressed," said Abrim. "Is it invisible?"

Rincewind risked a look behind him.

"I'm sure I had it when I came in," he said, and sagged.

It would be mistaken to say the Luggage was nowhere to be seen. It was somewhere to be seen, it was just that the place wasn't anywhere near Rincewind.

Abrim walked slowly around the table on which sat the hat, twirling his mustache.

"Once again," he said, "I ask you: this is an artifact of power, I feel it, and you must tell me what it does."

"Why don't you ask it?" said Rincewind.

"It refuses to tell me."

"Well, why do you want to know?"

Abrim laughed. It wasn't a nice sound. It sounded

as though he had had laughter explained to him, probably slowly and repeatedly, but had never heard anyone actually do it.

"You're a wizard," he said. "Wizardry is about power. I have taken an interest in magic myself. I have the talent, you know." The vizier drew himself up stiffly. "Oh, yes. But they wouldn't accept me at your University. They said I was mentally unstable, can you believe that?"

"No," said Rincewind, truthfully. Most of the wizards at Unseen had always seemed to him to be several bricks short of a shilling. Abrim seemed pretty normal wizard material.

Abrim gave him an encouraging smile.

Rincewind looked sideways at the hat. It said nothing. He looked back at the vizier. If the laughter had been weird, the smile made it sound as normal as birdsong. It looked as though the vizier had learned it from diagrams.

"Wild horses wouldn't get me to help you in any way," he said.

"Ah," said the vizier. "A challenge." He beckoned to the nearest guard.

"Do we have any wild horses in the stables?"

"Some fairly angry ones, master."

"Infuriate four of them and take them to the turnwise courtyard. And, oh, bring several lengths of chain."

"Right away, master."

"Um. Look," said Rincewind.

"Yes?" said Abrim.

"Well, if you put it like that . . ."

"You wish to make a point?"

"It's the Archchancellor's hat, if you must know," said Rincewind. "The symbol of wizardry."

"Powerful?"

Rincewind shivered. "Very," he said.

"Why is it called the Archchancellor's hat?"

"The Archchancellor is the most senior wizard, you see. The leader. But, look—"

Abrim picked up the hat and turned it around and around in his hands.

"It is, you might say, the symbol of office?"

"Absolutely, but look, if you put it on, I'd better warn you—"

Shut up.

Abrim leapt back, the hat dropping to the floor.

The wizard knows nothing. Send him away. We must negotiate.

The vizier stared down at the glittering octarines around the hat.

"I *negotiate?* With an item of apparel?"

I have much to offer, on the right head.

Rincewind was appalled. It has already been indicated that he had the kind of instinct for danger usually found only in certain small rodents, and it was currently battering on the side of his skull in an attempt to run away and hide somewhere.

"Don't listen!" he shouted.

Put me on, said the hat beguilingly, in an ancient voice that sounded as though the speaker had a mouthful of felt.

If there really was a school for viziers, Abrim had come top of the class.

"We'll talk first," he said. He nodded at the guards, and pointed to Rincewind.

"Take him away and throw him in the spider tank," he said.

"No, not spiders, on top of everything else!" moaned Rincewind.

The captain of the guard stepped forward and knuckled his forehead respectfully.

"Run out of spiders, master," he said.

"Oh." The vizier looked momentarily blank. "In that case, lock him in the tiger cage."

The guard hesitated, trying to ignore the sudden outburst of whimpering beside him. "The tiger's been ill, master. Backward and forward all night."

"Then throw this snivelling coward down the shaft of eternal fire!"

A couple of the guards exchanged glances over the head of Rincewind, who had sunk to his knees.

"Ah. We'll need a bit of notice of that, master—"

"—to get it going again, like."

The vizier's fist came down hard on the table. The captain of the guard brightened up horribly.

"There's the snake pit, master," he said. The other guards nodded. There was always the snake pit.

Four heads turned toward Rincewind, who stood up and brushed the sand off his knees.

"How do you feel about snakes?" said one of the guards.

"Snakes? I don't like snakes much—"

"The snake pit," said Abrim.

"Right. The snake pit," agreed the guards.

"—I mean, *some* snakes are okay—" Rincewind continued, as two guards grabbed him by the elbows.

In fact there was only one very cautious snake,

which remained obstinately curled up in a corner of the shadowy pit watching Rincewind suspiciously, possibly because he reminded it of a mongoose.

"Hi," it said eventually. "Are you a wizard?"

As a line of snake dialogue this was a considerable improvement on the normal string of esses, but Rincewind was sufficiently despondent not to waste time wondering and simply replied, "It's on my hat, can't you read?"

"In seventeen languages, actually. I taught myself."

"Really?"

"I sent off for courses. But I try not to read, of course. It's not in character."

"I suppose it wouldn't be." It was certainly the most cultured snake voice that Rincewind had ever heard.

"It's the same with the voice, I'm afraid," the snake added. "I shouldn't really be talking to you now. Not like this, anyway. I suppose I could grunt a bit. I rather think I should be trying to kill you, in fact."

"I have curious and unusual powers," said Rincewind. Fair enough, he thought, an almost total inability to master any form of magic is pretty unusual for a wizard and anyway, it doesn't matter about lying to a snake.

"Gosh. Well, I expect you won't be in here long, then."

"Hmm?"

"I expect you'll be levitating out of here like a shot, any minute."

Rincewind looked up at the fifteen-foot-deep walls of the snake pit, and rubbed his bruises.

"I might," he said cautiously.

"In that case, you wouldn't mind taking me with you, would you?"

"Eh?"

"It's a lot to ask, I know, but this pit is, well, it's the pits."

"Take you? But you're a snake, it's *your* pit. The idea is that you stay here and people come to you. I mean, I know about these things."

A shadow behind the snake unfolded itself and stood up.

"That's a pretty unpleasant thing to say about anyone," it said.

The figure stepped forward, into the pool of light.

It was a young man, taller than Rincewind. That is to say, Rincewind was sitting down, but the boy would have been taller than him even if he was standing up.

To say that he was lean would be to miss a perfect opportunity to use the word "emaciated." He looked as though toast racks and deckchairs had figured in his ancestry, and the reason it was so obvious was his clothes.

Rincewind looked again.

He had been right the first time.

The lank-haired figure in front of him was wearing the practically traditional garb for barbarian heroes—a few studded leather thongs, big furry boots, a little leather holdall and goosepimples. There was nothing unusual about that, you'd see a score of similarly-dressed adventurers in any street of Ankh-Morpork, except that you'd never see another one wearing—

The young man followed his gaze, looked down, and shrugged.

"I can't help it," he said. "I promised my mother."

"Woolly underwear?"

Strange things were happening in Al Khali that night. There was a certain silveriness rolling in from the sea, which baffled the city's astronomers, but that wasn't the strangest thing. There were little flashes of raw magic discharging off sharp edges, like static electricity, but that wasn't the strangest thing.

The strangest thing walked into a tavern on the edge of the city, where the everlasting wind blew the smell of the desert through every unglazed window, and sat down in the middle of the floor.

The occupants watched it for some time, sipping their coffee laced with desert *orakh*. This drink, made from cacti sap and scorpion venom, is one of the most virulent alcoholic beverages in the universe, but the desert nomads don't drink it for its intoxicating effects. They use it because they need something to mitigate the effect of Klatchian coffee.

Not because you could use the coffee to waterproof roofs. Not because it went through the untrained stomach lining like a hot ball bearing through runny butter. What it did was worse.

It made you knurd.*

---

* In a truly magical universe everything has its opposite. For example, there's anti-light. That's not the same as darkness, because darkness is merely the absence of light. Anti-light is what you get if you pass through darkness and *out the other side*. On the same basis, a state of knurdness isn't like sobriety. By comparison, sobriety is like having a bath in cotton wool. Knurdness strips away all illlusion, all the comforting pink fog in which people normally spend their lives, and lets them see and think clearly for the first time ever. Then, after they've screamed a bit, they make sure they never get knurd again.

The sons of the desert glanced suspiciously into their thimble-sized coffee-cups, and wondered whether they had overdone the orakh. Were they all seeing the same thing? Would it be foolish to pass a remark? These are the sort of things you need to worry about if you want to retain any credibility as a steely-eyed son of the deep desert. Pointing a shaking finger and saying, "Hey, look, a box just walked in here on hundreds of little legs, isn't that extraordinary!" would show a terrible and possibly fatal lack of machismo.

The drinkers tried not to catch one another's eye, even when the Luggage slid up to the row of orakh jars against the far wall. The Luggage had a way of standing still that was somehow even more terrible than watching it move about.

Finally one of them said, "I think it wants a drink."

There was a long silence, and then one of the others said, with the precision of a chess Grand Master making a killing move, "What does?"

The rest of the drinkers gazed impassively into their glasses.

There was no sound for a while other than the plopplopping of a gecko's footsteps across the sweating ceiling.

The first drinker said, "The demon that's just moved up behind you is what I was referring to, O brother of the sands."

The current holder of the All-Wadi Imperturbability Championship smiled glassily until he felt a tugging on his robe. The smile stayed where it was but the rest of his face didn't seem to want to be associated with it.

The Luggage was feeling crossed in love and was doing what any sensible person would do in these circumstances, which was get drunk. It had no money and no way of asking for what it wanted, but the Luggage somehow never had much difficulty in making itself understood.

The tavern keeper spent a very long lonely night filling a saucer with orakh, before the Luggage rather unsteadily walked out through one of the walls.

The desert was silent. It wasn't normally silent. It was normally alive with the chirruping of crickets, the buzz of mosquitoes, the hiss and whisper of hunting wings skimming across the cooling sands. But tonight it was silent with the thick, busy silence of dozens of nomads folding their tents and getting the hell out of it.

"I promised my mother," said the boy. "I get these colds, you see."

"Perhaps you should try wearing, well, a bit more clothing?"

"Oh, I couldn't do that. You've got to wear all this leather stuff."

"I wouldn't call it *all*," said Rincewind. "There's not enough of it to call it *all*. Why have you got to wear it?"

"So people know I'm a barbarian hero, of course."

Rincewind leaned his back against the fetid walls of the snake pit and stared at the boy. He looked at two eyes like boiled grapes, a shock of ginger hair, and a face that was a battleground between its native freckles and the dreadful invading forces of acne.

Rincewind rather enjoyed times like this. They convinced him that he wasn't mad because, if he *was* mad, that left no word at all to describe some of the people he met.

"Barbarian hero," he murmured.

"It's all right, isn't it? All this leather stuff was very expensive."

"Yes, but, look—what's your name, lad?"

"Nijel—"

"You see, Nijel—"

"Nijel the Destroyer," Nijel added.

"You see, Nijel—"

"—the Destroyer—"

"All right, the Destroyer—" said Rincewind desperately.

"—son of Harebut the Provision Merchant—"

"What?"

"You've got to be the son of someone," Nijel explained. "It says it here somewhere—" He half-turned and fumbled inside a grubby fur bag, eventually bringing out a thin, torn and grubby book.

"There's a bit in here about selecting your name," he muttered.

"How come you ended up in this pit, then?"

"I was intending to steal from Creosote's treasury, but I had an asthma attack," said Nijel, still fumbling through the crackling pages.

Rincewind looked down at the snake, which was still trying to keep out of everyone's way. It had a good thing going in the pit, and knew trouble when it saw it. It wasn't about to cause any irritation for anyone. It stared right back up at Rincewind and shrugged, which is pretty clever for a reptile with no shoulders.

"How long have you been a barbarian hero?"

"I'm just getting started. I've always wanted to be one, you see, and I thought maybe I could pick it up as I went along." Nijel peered short-sightedly at Rincewind. "That's all right, isn't it?"

"It's a desperate sort of life, by all accounts," Rincewind volunteered.

"Have you thought what it might be like selling groceries for the next fifty years?" Nijel muttered darkly.

Rincewind thought.

"Is lettuce involved?" he said.

"Oh yes," said Nijel, shoving the mysterious book back in his bag. Then he started to pay close attention to the pit walls.

Rincewind sighed. He liked lettuce. It was so incredibly boring. He had spent years in search of boredom, but had never achieved it. Just when he thought he had it in his grasp his life would suddenly become full of near-terminal interest. The thought that someone could voluntarily give up the prospect of being bored for fifty years made him feel quite weak. With fifty years ahead of him, he thought, he could elevate tedium to the status of an art form. There would be no end to the things he wouldn't do.

"Do you know any lamp wick jokes?" he said, settling himself comfortably on the sand.

"I don't think so," said Nijel politely, tapping a slab.

"I know hundreds. They are very droll. For example, do you know how many trolls it takes to change a lamp wick?"

"This slab moves," said Nijel. "Look, it's a sort of door. Give me a hand."

He pushed enthusiastically, his biceps standing out on his arms like peas on a pencil.

"I expect it's some sort of secret passage," he added. "Come on, use a bit of magic, will you? It's stuck."

"Don't you want to hear the rest of the joke?" said Rincewind, in a pained voice. It was warm and dry down here, with no immediate danger, not counting the snake, which was trying to look inconspicuous. Some people were never satisfied.

"I think not right at the moment," said Nijel. "I think I would prefer a bit of magical assistance."

"I'm not very good at it," said Rincewind. "Never got the hang of it, see, it's more than just pointing a finger at it and saying 'Kazam—'"

There was a sound like a thick bolt of octarine lightning zapping into a heavy rock slab and smashing it into a thousand bits of spitting, white-hot shrapnel, and no wonder.

After a while Nijel slowly got to his feet, beating out the small fires in his vest.

"Yes," he said, in the voice of one determined not to lose his self-control. "Well. Very good. We'll just let it cool down a bit, shall we? And then we, then we, we might as well be going."

He cleared his throat a bit.

"Nnh," said Rincewind. He was starting fixedly at the end of his finger, holding it out at arm's length in a manner that suggested he was very sorry he hadn't got longer arms.

Nijel peered into the smouldering hole.

"It seems to open into some kind of room," he said.

"Nnh."

"After you," said Nijel. He gave Rincewind a gentle push.

The wizard staggered forward, bumped his head on the rock and didn't appear to notice, and then rebounded into the hole.

Nijel patted the wall, and his brow wrinkled. "Can you feel something?" he said. "Should the stone be trembling?"

"Nnh."

"Are you all right?"

"Nnh."

Nijel put his ear to the stones. "There's a very strange noise," he said. "A sort of humming." A bit of dust shook itself free from the mortar over his head and floated down.

Then a couple of much heavier rocks danced free from the walls of the pits and thudded into the sand.

Rincewind had already staggered off down the tunnel, making little shocked noises and completely ignoring the stones that were missing him by inches and, in some cases, hitting him by kilograms.

If he had been in any state to notice it, he would have known what was happening. The air had a greasy feel and smelled like burning tin. Faint rainbows filmed every point and edge. A magical charge was building up somewhere very close to them, and it was a big one, and it was trying to earth itself.

A handy wizard, even one as incapable as Rincewind, stood out like a copper lighthouse.

Nijel blundered out of the rumbling, broiling dust and bumped into him standing, surrounded by an octarine corona, in another cave.

Rincewind looked terrible. Creosote would have probably noted his flashing eyes and floating hair.

He looked like someone who had just eaten a handful of pineal glands and washed them down with a pint of adrenochrome. He looked so high you could bounce intercontinental TV off him.

Every single hair stood out from his head, giving off little sparks. Even his skin gave the impression that it was trying to get away from him. His eyes appeared to be spinning horizontally; when he opened his mouth, peppermint sparks flashed from his teeth. Where he had trodden, stone melted or grew ears or turned into something small and scaly and purple and flew away.

"I say," said Nijel, "are you all right?"

"Nnh," said Rincewind, and the syllable turned into a large doughnut.

"You don't *look* all right," said Nijel with what might be called, in the circumstances, unusual perspicacity.

"Nnh."

"Why not try getting us out of here?" Nijel added, and wisely flung himself flat on the floor.

Rincewind nodded like a puppet and pointed his

loaded digit at the ceiling, which melted like ice under a blowlamp.

Still the rumbling went on, sending its disquieting harmonics dancing through the palace. It is a well-known factoid that there are frequencies that can cause panic, and frequencies that can cause embarrassing incontinence, but the shaking rock was resonating at the frequency that causes reality to melt and run out at the corners.

Nijel regarded the dripping ceiling and cautiously tasted it.

"Lime custard," he said, and added, "I suppose there's no chance of stairs, is there?"

More fire burst from Rincewind's ravaged fingers, coalescing into an almost perfect escalator, except that possibly no other moving staircase in the universe was floored with alligator skin.

Nijel grabbed the gently spinning wizard and leapt aboard.

Fortunately they had reached the top before the magic vanished, very suddenly.

Sprouting out of the center of the palace, shattering rooftops like a mushroom bursting through an ancient pavement, was a white tower taller than any other building in Al Khali.

Huge double doors had opened at its base and out of them, striding along as though they owned the place, were dozens of wizards. Rincewind thought he could recognize a few faces, faces which he'd seen before bumbling vaguely in lecture theaters or peering amiably at the world in the University grounds. They weren't faces built for evil. They didn't have a fang between them. But there was some common denominator among their expressions that could terrify a thoughtful person.

Nijel pulled back behind a handy wall. He found himself looking into Rincewind's worried eyes.

"Hey, that's magic!"

"I know," said Rincewind, "It's not right!" Nijel peered up at the sparkling tower.

"But—"

"It *feels* wrong," said Rincewind. "Don't ask me why."

Half a dozen of the Seriph's guards erupted from an arched doorway and plunged toward the wizards, their headlong rush made all the more sinister by their ghastly battle silences. For a moment their swords flashed in the sunlight, and then a couple of the wizards turned, extended their hands and—

Nijel looked away.

"Urgh," he said.

A few curved swords dropped onto the cobbles.

"I think we should very quietly go away," said Rincewind.

"But didn't you see what they just turned them into?"

"Dead people," said Rincewind. "I know. I don't want to think about it."

Nijel thought he'd never stop thinking about it, especially around 3 a.m. on windy nights. The point about being killed by magic was that it was much more *inventive* than, say, steel; there were all sorts of interesting new ways to die, and he couldn't put out of his mind the shapes he'd seen, just for an instant, before the wash of octarine fire had mercifully engulfed them.

"I didn't think wizards were like that," he said, as they hurried down a passageway. "I thought they were more, well, more silly than sinister. Sort of figures of fun."

"Laugh that one off, then," muttered Rincewind.

"But they just killed them, without even—"

"I wish you wouldn't go on about it. I saw it as well."

Nijel drew back. His eyes narrowed.

"You're a wizard, too," he said accusingly.

"Not that kind I'm not," said Rincewind shortly.

"What kind are you, then?"

"The non-killing kind."

"It was the way they looked at them as if it just didn't matter—" said Nijel, shaking his head. "That was the worst bit."

"Yes."

Rincewind dropped the single syllable heavily in front of Nijel's train of thought, like a tree trunk. The boy shuddered, but at least he shut up. Rincewind actually began to feel sorry for him, which was very unusual—he normally felt he needed all his pity for himself.

"Is that the first time you've seen someone killed?" he said.

"Yes."

"Exactly how long have you been a barbarian hero?"

"Er. What year is this?"

Rincewind peered around a corner, but such people as were around and vertical were far too busy panicking to bother about them.

"Out on the road, then?" he said quietly. "Lost

track of time? I know how it is. This is the Year of the Hyena."

"Oh. In that case, about—" Nijel's lips moved soundlessly—"about three days. Look," he added quickly, "how can people kill like that? Without even thinking about it?"

"I don't know," said Rincewind, in a tone of voice that suggested he *was* thinking about it.

"I mean, even when the vizier had me thrown in the snake pit, at least he seemed to be taking an interest."

"That's good. Everyone should have an interest."

"I mean, he even laughed!"

"Ah. A sense of humor, too."

Rincewind felt that he could see his future with the same crystal clarity that a man falling off a cliff sees the ground, and for much the same reason. So when Nijel said: "They just pointed their fingers without so much as—," Rincewind snapped: "Just shut up, will you? How do you think I feel about it? *I'm* a wizard, too!"

"Yes, well, *you'll* be all right then," muttered Nijel.

It wasn't a heavy blow, because even in a rage Rincewind still had muscles like tapioca, but it caught the side of Nijel's head and knocked him down more by the weight of surprise than its intrinsic energy.

"Yes, I'm a wizard all right," Rincewind hissed. "A wizard who isn't much good at magic! I've managed to survive up till now by not being important enough to die! And when all wizards are hated and feared, exactly how long do you think I'll last?"

"That's ridiculous!"

Rincewind couldn't have been more taken aback if Nijel had struck him.

"What?"

"Idiot! All you have to do is stop wearing that silly robe and get rid of that daft hat and no one will even know you're a wizard!"

Rincewind's mouth opened and shut a few times as he gave a very lifelike impression of a goldfish trying to grasp the concept of tap-dancing.

"Stop wearing the robe?" he said.

"Sure. All those tatty sequins and things, it's a total giveaway," said Nijel, struggling to his feet.

"Get rid of the hat?"

"You've got to admit that going around with 'wizzard' written on it is a bit of a heavy hint."

Rincewind gave him a worried grin.

"Sorry," he said, "I don't quite follow you—"

"Just get rid of them. It's easy enough, isn't it? Just drop them somewhere and then you could be a, a, well, whatever. Something that isn't a wizard."

There was a pause, broken only by the distant sounds of fighting.

"Er," said Rincewind, and shook his head. "You've lost me there . . ."

"Good grief, it's perfectly simple to understand!"

". . . not sure I quite catch your drift . . ." murmured Rincewind, his face ghastly with sweat.

"You can just *stop being a wizard*."

Rincewind's lips moved soundlessly as he replayed every word, one at a time, then all at once.

"What?" he said, and then he said, "Oh."

"Got it? Want to try it one more time?"

Rincewind nodded gloomily.

"I don't think you understand. A wizard isn't what you *do*, it's what you *are*. If I wasn't a wizard, I wouldn't be *anything*." He took off his hat and twiddled nervously with the loose star on its point, causing a few more cheap sequins to part company.

"I mean, it's got wizard written on my hat," he said. "It's very important—"

He stopped and stared at the hat.

"Hat," he said vaguely, aware of some importunate memory pressing its nose up against the windows of his mind.

"It's a *good* hat," said Nijel, who felt that something was expected of him.

"Hat," said Rincewind again, and then added, "the hat! We've got to get the hat!"

"You've got the hat," Nijel pointed out.

"Not this hat, the other hat. And Conina!"

He took a few random steps along a passageway, and then sidled back.

"Where do you suppose they are?" he said.

"Who?"

"There's a magic hat I've got to find. And a girl."

"Why?"

"It might be rather difficult to explain. I think there might be screaming involved somewhere."

Nijel didn't have much of a jaw but, such as it was, he stuck it out.

"There's a girl needs rescuing?" he said grimly.

Rincewind hesitated. "Someone will probably need rescuing," he admitted. "It might possibly be her. Or at least in her vicinity."

"Why didn't you say so? This is more like it, this is what I was expecting. This is what heroism is all about. Let's go!"

There was another crash, and the sound of people yelling.

"Where?" said Rincewind.

"Anywhere!"

Heroes usually have an ability to rush madly around crumbling palaces they hardly know, save everyone and get out just before the whole place blows up or sinks into the swamp. In fact Nijel and Rincewind visited the kitchens, assorted throne rooms, the stables (twice) and what seemed to Rincewind like several miles of corridor. Occasionally groups of black-clad guards would scurry past them, without so much as a second glance.

"This is ridiculous," said Nijel. "Why don't we ask someone? Are you all right?"

Rincewind leaned against a pillar decorated with embarrassing sculpture and wheezed.

"You could grab a guard and torture the information out of him," he said, gulping air. Nijel gave him an odd look.

"Wait here," he said, and wandered off until he found a servant industriously ransacking a cupboard.

"Excuse me," he said, "which way to the harem?"

"Turn left three doors down," said the man, without looking around.

"Right."

He wandered back again and told Rincewind.

"Yes, but did you torture him?"

"No."

"That wasn't very barbaric of you, was it?"

"Well, I'm working up to it," said Nijel. "I mean, I didn't say 'thank you'."

Thirty seconds later they pushed aside a heavy bead curtain and entered the seraglio of the Seriph of Al Khali.

There were gorgeous songbirds in cages of gold filigree. There were tinkling fountains. There were pots of rare orchids through which humming-birds skimmed like tiny, brilliant jewels. There were about twenty young women wearing enough clothes for, say, about half a dozen, huddled together in a silent crowd.

Rincewind had eyes for none of this. That is not to say that the sight of several dozen square yards of hip and thigh in every shade from pink to midnight black didn't start certain tides flowing deep in the crevasses of his libido, but they were swamped by the considerably bigger flood of panic at the sight of four guards turning toward him with scimitars in their hands and the light of murder in their eyes.

Without hesitation, Rincewind took a step backwards.

"Over to you, friend," he said.

"Right!"

Nijel drew his sword and held it out in front of him, his arms trembling at the effort.

There were a few seconds of total silence as everyone waited to see what would happen next. And then Nijel uttered the battle cry that Rincewind would never quite forget to the end of his life.

"Erm," he said, "excuse me . . ."

* * *

"It seems a shame," said a small wizard.

The others didn't speak. It *was* a shame, and there wasn't a man among them who couldn't hear the hot whine of guilt all down their backbones. But, as so often happens by that strange alchemy of the soul, the guilt made them arrogant and reckless.

"Just shut up, will you?" said the temporary leader. He was called Benado Sconner, but there is something in the air tonight that suggests that it is not worth committing his name to memory. The air is dark and heavy and full of ghosts.

The Unseen University isn't empty, there just aren't any people there.

But of course the six wizards sent to burn down the Library aren't afraid of ghosts, because they're so charged with magic that they practically buzz as they walk, they're wearing robes more splendid than any Archchancellor has worn, their pointy hats are more pointed than any hats have hitherto been, and the reason they're standing so close together is entirely coincidental.

"It's awfully dark in here," said the smallest of the wizards.

"It's midnight," said Sconner sharply, "and the only dangerous things in here are us. Isn't that right, boys?"

There was a chorus of vague murmurs. They were all in awe of Sconner, who was rumored to do positive-thinking exercises.

"And we're not scared of a few old books, are we, lads?" He glowered at the smallest wizard. "You're not, are you?" he added sharply.

"Me? Oh. No. Of course not. They're just paper, like *he* said," said the wizard quickly.

"Well, then."

"There's ninety thousand of them, mind," said another wizard.

"I always heard there was no end to 'em," said another. "It's all down to dimensions, I heard, like what we see is only the tip of the whatever, you know, the thing that is mostly underwater—"

"Hippopotamus?"

"Alligator?"

"Ocean?"

"Look, just shut up, all of you!" shouted Sconner. He hesitated. The darkness seemed to suck at the sound of his voice. It packed the air like feathers.

He pulled himself together a bit.

"Right, then," he said, and turned toward the forbidding doors of the Library.

He raised his hands, made a few complicated gestures in which his fingers, in some eye-watering way, appeared to pass through each other, and shattered the doors into sawdust.

The waves of silence poured back again, strangling the sound of falling woodchips.

There was no doubt that the doors were smashed. Four forlorn hinges hung trembling from the frame, and a litter of broken benches and shelves lay in the wreckage. Even Sconner was a little surprised.

"There," he said. "It's as easy as that. You see? Nothing happened to me. Right?"

There was a shuffling of curly-toed boots. The darkness beyond the doorway was limned with the indistinct, eye-aching glow of thaumaturgic radiation as possibility particles exceeded the speed of reality in a strong magical field.

"Now then," said Sconner, brightly, "who would like the honor of setting the fire?"

Ten silent seconds later he said, "In that case I will do it myself. Honestly, I might as well be talking to the wall."

He strode through the doorway and hurried across the floor to the little patch of starlight that lanced down from the glass dome high above the center of the Library (although, of course, there has always been considerable debate about the precise geography of the place; heavy concentrations of magic distort time and space, and it is possible that the Library doesn't even have an edge, never mind a center).

He stretched out his arms.

"There. See? Absolutely nothing has happened. Now come on in."

The other wizards did so, with great reluctance and a tendency to duck as they passed through the ravished arch.

"Okay," said Sconner, with some satisfaction. "Now, has everyone got their matches as instructed? Magical fire won't work, not on these books, so I want everyone to—"

"Something moved up there," said the smallest wizard.

Sconner blinked.

"What?"

"Something moved up by the dome," said the wizard, adding by way of explanation, "I saw it."

Sconner squinted upwards into the bewildering shadows, and decided to exert a bit of authority.

"Nonsense," he said briskly. He pulled out a bundle of foul-smelling yellow matches, and said, "Now, I want you all to pile—"

"I did see it, you know," said the small wizard, sulkily.

"All right, what did you see?"

"Well, I'm not exactly—"

"You don't know, do you?" snapped Sconner.

"I saw *someth*—"

"You don't know!" repeated Sconner, "You're just seeing shadows, just trying to undermine my authority, isn't that it?" Sconner hesitated, and his eyes glazed momentarily. "I am calm," he intoned, "I am totally in control. I will not let—"

"It *was*—"

"Listen, shortarse, you can just jolly well shut up, all right?"

One of the other wizards, who had been staring upwards to conceal his embarrassment, gave a strangled little cough.

"Er, Sconner—"

"And that goes for you too!" Sconner pulled himself to his full, bristling height and flourished the matches.

"As *I* was saying," he said, "I want you to light the matches and—I suppose I'll have to show you how to light matches, for the benefit of shortarse there—and *I'm not out of the window, you know*. Good grief. Look at me. You take a match—"

He lit a match, the darkness blossomed into a ball of sulphurous white light, and the Librarian dropped on him like the descent of Man.

They all knew the Librarian, in the same definite but diffused way that people know walls and floors and all the other minor but necessary scenery on the stage of life. If they recall him at all, it was as a sort of gentle mobile sigh, sitting under his desk repairing books, or knuckling his way among the shelves in search of secret smokers. Any wizard unwise enough to hazard a clandestine rollup wouldn't know anything about it until a soft leathery hand reached up and removed the offending homemade, but the Librarian never made a fuss, he just looked extremely hurt and sorrowful about the whole sad business and then ate it.

Whereas what was now attempting with considerable effort to unscrew Sconner's head by the ears was a screaming nightmare with its lips curled back to reveal long yellow fangs.

The terrified wizards turned to run and found themselves bumping into bookshelves that had unaccountably blocked the aisles. The smallest wizard yelped and rolled under a table laden with atlases, and lay with his hands over his ears to block out the dreadful sounds as the remaining wizards tried to escape.

Eventually there was nothing but silence, but it was that particularly massive silence created by something moving very stealthily, as it might be, in search of something else. The smallest wizard ate the tip of his hat out of sheer terror.

The silent mover grabbed him by the leg and pulled him gently but firmly out into the open, where he gibbered a bit with his eyes shut and then, when ghastly teeth failed to meet in his throat, ventured a quick glance.

The Librarian picked him up by the scruff of his neck and dangled him reflectively a foot off the ground, just out of reach of a small and elderly wire-haired terrier who was trying to remember how to bite people's ankles.

"Er—" said the wizard, and was then thrown in an almost flat trajectory through the broken doorway, where his fall was broken by the floor.

After a while a shadow next to him said, "Well, that's it, then. Anyone seen that daft bastard Sconner?"

And a shadow on the other side of him said, "I think my neck's broken."

"Who's that?"

"*That daft bastard*," said the shadow, nastily.

"Oh. Sorry, Sconner."

Sconner stood up, his whole body now outlined in magical aura. He was trembling with rage as he raised his hands.

"I'll show that wretched throwback to respect his evolutionary superiors—" he snarled.

"Get him, lads!"

And Sconner was borne to the flagstones again under the weight of all five wizards.

"Sorry, but—"

"—you know that if you use—"

"—magic near the Library, with all the magic that's in there—"

"—get one thing wrong and it's a critical Mass and then—"

"BANG! Goodnight, world!"

Sconner growled. The wizards sitting on him decided that getting up was not the wisest thing they could do at this point.

Eventually he said, "Right. You're right. Thank you. It was wrong of me to lose my temper like that. Clouded my judgment. Essential to be dispassionate. You're absolutely right. Thank you. Get off."

They risked it. Sconner stood up.

"That monkey," he said, "has eaten its last banana. Fetch—"

"Er. Ape, Sconner," said the smallest wizard, unable to stop himself. "It's an ape, you see. Not a monkey . . ."

He wilted under the stare.

"Who cares? Ape, monkey, what's the difference?" said Sconner. "What's the difference, Mr. Zoologist?"

"I don't know, Sconner," said the wizard meekly. "I think it's a class thing."

"Shut up."

"Yes, Sconner."

"You ghastly little man," said Sconner.

He turned and added, in a voice as level as a sawblade: "I am perfectly controlled. My mind is as cool as a bald mammoth. My intellect is absolutely in charge. Which one of you sat on my head? No, I must not get angry. I am *not* angry. I am thinking positively. My faculties are fully engaged—do any of you wish to argue?"

"No, Sconner," they chorused.

"Then get me a dozen barrels of oil and all the kindling you can find! That ape's gonna *fry*!"

From high in the Library roof, home of owls and bats and other things, there was a clink of chain and the sound of glass being broken as respectfully as possible.

"They don't look very worried," said Nijel, slightly affronted.

"How can I put this?" said Rincewind. "When they come to write the list of Great Battle Cries of the World, 'Erm, excuse me' won't be one of them."

He stepped to one side. "I'm not with him," he said earnestly to a grinning guard. "I just met him, somewhere. In a pit." He gave a little laugh. "This sort of thing happens to me all the time," he said.

The guards stared through him.

"Erm," he said.

"Okay," he said.

He sidled back to Nijel.

"Are you any good with that sword?"

Without taking his eyes off the guards, Nijel fumbled in his pack and handed Rincewind the book.

"I've read the whole of chapter three," he said. "It's got illustrations."

Rincewind turned over the crumpled pages. The book had been used so hard you could have shuffled it, but what was probably once the front cover showed a rather poor woodcut of a muscular man. He had arms like two bags full of footballs, and he was standing knee-deep in languorous women and slaughtered victims with a smug expression on his face.

About him was the legend: *Inne Juste 7 Dayes I wille make You a Barbearian Hero*! Below it, in a slightly smaller type, was the name: *Cohen the Barbarean*. Rincewind rather doubted it. He had met Cohen and, while he could read after a fashion, the old boy had never really mastered the pen and still signed his name with an "X," which he usually spelled wrong. On the other hand, he gravitated rapidly to anything with money in it.

Rincewind looked again at the illustration, and then at Nijel.

"Seven days?"

"Well, I'm a slow reader."

"Ah," said Rincewind.

"And I didn't bother with chapter six, because I promised my mother I'd stick with just the looting and pillaging, until I find the right girl."

"And this book teaches you how to be a hero?"

"Oh, yes. It's very good." Nijel gave him a worried glance. "That's all right, isn't it? It cost a lot of money."

"Well, er. I suppose you'd better get on with it, then."

Nijel squared his, for want of a better word, shoulders, and waved his sword again.

"You four had better just jolly well watch out," he said, "or . . . hold on a moment." He took the book from Rincewind and riffled through the pages until he found what he was looking for, and continued, "Yes, or 'the chill winds of fate will blow through your bleached skeletons/the legions of Hell will drown your living soul in acid.' There. How d'you like them . . . excuse me a moment . . . apples?"

There was a metallic chord as four men drew their swords in perfect harmony.

Nijel's sword became a blur. It made a complicated figure eight in the air in front of him, spun over his arm, flicked from hand to hand behind his back, seemed to orbit his chest twice, and leapt like a salmon.

One or two of the harem ladies broke into spontaneous applause. Even the guards looked impressed. "That's a Triple Orcthrust with Extra Flip," said Nijel proudly. "I broke a lot of mirrors learning that. Look, they're stopping."

"They've never seen anything like it, I imagine," said Rincewind weakly, judging the distance to the doorway.

"I should think not."

"Especially the last bit, where it stuck in the ceiling."

Nijel looked upwards.

"Funny," he said, "it always did that at home, too. I wonder what I'm doing wrong."

"Search me."

"Gosh, I'm sorry," said Nijel, as the guards seemed to realize that the entertainment was over and closed in for the kill.

"Don't blame youself—" said Rincewind, as Nijel reached up and tried unsuccessfully to free the blade.

"Thank you."

"—I'll do it for you."

Rincewind considered his next step. In fact, he considered several steps. But the door was too far away and anyway, by the sound of it, things were not a lot healthier out there.

There was only one thing for it. He'd have to try magic.

He raised his hand and two of the men fell over. He raised his other hand and the other two fell over.

Just as he was beginning to wonder about this, Conina stepped daintily over the prone bodies, idly rubbing the sides of her hands.

"I thought you'd never turn up," she said. "Who's your friend?"

As has already been indicated, the Luggage seldom shows any sign of emotion, or at least any emotion less extreme than blind rage and hatred, and therefore it is hard to gauge its feelings when it woke up, a few miles outside Al Khali, on its lid in a dried-up wadi with its legs in the air.

Even a few minutes after dawn the air was like the breath of a furnace. After a certain amount of rocking the Luggage managed to get most of its feet pointing the right way, and stood doing a complicated slow-motion jig to keep as few of them on the burning sand as possible.

It wasn't lost. It always knew exactly where it was. It was always *here*.

It was just that everywhere else seemed to have been temporarily mislaid.

After some deliberation the Luggage turned and walked very slowly, into a boulder.

It backed away and sat down, rather puzzled. It

felt as though it had been stuffed with hot feathers, and it was dimly aware of the benefits of shade and a nice cool drink.

After a few false starts it walked to the top of a nearby sand dune, which gave it an unrivalled view of hundreds of other dunes.

Deep in its heartwood the Luggage was troubled. It had been spurned. It had been told to go *away*. It had been rejected. It had also drunk enough orakh to poison a small country.

If there is one thing a travel accessory needs more than anything else, it is someone to belong to. The Luggage set off unsteadily across the scorching sand, full of hope.

"I don't think we've got time for introductions," said Rincewind, as a distant part of the palace collapsed with a thump that vibrated the floor. "It's time we were—"

He realized he was talking to himself.

Nijel let go of the sword.

Conina stepped forward.

"Oh, no," said Rincewind, but it was far too late. The world had suddenly separated into two parts—the bit which contained Nijel and Conina, and the bit which contained everything else. The air between them crackled. Probably, in their half, a distant orchestra was playing, bluebirds were tweeting, little pink clouds were barrelling through the sky, and all the other things that happen at times like this. When that sort of thing is going on, mere collapsing palaces in the next world don't stand a chance.

"Look, perhaps we can just get the introductions over with," said Rincewind desperately. "Nijel—"

"—the Destroyer—" said Nijel dreamily.

"All right, Nijel the Destroyer," said Rincewind, and added, "Son of Harebut the—"

"Mighty," said Nijel. Rincewind gaped a bit, and then shrugged.

"Well, whoever," he conceded. "Anyway, this is Conina. Which is rather a coincidence, because you'll be interested to know that her father was mmph."

Conina, without turning her gaze, had extended a hand and held Rincewind's face in a gentle grip which, with only a slight increase in finger pressure, could have turned his head into a bowling ball.

"Although I could be mistaken," he added, when she took her hand away. "Who knows? Who cares? What does it matter?"

They didn't take any notice.

"I'll just go and see if I can find the hat, shall I?" he said.

"Good idea," murmured Conina.

"I expect I shall get murdered, but I don't mind," said Rincewind.

"Jolly good," said Nijel.

"I don't expect anyone will even notice I'm gone," said Rincewind.

"Fine, fine," said Conina.

"I shall be chopped into small pieces, I expect," said Rincewind, walking toward the door at the speed of a dying snail.

Conina blinked.

"What hat?" she said, and then, "Oh, that hat."

"I suppose there's no possible chance that you two might be of some assistance?" Rincewind ventured.

Somewhere inside Conina and Nijel's private world the bluebirds went to roost, the little pink clouds drifted away and the orchestra packed up and sneaked off to do a private gig at a nightclub somewhere. A bit of reality reasserted itself.

Conina dragged her admiring gaze away from Nijel's rapt face and turned it onto Rincewind, where it grew slightly cooler.

She sidled across the floor and grabbed the wizard by the arm.

"Look," she said, "you won't tell him who I *really* am, will you? Only boys get funny ideas and—well, anyway, if you do I will personally break all your—"

"I'll be far too busy," said Rincewind, "what with you helping me get the hat and everything. Not that I can imagine what you see in him," he added, haughtily.

"He's nice. I don't seem to meet many nice people."

"Yes, well—"

"He's looking at us!"

"So what? You're not frightened of him, are you?"

"Suppose he talks to me!"

Rincewind looked blank. Not for the first time in his life, he felt that there were whole areas of human experience that had passed him by, if areas could pass by people. Maybe *he* had passed *them* by. He shrugged.

"Why did you let them take you off to the harem without a fight?" he said.

"I've always wanted to know what went on in one."

There was a pause. "Well?" said Rincewind.

"Well, we all sat round, and then after a bit the Seriph came in, and then he asked me over and said that since I was new it would be my turn, and then, you'll never guess what he wanted me to do. The girls said it's the only thing he's interested in."

"Er."

"Are you all right?"

"Fine, fine," Rincewind muttered.

"Your face has gone all shiny."

"No, I'm fine, fine."

"He asked me to tell him a story."

"What about?" said Rincewind suspiciously.

"The other girls said he prefers something with rabbits in it."

"Ah. Rabbits."

"Small fluffy white ones. But the only stories I know are the ones father taught me when I was little, and I don't think they're really suitable."

"Not many rabbits?"

"Lots of arms and legs being chopped off," said Conina, and sighed. "That's why you mustn't tell *him* about me you see? I'm just not cut out for a normal life."

"Telling stories in a harem isn't bloody normal," said Rincewind. "It'll never catch on."

"He's looking at us again!" Conina grabbed Rincewind's arm.

He shook her off. "Oh, good grief," he said, and hurried across the room to Nijel, who grabbed his other arm.

"You haven't been telling her about me, have you?" he demanded. "I'll never live it down if you've told her that I'm only just learning how—"

"Nonono. She just wants you to help us. It's a sort of quest."

Nijel's eyes gleamed.

"You mean a geas?" he said.

"Pardon?"

"It's in the book. To be a proper hero it says you've got to labor under a geas."

Rincewind's forehead wrinkled. "Is it a sort of bird?"

"I think it's more a sort of obligation, or something," said Nijel, but without much certainty.

"Sounds more like a kind of bird to me," said Rincewind, "I'm sure I read it in a bestiary once. Large. Couldn't fly. Big pink legs, it had." His face went blank as his ears digested what they had just heard his lips say.

Five seconds later they were out of the room, leaving behind four prone guards and the harem ladies themselves, who settled down for a bit of storytelling.

The desert rimwards of Al Khali is bisected by the river Tsort, famed in myth and lies, which insinuates its way through the brown landscapes like a long damp descriptive passage punctuated with sandbanks. And every sandbank is covered with sunbaked logs, and most of the logs are the kind of logs that have teeth, and most of the logs opened one lazy eye at the distant sounds of splashing from upstream, and suddenly most of the logs had legs. A dozen scaly bodies slipped into the turbid waters, which rolled over them again. The dark waters were unruffled, except for a few inconsequential V-shaped ripples.

The Luggage paddled gently down the stream. The water was making it feel a little better. It spun gently in the weak current, the focus of several mysterious little swirls that sped across the surface of the water.

The ripples converged.

The Luggage jerked. Its lid flew open. It shot under the surface with a brief, despairing creak.

The chocolate-colored waters of the Tsort rolled back again. They were getting good at it.

And the tower of sourcery loomed over Al Khali like a vast and beautiful fungus, the kind that appear in books with little skull-and-crossbones symbols beside them.

The Seriph's guard had fought back, but there were now quite a lot of bewildered frogs and newts around the base of the tower, and they were the fortunate ones. They still had arms and legs, of a sort, and most of their essential organs were still on the inside. The city was under the rule of sourcery . . . martial lore.

Some of the buildings nearest the base of the tower were already turning into the bright white marble that the wizards obviously preferred.

The trio stared out through a hole in the palace walls.

"Very impressive," said Conina critically. "Your wizards are more powerful than I thought."

"Not *my* wizards," said Rincewind. "I don't know

whose wizards they are. I don't like it. All the wizards *I* knew couldn't stick one brick on another."

"I don't like the idea of wizards ruling everybody," said Nijel. "Of course, as a hero I am philosophically against the whole idea of wizardry in any case. The time will come when," his eyes glazed slightly, as if he was trying to remember something he'd seen somewhere, "the time will come when all wizardry has gone from the face of the world and the sons of, of—anyway, we can all be a bit more practical about things," he added lamely.

"Read it in a book, did you?" said Rincewind sourly. "Any geas in it?"

"He's got a point," said Conina. "I've nothing against wizards, but it's not as if they do much good. They're just a bit of decoration, really. Up to now."

Rincewind pulled off his hat. It was battered, stained and covered with rock dust, bits of it had been sheared off, the point was dented and the star was shedding sequins like pollen, but the word 'Wizzard' was still just readable under the grime.

"See this?" he demanded, red in the face. "Do you see it? Do you? What does it tell you?"

"That you can't spell?" said Nijel.

"What? No! It says I'm a wizard, that's what! Twenty years behind the staff, and proud of it! I've done my time, I have! I've pas—I've sat dozens of exams! If all the spells I've read were piled on top of one another, they'd . . . it'd . . . you'd have a lot of spells!"

"Yes, but—" Conina began.

"*Yes?*"

"You're not actually very good at them, are you?"

Rincewind glared at her. He tried to think of what to say next, and a small receptor area opened in his mind at the same time as an inspiration particle, its path bent and skewed by a trillion random events, screamed down through the atmosphere and burst silently just at the right spot.

"Talent just defines what you do," he said. "It doesn't define what you are. Deep down, I mean. When you know what you are, you can do anything."

He thought a bit more and added, "That's what makes sourcerers so powerful. The important thing is to know what you really are."

There was a pause full of philosophy.

"Rincewind?" said Conina, kindly.

"Hmm?" said Rincewind, who was still wondering how the words got into his head.

"You really are an idiot. Do you know that?"

"You will all stand very still."

Abrim the vizier stepped out of a ruined archway. He was wearing the Archchancellor's hat.

The desert fried under the flame of the sun. Nothing moved except the shimmering air, hot as a stolen volcano, dry as a skull.

A basilisk lay panting in the baking shade of a rock, dribbling corrosive yellow slime. For the last five minutes its ears had been detecting the faint thump of hundreds of little legs moving unsteadily over the dunes, which seemed to indicate that dinner was on the way.

It blinked its legendary eyes and uncoiled twenty feet of hungry body, winding out and onto the sand like fluid death.

The Luggage staggered to a halt and raised its lid threateningly. The basilisk hissed, but a little uncertainly, because it had never seen a walking box before, and certainly never one with lots of alligator teeth stuck in its lid. There were also scraps of leathery hide adhering to it, as though it had been involved in a fight in a handbag factory, and in a way that the basilisk wouldn't have been able to describe even if it could talk, it appeared to be glaring.

Right, the reptile thought, if that's the way you want to play it.

It turned on the Luggage a stare like a diamond drill, a stare that nipped in via the staree's eyeballs and flayed the brain from the inside, a stare that tore the frail net curtains on the windows of the soul, a stare that—

The basilisk realized something was very wrong. An entirely new and unwelcome sensation started to arise just behind its saucer-shaped eyes. It started small, like the little itch in those few square inches of back that no amount of writhing will allow you to scratch, and grew until it became a second, red-hot, internal sun.

The basilisk was feeling a terrible, overpowering and irresistible urge to blink . . .

It did something incredibly unwise.

It blinked.

"He's talking through his hat," said Rincewind.

"Eh?" said Nijel, who was beginning to realize that the world of the barbarian hero wasn't the clean, simple place he had imagined in the days when the most exciting thing he had ever done was stack parsnips.

"The hat's talking through him, you mean," said Conina, and she backed away too, as one tends to do in the presence of horror.

"Eh?"

"I will not harm you. You have been of some service," said Abrim, stepping forward with his hands out. *"But you are right. He thought he could gain power through wearing me. Of course, it is the other way around. An astonishingly devious and clever mind."*

"So you tried his head on for size?" said Rincewind. He shuddered. *He'd* worn the hat. Obviously he didn't have the right kind of mind. Abrim did have the right kind of mind, and now his eyes were gray and colorless, his skin was pale and he walked as though his body was hanging down from his head.

Nijel had pulled out his book and was riffling feverishly through the pages.

"What on earth are you doing?" said Conina, not taking her eyes off the ghastly figure.

"I'm looking up the Index of Wandering Monsters," said Nijel. "Do you think it's an Undead? They're awfully difficult to kill, you need garlic and—"

"You won't find this in there," said Rincewind slowly. "It's—it's a vampire hat."

"Of course, it might be a Zombie," said Nijel, running his finger down a page. "It says here you need black pepper and sea salt, but—"

"You're supposed to fight the bloody things, not eat them," said Conina.

"This is a mind I can use," said the hat. *"Now I can fight back. I shall rally wizardry. There is room for only one magic in this world, and I embody it. Sourcery beware!"*

"Oh, no," said Rincewind under his breath.

"Wizardry has learned a lot in the last twenty centuries. This upstart can be beaten. You three will follow me."

It wasn't a request. It wasn't even an order. It was a sort of forecast. The voice of the hat went straight to the hindbrain without bothering to deal with the consciousness, and Rincewind's legs started to move of their own accord.

The other two also jerked forward, walking with the awkward doll-like jerking that suggested that they, too, were on invisible strings.

"Why the oh, no?" said Conina, "I mean, 'Oh, no' on general principles I can understand, but was there any particular reason?"

"If we get a chance we must run," said Rincewind.

"Did you have anywhere in mind?"

"It probably won't matter. We're doomed anyway."

"Why?" said Nijel.

"Well," said Rincewind, "have you ever heard of the Mage Wars?"

There were a lot of things on the Disc that owed their origin to the Mage Wars. Sapient pearwood was one of them.

The original tree was probably perfectly normal and spent its days drinking groundwater and eating sunshine in a state of blessed unawareness and then the magic wars broke around it and pitchforked its genes into a state of acute perspicacity.

It also left it ingrained, as it were, with a bad temper. But sapient pearwood got off lightly.

Once, when the level of background magic on the Disc was young and high and found every opportunity to burst on the world, wizards were all as powerful as sourcerers and built their towers on every hilltop. And if there was one thing a really powerful wizard can't stand, it is another wizard. His instinctive approach to diplomacy is to hex 'em till they glow, then curse them in the dark.

That could only mean one thing. All right, two things. Three things.

All-out. Thaumaturgical. War.

And there were of course no alliances, no sides, no deals, no mercy, no cease. The skies twisted, the seas boiled. The scream and whizz of fireballs turned the night into day, but that was all right because the ensuing clouds of black smoke turned the day into night. The landscape rose and fell like a honeymoon duvet, and the very fabric of space itself was tied in multidimensional knots and bashed on a flat stone down by the river of Time. For example, a popular spell at the time was Pelepel's Temporal Compressor, which on one occasion resulted in a race of giant reptiles being created, evolving, spreading, flourishing and then being destroyed in the space of about five minutes, leaving only its bones in the earth to mislead forthcoming generations completely. Trees swam, fishes walked, mountains strolled down to the shops for a packet of cigarettes, and the mutability of existence was such that the first thing any cautious person would do when they woke up in the mornings was count their arms and legs.

That was, in fact, the problem. All the wizards were pretty evenly matched and in any case lived in high towers well protected with spells, which meant that most magical weapons rebounded and landed on the common people who were trying to scratch an honest living from what was, temporarily, the soil, and lead ordinary, decent (but rather short) lives.

But still the fighting raged, battering the very structure of the universe of order, weakening the walls of reality and threatening to topple the whole rickety edifice of time and space into the darkness of the Dungeon Dimensions . . .

One story said that the gods stepped in, but the gods don't usually take a hand in human affairs unless it amuses them. Another one—and this was the one that the wizards themselves told, and wrote down in their books—was that the wizards themselves got together and settled their differences amicably for the good of mankind. And this was generally accepted as the true account, despite being as internally likely as a lead lifebelt.

The truth isn't easily pinned to a page. In the bathtub of history the truth is harder to hold than the soap, and much more difficult to find . . .

"What happened, then?" said Conina.

"It doesn't matter," said Rincewind, mournfully. "It's going to start all over again. I can feel it. I've got this instinct. There's too much magic flowing into the world. There's going to be a horrible war.

It's all going to happen. The Disc is too old to take it this time. Everything's been worn too thin. Doom, darkness and destruction bear down on us. The Apocralypse is nigh."

"Death walks abroad," added Nijel helpfully.

"What?" snapped Rincewind, angry at being interrupted.

"I said, Death walks abroad," said Nijel.

"Abroad I don't mind," said Rincewind. "They're all foreigners. It's Death walking around here I'm not looking forward to."

"It's only a metaphor," said Conina.

"That's all you know. I've met him."

"What did he look like?" said Nijel.

"Put it like this—"

"Yes?"

"He didn't need a hairdresser."

Now the sun was a blowlamp nailed to the sky, and the only difference between the sand and red-hot ash was the color.

The Luggage plodded erratically across the burning dunes. There were a few traces of yellow slime rapidly drying on its lid.

The lonely little oblong was watched, from atop of a stone pinnacle the shape and temperature of a firebrick, by a chimera.* The chimera was an

---

* For a description of the chimera we shall turn to Broomfog's famous bestiary *Anima Unnaturale:* "It have thee legges of an mermade, the hair of an tortoise, the teeth of an fowel, and the winges of an snake. Of course, I have only my worde for it, the beast having the breathe of an furnace and the temperament of an rubber balloon in a hurricane."

extremely rare species, and this particular one wasn't about to do anything to help matters.

It judged its moment carefully, kicked away with its talons, folded its leathery wings and plummeted down toward its victim.

The chimera's technique was to swoop low over the prey, lightly boiling it with its fiery breath, and then turn and rend its dinner with its teeth. It managed the fire part but then, at the point where experience told the creature it should be facing a stricken and terrified victim, found itself on the ground in the path of a scorched and furious Luggage.

The only thing incandescent about the Luggage was its rage. It had spent several hours with a headache, during which it had seemed the whole world had tried to attack it. It had had enough.

When it had stamped the unfortunate chimera into a greasy puddle on the sand it paused for a moment, apparently considering its future. It was becoming clear that not belonging to anyone was a lot harder than it had thought. It had vague, comforting recollections of service and a wardrobe to call its own.

It turned around very slowly, pausing frequently to open its lid. It might have been sniffing the air, if it had a nose. At last it made up its mind, if it had a mind.

The hat and its wearer also strode purposefully across the rubble that had been the legendary Rhoxie to the foot of the tower of sourcery, their unwilling entourage straggling along behind them.

There were doors at the foot of the tower. Unlike

those of Unseen University, which were usually propped wide open, they were tightly shut. They seemed to glow.

"You three are privileged to be here," said the hat through Abrim's slack mouth. *"This is the moment when wizardry stops running,"* he glanced witheringly at Rincewind, *"and starts fighting back. You will remember it for the rest of your lives."*

"What, until lunchtime?" said Rincewind weakly.

"Watch closely," said Abrim. He extended his hands.

"If we get a chance," whispered Rincewind to Nijel, "we run, right?"

"Where to?"

"From," said Rincewind, "the important word is *from*."

"I don't trust this man," said Nijel. "I try not to judge from first impressions, but I definitely think he's up to no good."

"He had you thrown in a snake pit!"

"Perhaps I should have taken the hint."

The vizier started to mutter. Even Rincewind, whose few talents included a gift for languages, didn't recognize it, but it sounded like the kind of language designed specifically for muttering, the words curling out like scythes at ankle height, dark and red and merciless. They made complicated swirls in the air, and then drifted gently toward the doors of the tower.

Where they touched the white marble it turned black and crumbled.

As the remains drifted to the ground a wizard stepped through and looked Abrim up and down.

Rincewind was used to the dressy ways of wizards,

but this one was really impressive, his robe so padded and crenellated and buttressed in fantastic folds and creases that it had probably been designed by an architect. The matching hat looked like a wedding cake that had collided intimately with a Christmas tree.

The actual face, peering through the small gap between the baroque collar and the filigreed fringe of the brim, was a bit of a disappointment. At some time in the past it had thought its appearance would be improved by a thin, scruffy mustache. It had been wrong.

"That was our bloody door!" it said. "You're really going to regret this!"

Abrim folded his arms.

This seemed to infuriate the other wizard. He flung up his arms, untangled his hands from the lace on his sleeves, and sent a flare screaming across the gap.

It struck Abrim in the chest and rebounded in a gout of incandescence, but when the blue afterimages allowed Rincewind to see he saw Abrim, unharmed.

His opponent frantically patted out the last of the little fires in his own clothing and looked up with murder in his eyes.

"You don't seem to understand," he rasped. "It's sourcery you're dealing with now. You can't fight sourcery."

"*I can* use *sourcery*," said Abrim.

The wizard snarled and lofted a fireball, which burst harmlessly inches from Abrim's dreadful grin.

A look of acute puzzlement passed across the

other one's face. He tried again, sending lines of blue-hot magic lancing straight from infinity toward Abrim's heart. Abrim waved them away.

"Your choice is simple," he said. *"You can join me, or you can die."*

It was at this point that Rincewind became aware of a regular scraping sound close to his ear. It had an unpleasant metallic ring.

He half-turned, and felt the familiar and very uncomfortable prickly feeling of Time slowing down around him.

Death paused in the act of running a whetstone along the edge of his scythe and gave him a nod of acknowledgment, as between one professional and another.

He put a bony digit to his lips, or rather, to the place where his lips would have been if he'd had lips.

All wizards can see Death, but they don't necessarily want to.

There was a popping in Rincewind's ears and the specter vanished.

Abrim and the rival wizard were surrounded by a corona of randomized magic, and it was evidently having no effect on Abrim. Rincewind drifted back into the land of the living just in time to see the man reach out and grab the wizard by his tasteless collar.

"You cannot defeat me," he said in the hat's voice. *"I have had two thousand years of harnessing power to my own ends. I can draw my power from your power. Yield to me or you won't even have time to regret it."*

The wizard struggled and, unfortunately, let pride win over caution.

"Never!" he said.

"*Die*," suggested Abrim.

Rincewind had seen many strange things in his life, most of them with extreme reluctance, but he had never seen anyone actually killed by magic.

Wizards didn't kill ordinary people because a) they seldom noticed them and b) it wasn't considered sporting and c) besides, who'd do all the cooking and growing food and things. And killing a brother wizard with magic was well-nigh impossible on account of the layers of protective spells that any cautious wizard maintained about his person at all times.* The first thing a young wizard learns at Unseen University—apart from where his peg is, and which way to the lavatory—is that he must protect himself at all times.

Some people think this is paranoia, but it isn't. Paranoids only think everyone is out to get them. Wizards *know* it.

The little wizard was wearing the psychic equivalent of three feet of tempered steel and it was being melted like butter under a blowlamp. It streamed away, vanished.

If there are words to describe what happened to the wizard next then they're imprisoned inside a wild thesaurus in the Unseen University Library. Perhaps it's best left to the imagination, except that anyone able to imagine the kind of shape that Rincewind saw writhing painfully for a few seconds

---

* Of course, wizards often killed one another by ordinary, nonmagical means, but this was perfectly allowable and death by assassination was considered natural causes for a wizard.

before it mercifully vanished must be a candidate for the famous white canvas blazer with the optional long sleeves.

"*So perish all enemies,*" said Abrim.

He turned his face up to the heights of the tower.

"*I challenge,*" he said. "*And those who will not face me must follow me, according to the Lore.*"

There was a long, thick pause caused by a lot of people listening very hard. Eventually, from the top of the tower, a voice called out uncertainly, "Whereabouts in the Lore?"

"*I embody the Lore.*"

There was a distant whispering and then the same voice called out, "The Lore is dead. Sourcery is above the Lo—"

The sentence ended in a scream because Abrim raised his left hand and sent a thin beam of green light in the precise direction of the speaker.

It was at about this moment that Rincewind realized that he could move his limbs himself. The hat had temporarily lost interest in them. He glanced sideways at Conina. In instant, unspoken agreement they each grasped one of Nijel's arms and turned and ran, and didn't stop until they'd put several walls between them and the tower. Rincewind ran expecting something to hit him in the back of the neck. Possibly the world.

All three landed in the rubble and lay there panting.

"You needn't have done that," muttered Nijel. "I was just getting ready to really give him a seeing-to. How can I ever—"

There was an explosion behind them and shafts of multicolored fire screamed overhead, striking sparks off the masonry. Then there was a sound like an enormous cork being pulled out of a small bottle, and a peal of laughter that, somehow, wasn't very amusing. The ground shook.

"What's going on?" said Conina.

"Magical war," said Rincewind.

"Is that good?"

"No."

"But surely you want wizardry to triumph?" said Nijel.

Rincewind shrugged, and ducked as something unseen and big whirred overhead making a noise like a partridge.

"I've never seen wizards fight," said Nijel. He started to scramble up the rubble and screamed as Conina grabbed him by the leg.

"I don't think that would be a good idea," she said. "Rincewind?"

The wizard shook his head gloomily, and picked up a pebble. He tossed it up above the ruined wall, where it turned into a small blue teapot. It smashed when it hit the ground.

"The spells react with one another," he said. "There's no telling what they'll do."

"But we're safe behind this wall?" said Conina.

Rincewind brightened a bit. "Are we?" he said.

"I was asking you."

"Oh. No. I shouldn't think so. It's just ordinary stone. The right spell and . . . phooey."

"Phooey?"

"Right."

"Shall we run away again?"

"It's worth a try."

They made it to another upright wall a few seconds before a randomly spitting ball of yellow fire landed where they had been lying and turned the ground into something awful. The whole area around the tower was a tornado of sparkling air.

"We need a plan," said Nijel.

"We could try running again," said Rincewind.

"That doesn't solve anything!"

"Solves most things," said Rincewind.

"How far do we have to go to be safe?" said Conina.

Rincewind risked a look around the wall.

"Interesting philosophical question," he said. "I've been a long way, and I've never been safe."

Conina sighed and stared at a pile of rubble nearby. She stared at it again. There was something odd there, and she couldn't quite put her finger on it.

"I could rush at them," said Nijel, vaguely. He stared yearningly at Conina's back.

"Wouldn't work," said Rincewind. "Nothing works against magic. Except stronger magic. And then the only thing that beats stronger magic is even stronger magic. And next thing you know . . ."

"Phooey?" suggested Nijel.

"It happened before," said Rincewind. "Went on for thousands of years until not a—"

"Do you know what's odd about that heap of stone?" said Conina.

Rincewind glanced at it. He screwed up his eyes.

"What, apart from the legs?" he said.

It took several minutes to dig the Seriph out. He was still clutching a wine bottle, which was almost empty, and blinked at them all in vague recognition.

"Powerful," he said, and then after some effort added, "stuff, this vintage. Felt," he continued, "as though the place fell on me."

"It did," said Rincewind.

"Ah. That would be it, then." Creosote focused on Conina, after several attempts, and rocked backwards. "My word," he said, "the young lady again. Very impressive."

"I say—" Nijel began.

"Your hair," said the Seriph, rocking slowly forward again, "is like, is like a flock of goats that graze upon the side of Mount Gebra."

"Look here—"

"Your breasts are like, like," the Seriph swayed sideways a little, and gave a brief, sorrowful glance at the empty bottle, "are like the jewelled melons in the fabled gardens of dawn."

Conina's eyes widened. "They are?" she said.

"No," said the Seriph, "doubt about it. I know jewelled melons when I see them. As the white does in the meadows of the water margin are your thighs, which—"

"Erm, excuse me—" said Nijel, clearing his throat with malice aforethought.

Creosote swayed in his direction.

"Hmm?" he said.

"Where I come from," said Nijel stonily, "we don't talk to ladies like that."

Conina sighed as Nijel shuffled protectively in front of her. It was, she reflected, absolutely true.

"In fact," he went on, sticking out his jaw as far as

possible, which still made it appear like a dimple, "I've a jolly good mind—"

"Open to debate," said Rincewind, stepping forward. "Er, sir, sire, we need to get out. I suppose you wouldn't know the way?"

"Thousands of rooms," said the Seriph, "in here, you know. Not been out in years." He hiccuped. "Decades. Ians. Never been out, in fact." His face glazed over in the act of composition. "The bird of Time has but, um, a little way to walk and lo! the bird is on its feet."

"It's a geas," muttered Rincewind.

Creosote swayed at him. "Abrim does all the ruling, you see. Terrible hard work."

"He's not," said Rincewind, "making a very good job of it just at present."

"And we'd sort of like to get away," said Conina, who was still turning over the phrase about the goats.

"And I've got this geas," said Nijel, glaring at Rincewind.

Creosote patted him on the arm.

"That's nice," he said. "Everyone should have a pet."

"So if you happen to know if you own any stables or anything . . ." prompted Rincewind.

"Hundreds," said Creosote. "I own some of the finest, most . . . finest horses in the world." His brow wrinkled. "So they tell me."

"But you wouldn't happen to know where they are?"

"Not as such," the Seriph admitted. A random spray of magic turned the nearby wall into arsenic meringue.

"I think we might have been better off in the snake pit," said Rincewind, turning away.

Creosote took another sorrowful glance at his empty wine bottle.

"I know where there's a magic carpet," he said.

"No," said Rincewind, raising his hands protectively. "Absolutely not. Don't even—"

"It belonged to my grandfather—"

"A real magic carpet?" said Nijel.

"Listen," said Rincewind urgently. "I get vertigo just listening to tall stories."

"Oh, quite," the Seriph burped gently, "genuine. Very pretty pattern." He squinted at the bottle again, and sighed. "It was a lovely blue color," he added.

"And you wouldn't happen to know where it is?" said Conina slowly, in the manner of one creeping up very carefully to a wild animal that might take fright at any moment.

"In the treasury. I know the way *there*. I'm extremely rich, you know. Or so they tell me." He lowered his voice and tried to wink at Conina, eventually managing it with both eyes. "We could sit on it," he said, breaking into a sweat. "And you could tell me a story . . ."

Rincewind tried to scream through gritted teeth.

His ankles were already beginning to sweat.

"I'm not going to ride on a magic carpet!" he hissed. "I'm afraid of grounds!"

"You mean heights," said Conina. "And stop being silly."

"I know what I mean! It's the grounds that kill you!"

* * *

The battle of Al Khali was a hammer-headed cloud, in whose roiling depths weird shapes could be heard and strange sounds were seen. Occasional misses seared across the city. Where they landed things were . . . *different*.

For example, a large part of the *soak* had turned into an impenetrable forest of giant yellow mushrooms. No one knew what effect this had on its inhabitants, although possibly they hadn't noticed.

The temple of Offler the Crocodile God, patron deity of the city, was now a rather ugly sugary thing constructed in five dimensions. But this was no problem because it was being eaten by a herd of giant ants.

On the other hand, not many people were left to appreciate this statement against uncontrolled civic alteration, because most of them were running for their lives. They fled across the fertile fields in a steady stream. Some had taken to boats, but this method of escape had ceased when most of the harbor area turned into a swamp in which, for no obvious reason, a couple of small pink elephants were building a nest.

Down below the panic on the roads the Luggage paddled slowly up one of the reed-lined drainage ditches. A little way ahead of it a moving wave of small alligators, rats and snapping turtles was pouring out of the water and scrambling frantically up the bank, propelled by some vague but absolutely accurate animal instinct.

The Luggage's lid was set in an expression of grim determination. It didn't want much out of the world, except for the total extinction of every other lifeform, but what it needed more than anything else now was its owner.

It was easy to see that the room was a treasury by its incredible emptiness. Doors hung off hooks. Barred alcoves had been smashed in. Lots of smashed chests lay around, and this gave Rincewind a pang of guilt and he wondered, for about two seconds, where the Luggage had got to.

There was a respectful silence, as there always is when large sums of money have just passed away. Nijel wandered off and prodded some of the chests in a forlorn search for secret drawers, as per the instructions in Chapter Eleven.

Conina reached down and picked up a small copper coin.

"How horrible," said Rincewind eventually. "A treasury with no treasure in it."

The seriph stood and beamed. "Not to worry," he said.

"But all your money has been stolen!" said Conina.

"The servants, I expect," said Creosote. "Very disloyal of them."

Rincewind gave him an odd look. "Doesn't it worry you?"

"Not much. I never really spent anything. I've often wondered what being poor was like."

"You're going to get a huge opportunity to find out."

"Will I need training?"

"It comes naturally," said Rincewind. "You pick it up as you go along." There was a distant explosion and part of the ceiling turned to jelly.

"Erm, excuse me," said Nijel, "this carpet . . ."

"Yes," said Conina, "the carpet."

Creosote gave them a benevolent, slightly tipsy smile.

"Ah, yes. The carpet. Push the nose of the statue behind you, peach-buttocked jewel of the desert dawn."

Conina, blushing, performed this act of minor sacrilege on a large green statue of Offler the Crocodile God.

Nothing happened. Secret compartments assiduously failed to open.

"Um. Try the left hand."

She gave it an experimental twist. Creosote scratched his head.

"Maybe it was the right hand . . ."

"I should try and remember, if I were you," said Conina sharply, when that didn't work either. "There aren't many bits left that I'd care to pull."

"What's that thing there?" said Rincewind.

"You're really going to hear about it if it isn't the tail," said Conina, and gave it a kick.

There was a distant metallic groaning noise, like a saucepan in pain. The statue shuddered. It was followed by a few heavy clonks somewhere inside the wall, and Offler the Crocodile God grated ponderously aside. There was a tunnel behind him.

"My grandfather had this built for our more interesting treasure," said Creosote. "He was very"—he groped for a word—"ingenious."

"If you think I'm setting foot in there—" Rincewind began.

"Stand aside," said Nijel, loftily. "I will go first."

"There could be traps—" said Conina doubtfully. She shot the Seriph a glance.

"Oh, probably, O gazelle of Heaven," he said. "I haven't been in there since I was six. There were some slabs you shouldn't tread on, I think."

"Don't worry about that," said Nijel, peering into the gloom of the tunnel. "I shouldn't think there's a booby trap that *I* couldn't spot."

"Had a lot of experience at this sort of thing, have you?" said Rincewind sourly.

"Well, I know Chapter Fourteen by heart. It had illustrations," said Nijel, and ducked into the shadows.

They waited for several minutes in what would have been a horrified hush if it wasn't for the muffled grunts and occasional thumping noises from the tunnel. Eventually Nijel's voice echoed back down to them from a distance.

"There's absolutely nothing," he said. "I've tried everything. It's as steady as a rock. Everything must have seized up, or something."

Rincewind and Conina exchanged glances.

"He doesn't know the first thing about traps," she said. "When I was five, my father made me walk all the way down a passage that he'd rigged up, just to teach me—"

"He got through, didn't he?" said Rincewind.

There was a noise like a damp finger dragged across glass, but amplified a billion times, and the floor shook.

"Anyway, we haven't got a lot of choice," he added, and ducked into the tunnel. The others followed him. Many people who had gotten to know Rincewind had come to treat him as a sort of two-legged miner's canary* and tended to assume that if Rincewind was still upright and not actually running then some hope remained.

"This is fun," said Creosote. "Me, robbing my own treasury. If I catch myself I can have myself flung into the snake pit."

"But you could throw yourself on your mercy," said Conina, running a paranoid eye over the dusty stonework.

"Oh, no. I think I would have to teach me a lesson, as an example to myself."

There was a little click above them. A small slab slid aside and a rusty metal hook descended slowly and jerkily. Another bar creaked out of the wall and tapped Rincewind on the shoulder. As he swung around, the first hook hung a yellowing notice on his back and retracted into the roof.

"What'd it do? What'd it do?" screamed Rincewind, trying to read his own shoulderblades.

"It says, *Kick Me*," said Conina.

A section of wall slid up beside the petrified wizard. A large boot on the end of a complicated series of metal joints gave a half-hearted wobble and then the whole thing snapped at the knee.

The three of them looked at it in silence. Then Conina said, "We're dealing here with a warped brain, I can tell."

Rincewind gingerly unhooked the sign and let it drop. Conina pushed past him and stalked along the passage with an air of angry caution, and when a

---

* All right. But you've got the general idea.

metal hand extended itself on a spring and waggled in a friendly fashion she didn't shake it but instead traced its moulting wiring to a couple of corroded electrodes in a big glass jar.

"Your grandad was a man with a sense of humor?" she said.

"Oh, yes. Always liked a chuckle," said Creosote.

"Oh, good," said Conina. She prodded gingerly at a flagstone which, to Rincewind, looked no different to any of its fellows. With a sad little springy noise a moulting feather duster wobbled out of the wall at armpit height.

"I think I would have quite liked to meet the old Seriph," she said, through gritted teeth, "although not to shake him by the hand. You'd better give me a leg up here, wizard."

"Pardon?"

Conina pointed irritably to a half-open stone doorway just ahead of them.

"I want to look up there," she said. "You just put your hands together for me to stand on, right? How do you manage to be so useless?"

"Being useful always gets me into trouble," muttered Rincewind, trying to ignore the warm flesh brushing against his nose.

He could hear her rooting around above the door.

"I thought so," she said.

"What is it? Fiendishly sharp spears poised to drop?"

"No."

"Spiked grill ready to skewer—?"

"It's a bucket," said Conina flatly, giving it a push.

"What, of scalding, poisonous—?"

"Whitewash. Just a lot of old, dried-up white-wash." Conina jumped down.

"That's grandfather for you," said Creosote. "Never a dull moment."

"Well, I've just about had enough," Conina said firmly, and pointed to the far end of the tunnel. "Come on, you two."

They were about three feet from the far end when Rincewind felt a movement in the air above him. Conina struck him in the small of the back, shoving him forward into the room beyond. He rolled when he hit the floor, and something nicked his foot at the same time as a loud thump deafened him.

The entire roof, a huge block of stone four feet thick, had dropped into the tunnel.

Rincewind crawled forward through the dust clouds and, with a trembling finger, traced the lettering on the side of the slab.

"*Laugh This One Off*," he said.

He sat back.

"That's grandad," said Creosote happily, "always a—"

He intercepted Conina's gaze, which had the force of a lead pipe, and wisely shut up.

Nijel emerged from the clouds, coughing.

"I say, what happened?" he said. "Is everyone all right? It didn't do that when I went through."

Rincewind sought for a reply, and couldn't find anything better than, "Didn't it?"

Light filtered into the deep room from tiny barred windows up near the roof. There was no way out except by walking through the several hundred tons of stone that blocked the tunnel or, to put it in another way, which was the way Rincewind put it, they were undoubtedly trapped. He relaxed a bit.

At least there was no mistaking the magic carpet. It lay rolled up on a raised slab in the middle of the room. Next to it was a small, sleek oil lamp and—Rincewind craned to see—a small gold ring. He groaned. A faint octarine corona hung over all three items, indicating that they were magical.

When Conina unrolled the carpet a number of small objects tumbled onto the floor, including a brass herring, a wooden ear, a few large square sequins and a lead box with a preserved soap bubble in it.

"What on earth are they?" said Nijel.

"Well," said Rincewind, "before they tried to eat that carpet, they were probably moths."

"Gosh."

"That's what you people never understand," said Rincewind, wearily. "You think magic is just something you can pick up and use, like a, a—"

"Parsnip?" said Nijel.

"Wine bottle?" said the Seriph.

"Something like that," said Rincewind cautiously, but rallied somewhat and went on, "But the truth is, is—"

"Not like that?"

"More like a wine bottle?" said the Seriph hopefully.

"Magic *uses* people," said Rincewind hurriedly. "It affects you as much as you affect it, sort of thing. You can't mess around with magical things without it affecting you. I just thought I'd better warn you."

"Like a wine bottle," said Creosote, "that—"

"—*drinks you back*," said Rincewind. "So you can put down that lamp and ring for a start, and for goodness' sake don't rub anything."

"My grandfather built up the family fortunes with them," said Creosote wistfully. "His wicked uncle locked him in a cave, you know. He had to set himself up with what came to hand. He had nothing in the whole world but a magic carpet, a magic lamp, a magic ring and a grotto full of assorted jewels."

"Came up the hard way, did he?" said Rincewind.

Conina spread the carpet on the floor. It had a complex pattern of golden dragons on a blue background. They were extremely complicated dragons, with long beards, ears and wings, and they seemed to be frozen in motion, caught in transition from one state to another, suggesting that the loom which wove them had rather more dimensions than the usual three, but the worst thing about it was that if you looked at it long enough the pattern became blue dragons on a gold background, and a terrible feeling stole over you that if you kept on trying to see both types of dragon at once your brains would trickle out of your ears.

Rincewind tore his gaze away with some difficulty as another distant explosion rocked the building.

"How does it work?" he said.

Creosote shrugged. "I've never used it," he said. "I suppose you just say 'up' and 'down' and things like that."

"How about 'fly through the wall'?" said Rincewind.

All three of them looked up at the high, dark and, above all, solid walls of the room.

"We could try sitting on it and saying 'rise,'" Nijel volunteered. "And then, before we hit the roof, we could say, well, 'stop.'" He considered this for a bit, and then added, "If that's the word."

"Or, 'drop,'" said Rincewind, "or 'descend,' 'dive,' 'fall,' 'sink.' Or 'plunge.'"

"'Plummet,'" suggested Conina gloomily.

"Of course," said Nijel, "with all this wild magic floating around, you could try using some of it."

"Ah—" said Rincewind, and, "Well—"

"You've got 'wizzard' written on your hat," said Creosote.

"Anyone can write things on their hat," said Conina. "You don't want to believe everything you read."

"Now hold on a minute," said Rincewind hotly.

They held on a minute.

They held on for a further seventeen seconds.

"Look, it's a lot harder than you think," he said.

"What did I tell you?" said Conina. "Come on, let's dig the mortar out with our fingernails."

Rincewind waved her into silence, removed his hat, pointedly blew the dust off the star, put the hat on again, adjusted the brim, rolled up his sleeves, flexed his fingers and panicked.

In default of anything better to do, he leaned against the stone.

It was vibrating. It wasn't that it was being shaken; it felt like the throbbing was coming from inside the wall.

It was very much the same sort of trembling he

had felt back at the University, just before the sourcerer arrived. The stone was definitely very unhappy about something.

He sidled along the wall and put his ear to the next stone, which was a smaller, wedge-shaped stone cut to fit an angle of the wall, not a big, distinguished stone, but a bantam stone, patiently doing its bit for the greater good of the wall as a whole. It was also shaking.

"Shh!" said Conina.

"I can't hear anything," said Nijel loudly. Nijel was one of those people who, if you say 'don't look now,' would immediately swivel his head like an owl on a turntable. These are the same people who, when you point out, say, an unusual crocus just beside them, turn around aimlessly and put their foot down with a sad little squashy noise. If they were lost in a trackless desert you could find them by putting down, somewhere on the sand, something small and fragile like a valuable old mug that had been in your family for generations, and then hurrying back as soon as you heard the crash.

Anyway.

"That's the point! What happened to the war?"

A little cascade of mortar poured down from the ceiling onto Rincewind's hat.

"Something's acting on the stones," he said quietly. "They're trying to break free."

"We're right underneath quite a lot of them," observed Creosote.

There was a grinding noise above them and a shaft of daylight lanced down. To Rincewind's surprise it wasn't accompanied by sudden death from crushing. There was another silicon creak, and the hole grew. The stones were falling out, and they were falling *up*.

"I think," he said, "that the carpet might be worth a try at this point."

The wall beside him shook itself like a dog and drifted apart, its masonry giving Rincewind several severe blows as it soared away.

The four of them landed on the blue and gold carpet in a storm of flying rock.

"We've got to get out of here," said Nijel, keeping up his reputation for acute observation.

"Hang on," said Rincewind. "I'll say—"

"You won't," snapped Conina, kneeling beside him. "*I'll* say. I don't trust you."

"But you've—"

"Shut up," said Conina. She patted the carpet.

"Carpet—rise," she commanded.

There was a pause.

"Up."

"Perhaps it doesn't understand the language," said Nijel.

"Lift. Levitate. Fly."

"Or it could be, say, sensitive to one particular voice—"

"Shut. Up."

"You tried up," said Nijel. "Try ascend."

"Or soar," said Creosote. Several tons of flagstone swooped past an inch from his head.

"If it was going to answer to them it would have done so, wouldn't it?" said Conina. The air around her was thick with dust as the flying stones ground together. She thumped the carpet.

"Take off, you blasted mat! Arrgh!"

A piece of cornice clipped her shoulder. She rubbed the bruise irritably, and turned to Rincewind, who was sitting with his knees under his chin and his hat pulled down over his head.

"Why doesn't it work?" she said.

"You're not saying the right words," he said.

"It doesn't understand the language?"

"Language hasn't got anything to do with it. You've neglected something fundamental."

"Well?"

"Well what?" sniffed Rincewind.

"Look, this isn't the time to stand on your dignity!"

"You keep on trying, don't you mind me."

"Make it fly!"

Rincewind pulled his hat further over his ears.

"Please?" said Conina.

The hat rose a bit.

"We'd all be terribly bucked," said Nijel.

"Hear, hear," said Creosote.

The hat rose some more. "You're quite sure?" said Rincewind.

"Yes!"

Rincewind cleared his throat.

"Down," he commanded.

The carpet rose from the ground and hovered expectantly a few feet over the dust.

"How did—" Conina began, but Nijel interrupted her.

"Wizards are privy to arcane knowledge, that's probably what it is," he said. "Probably the carpet's got a geas on it to do the opposite of anything that's said. Can you make it go up further?"

"Yes, but I'm not going to," said Rincewind. The carpet drifted slowly forward and, as happens so often at times like this, a rolling of masonry bounced right across the spot where it had lain.

A moment later they were out in the open air, the storm of stone behind them.

The palace was pulling itself to pieces, and the pieces were funnelling up into the air like a volcanic eruption in reverse. The sourcerous tower had completely disappeared, but the stones were dancing toward the spot where it had stood and . . .

"They're building another tower!" said Nijel.

"Out of my palace, too," said Creosote.

"The hat's won," said Rincewind. "That's why it's building its own tower. It's a sort of reaction. Wizards always used to build a tower around themselves, like those . . . what do you call those things you find at the bottom of rivers?"

"Frogs."

"Stones."

"Unsuccessful gangsters."

"Caddis flies is what I meant," said Rincewind. "When a wizard set out to fight, the first thing he always did was build a tower."

"It's very big," said Nijel.

Rincewind nodded glumly.

"Where are we going?" said Conina.

Rincewind shrugged.

"Away," he said.

The outer palace wall drifted just below them. As they passed over it began to shake, and small bricks began to loop toward the storm of flying rock that buzzed around the new tower.

Eventually Conina said, "All right. How did you get the carpet to fly? Does it really do the opposite of what you command?"

"No. I just paid attention to certain fundamental details of laminar and spatial arrangements."

"You've lost me there," she admitted.

"You want it in non-wizard talk?"

"Yes."

"You put it on the floor upside down," said Rincewind.

Conina sat very still for a while. Then she said, "I must say this is very comfortable. It's the first time I've ever flown on a carpet."

"It's the first time I've ever flown one," said Rincewind vaguely.

"You do it very well," she said.

"Thank you."

"You said you were frightened of heights."

"Terrified."

"You don't show it."

"I'm not thinking about it."

Rincewind turned and looked at the tower behind them. It had grown quite a lot in the last minute, blossoming at the top into a complexity of turrets and battlements. A swarm of tiles was hovering over it, individual tiles swooping down and clinking into place like ceramic bees on a bombing run. It was impossibly high—the stones at the bottom would have been crushed if it wasn't for the magic that crackled through them.

Well, that was just about *it* as far as organized wizardry was concerned. Two thousand years of peaceful magic had gone down the drain, the towers were going up again, and with all this new raw magic floating around something was going to get very seriously hurt. Probably the universe. Too much magic could wrap time and space around itself, and that wasn't good news for the kind of person who had grown used to things like effects following things like causes.

And, of course, it would be impossible to explain things to his companions. They didn't seem to grasp ideas properly; more particularly, they didn't seem able to get the hang of doom. They suffered from the terrible delusion that something could be done. They seemed prepared to make the world the way they wanted it or die in the attempt, and the trouble with dying in the attempt was that you died in the attempt.

The whole point about the old University organization was that it kept a sort of peace between wizards who got along with one another about as easily as cats in a sack, and now the gloves were off anyone who tried to interfere was going to end up severely scratched. This wasn't the old, gentle, rather silly magic that the Disc was used to; this was magic war, white-hot and searing.

Rincewind wasn't very good at precognition; in fact he could barely see into the present. But he knew with weary certainty that at some point in the very near future, like thirty seconds or so, someone would say: "Surely there's something we could do?"

The desert passed below them, lit by the low rays of the setting sun.

"There don't seem to be many stars," said Nijel. "Perhaps they're scared to come out."

Rincewind looked up. There was a silver haze high in the air.

"It's raw magic settling out of the atmosphere," he said. "It's saturated."

Twenty-seven, twenty-eight, twen—

"Surely there's—" Conina began.

"There isn't," said Rincewind flatly, but with just the faintest twinge of satisfaction. "The wizards will fight each other until there's one victor. There isn't anything anyone else can do."

"I could do with a drink," said Creosote. "I suppose we couldn't stop somewhere where I could buy an inn?"

"What with?" said Nijel. "You're poor, remember?"

"Poor I don't mind," said the Seriph. "It's sobriety that is giving me difficulties."

Conina prodded Rincewind gently in the ribs.

"Are you steering this thing?" she said.

"No."

"Then where is it going?"

Nijel peered downwards.

"By the look of it," he said, "it's going hubwards. Towards the Circle Sea."

"*Someone* must be guiding it."

Hallo, said a friendly voice in Rincewind's head.

You're not my conscience again, are you? thought Rincewind.

I'm feeling really bad.

Well, I'm sorry, Rincewind thought, but none of this is my fault. I'm just a victim of circuses. I don't see why I should take the blame.

Yes, but you could do something about it.

Like what?

You could destroy the sourcerer. All this would collapse then.

I wouldn't stand a chance.

Then at least you could die in the attempt. That might be preferable to letting magical war break out.

"Look, just shut up, will you?" said Rincewind.

"What?" said Conina.

"Um?" said Rincewind, vaguely. He looked down blankly at the blue and gold pattern underneath him, and added, "You're flying this, aren't you? Through me! That's sneaky!"

"What are you talking about?"

"Oh. Sorry. Talking to myself."

"I think," said Conina, "that we'd better land."

They glided down toward a crescent of beach where the desert reached the sea. In a normal light it would have been blinding white with a sand made up of billions of tiny shell fragments, but at this time of day it was blood-red and primordial. Ranks of driftwood, carved by the waves and bleached by the sun, were piled up on the tideline like the bones of ancient fish or the biggest floral art accessory counter in the universe. Nothing stirred, apart from the waves. There were a few rocks around, but they were firebrick hot and home to no mollusc or seaweed.

Even the sea looked arid. If any proto-amphibian emerged onto a beach like this, it would have given up there and then, gone back into the water and told all its relatives to forget the legs, it wasn't worth it. The air felt as though it had been cooked in a sock.

Even so, Nijel insisted that they light a fire.

"It's more friendly," he said. "Besides, there could be monsters."

Conina looked at the oily wavelets, rolling up the beach in what appeared to be a half-hearted attempt to get out of the sea.

"In that?" she said.

"You never can tell."

Rincewind mooched along the waterline, distractedly picking up stones and throwing them in the sea. One or two were thrown back.

After a while Conina got a fire going, and the bone-dry, salt-saturated wood sent blue and green flames roaring up under a fountain of sparks. The wizard went and sat in the dancing shadows, his back against a pile of whitened wood, wrapped in a cloud of such impenetrable gloom that even Creosote stopped complaining of thirst and shut up.

Conina woke up after midnight. There was a crescent moon on the horizon and a thin, chilly mist covered the sand. Creosote was snoring on his back. Nijel, who was theoretically on guard, was sound asleep.

Conina lay perfectly still, every sense seeking out the thing that had awaken her.

Finally she heard it again. It was a tiny, diffident clinking noise, barely audible above the muted slurp of the sea.

She got up, or rather, she slid into the vertical as bonelessly as a jellyfish, and flicked Nijel's sword out of his unresisting hand. Then she sidled through the mist without causing so much as an extra swirl.

The fire sank down further into its bed of ash.

After a while Conina came back, and shook the other two awake.

"Warrizit?"

"I think you ought to see this," she hissed. "I think it could be important."

"I just shut my eyes for a second—" Nijel protested.

"Never mind about that. Come on."

Creosote squinted around the impromptu campsite.

"Where's the wizard fellow?"

"You'll see. And don't make a noise. It could be dangerous."

They stumbled after her knee-deep in vapor, toward the sea.

Eventually Nijel said, "Why dangerous—"

"Shh! Did you hear it?"

Nijel listened.

"Like a sort of ringing noise?"

"Watch . . ."

Rincewind walked jerkily up the beach, carrying a large round rock in both hands. He walked past them without a word, his eyes staring straight ahead.

They followed him along the cold beach until he reached a bare area between the dunes, where he stopped and, still moving with all the grace of a clothes horse, dropped the rock. It made a clinking noise.

There was a wide circle of other stones. Very few of them had actually stayed on top of another one.

The three of them crouched down and watched him.

"Is he asleep?" said Creosote.

Conina nodded.

"What's he trying to do?"

"I think he's trying to build a tower."

Rincewind lurched back into the ring of stones and, with great care, placed another rock on empty air. It fell down.

"He's not very good at it, is he," said Nijel.

"It is very sad," said Creosote.

"Maybe we ought to wake him up," said Conina. "Only I heard that if you wake up sleepwalkers their legs fall off, or something. What do you think?"

"Could be risky, with wizards," said Nijel.

They tried to make themselves comfortable on the chilly sand.

"It's rather pathetic, isn't it?" said Creosote. "It's not as if he's really a proper wizard."

Conina and Nijel tried to avoid one another's gaze. Finally the boy coughed, and said, "I'm not exactly a barbarian hero, you know. You may have noticed."

They watched the toiling figure of Rincewind for a while, and then Conina said, "If it comes to that, I think I lack a certain something when it comes to hairdressing."

They both stared fixedly at the sleepwalker, busy with their own thoughts and red with mutual embarrassment.

Creosote cleared his throat.

"If it makes anyone feel better," he said, "I sometimes perceive that my poetry leaves a lot to be desired."

Rincewind carefully tried to balance a large rock on a small pebble. It fell off, but he appeared to be happy with the result.

"Speaking as a poet," said Conina carefully, "what would you say about this situation?"

Creosote shifted uneasily. "Funny old thing, life," he said.

"Pretty apt."

Nijel lay back and looked up at the hazy stars. Then he sat bolt upright.

"Did you see that?" he demanded.

"What?"

"It was a sort of flash, a kind of—"

The hubward horizon exploded into a silent flower of color, which expanded rapidly through all the hues of the conventional spectrum before flashing into brilliant octarine. It etched itself on their eyeballs before fading away.

After a while there was a distant rumble.

"Some sort of magical weapon," said Conina, blinking. A gust of warm wind picked up the mist and streamed it past them.

"Blow this," said Nijel, getting to his feet. "I'm going to wake him up, even if it means we end up carrying him."

He reached out for Rincewind's shoulder just as something went past very high overhead, making a noise like a flock of geese on nitrous oxide. It disappeared into the desert behind them. Then there was a sound that would have set false teeth on edge, a flash of green light, and a thump.

"I'll wake him up," said Conina. "You get the carpet."

She clambered over the ring of rocks and took the sleeping wizard gently by the arm, and this would have been a textbook way of waking a somnambulist if Rincewind hadn't dropped the rock he was carrying on his foot.

He opened his eyes.

"Where am I?" he said.

"On the beach. You've been . . . er . . . dreaming."

Rincewind blinked at the mist, the sky, the circle of stones, Conina, the circle of stones again, and finally back at the sky.

"What's been happening?" he said.

"Some sort of magical fireworks."

"Oh. It's started, then."

He lurched unsteadily out of the circle, in a way that suggested to Conina that perhaps he wasn't quite awake yet, and staggered back toward the remains of the fire. He walked a few steps and then appeared to remember something.

He looked down at his foot, and said, "Ow."

He'd almost reached the fire when the blast from the last spell reached them. It had been aimed at the tower in Al Khali, which was twenty miles away, and by now the wavefront was extremely diffuse. It was hardly affecting the nature of things as it surged over the dunes with a faint sucking noise; the fire burned red and green for a second, one of Nijel's sandals turned into a small and irritated badger, and a pigeon flew out of the Seriph's turban.

Then it was past and boiling out over the sea.

"What was *that*?" said Nijel. He kicked the badger, who was sniffing at his foot.

"Hmm?" said Rincewind.

"*That!*"

"Oh, that," said Rincewind. "Just the backwash of a spell. They probably hit the tower in Al Khali."

"It must have been pretty big to affect us here."

"It probably was."

"Hey, that was my palace," said Creosote weakly. "I mean, I know it was a lot, but it was all I had."

"Sorry."

"But there were people in the city!"

"They're probably all right," said Rincewind.

"Good."

"Whatever they are."

"What?"

Conina grabbed his arm. "Don't shout at him," she said. "He's not himself."

"Ah," said Creosote dourly, "an improvement."

"I say, that's a bit unfair," Nijel protested. "I mean, he got me out of the snake pit and, well, he knows a lot—"

"Yes, wizards are good at getting you out of the sort of trouble that only wizards can get you into," said Creosote. "Then they expect you to thank them."

"Oh, I think—"

"It's got to be said," said Creosote, waving his hands irritably. He was briefly illuminated by the passage of another spell across the tormented sky.

"Look at that!" he snapped. "Oh, he *means* well. They all mean well. They probably all think the Disc would be a better place if they were in charge. Take it from me, there's nothing more terrible than someone out to do the world a favor. Wizards! When all's said and done, what good are they? I mean, can you name me something worthwhile any wizard's done?"

"I think that's a bit cruel," said Conina, but with

an edge in her voice that suggested that she could be open to persuasion on the subject.

"Well, they make me sick," muttered Creosote, who was feeling acutely sober and didn't like it much.

"I think we'll all feel better if we try to get a bit more sleep," said Nijel diplomatically. "Things always look better by daylight. Nearly always, anyway."

"My mouth feels all horrible, too," muttered Creosote, determined to cling onto the remnant of his anger.

Conina turned back to the fire, and became aware of a gap in the scenery. It was Rincewind-shaped.

"He's gone!"

In fact Rincewind was already half a mile out over the dark sea, squatting on the carpet like an angry buddha, his mind a soup of rage, humiliation and fury, with a side order of outrage.

He hadn't wanted much, ever. He'd stuck with wizardry even though he wasn't any good at it, he'd always done his best, and now the whole world was conspiring against him. Well, he'd show them. Precisely who 'they' were and what they were going to be shown was merely a matter of detail.

He reached up and touched his hat for reassurance, even as it lost its last few sequins in the slipstream.

The Luggage was having problems of its own.

The area around the tower of Al Khali, under the relentless magical bombardment, was already drifting beyond that reality horizon where time, space and matter lose their separate identities and start wearing one another's clothes. It was quite impossible to describe.

Here is what it looked like.

It looked like a piano sounds shortly after being dropped down a well. It tasted yellow, and felt Paisley. It smelled like a total eclipse of the moon. Of course, nearer to the tower it got *really* weird.

Expecting anything unprotected to survive in that would be like expecting snow on a supernova. Fortunately the Luggage didn't know this, and slid through the maelstrom with raw magic crystallizing on its lid and hinges. It was in a foul mood but, again, there was nothing very unusual about this, except that the crackling fury earthing itself spectacularly all over the Luggage in a multi-colored corona gave it the appearance of an early and very angry amphibian crawling out of a burning swamp.

It was hot and stuffy inside the tower. There were no internal floors, just a series of walkways around the walls. They were lined with wizards, and the central space was a column of octarine light that creaked loudly as they poured their power into it. At its base stood Abrim, the octarine gems on the hat blazing so brightly that they looked more like holes cut through into a different universe where, in defiance of probability, they had come out inside a sun.

The vizier stood with his hands out, fingers splayed, eyes shut, mouth a thin line of concentration, balancing the forces. Usually a wizard could control power only to the extent of his own physical capability, but Abrim was learning fast.

You made yourself the pinch in the hourglass, the fulcrum on the balance, the roll around the sausage.

Do it right and you *were* the power, it was part of you and you were capable of—

Has it been pointed out that his feet were several inches off the ground? His feet were several inches off the ground.

Abrim was pulling together the potency for a spell that would soar away into the sky and beset the Ankh tower with a thousand screaming demons when there came a thunderous knock at the door.

There is a mantra to be said on these occasions. It doesn't matter if the door is a tent flap, a scrap of hide on a windblown yurt, three inches of solid oak with great iron nails in it or a rectangle of chipboard with mahogany veneer, a small light over it made of horrible bits of colored glass and a bellpush that plays a choice of twenty popular melodies that no music lover would want to listen to even after five years' sensory deprivation.

One wizard turned to another and duly said: "I wonder who that can be at this time of night?"

There was another series of thumps on the woodwork.

"There can't be anyone alive out there," said the other wizard, and he said it nervously, because if you ruled out the possibility of it being anyone alive that always left the suspicion that perhaps it was someone dead.

This time the banging rattled the hinges.

"One of us had better go out," said the first wizard.

"Good man."

"Ah. Oh. Right."

He set off slowly down the short, arched passage.

"I'll just go and see who it is, then?" he said.

"First class."

It was a strange figure that made its hesitant way to the door. Ordinary robes weren't sufficient protection in the high-energy field inside tower, and over his brocade and velvet the wizard wore a thick, padded overall stuffed with rowan shavings and embroidered with industrial-grade sigils. He'd affixed a smoked glass visor to his pointy hat and his gauntlets, which were extremely big, suggested that he was a wicket keeper in a game of cricket played at supersonic speeds. The actinic flashes and pulsations from the great work in the main hall cast harsh shadows around him as he fumbled for the bolts.

He pulled down the visor and opened the door a fraction.

"We don't want any—" he began, and ought to have chosen his words better, because they were his epitaph.

It was some time before his colleague noticed his continued absence, and wandered down the passage to find him. The door had been thrown wide open, the thaumatic inferno outside roaring against the web of spells that held it in check. In fact the door hadn't been pushed *completely* back; he pulled it aside to see why, and gave a little whimper.

There was a noise behind him. He turned around.

"Wha—" he began, which is a pretty poor syllable on which to end a life.

*   *   *

High over the Circle Sea Rincewind was feeling like a bit of an idiot.

This happens to everyone sooner or later.

For example, in a tavern someone jogs your elbow and you turn around quickly and give a mouthful of abuse to, you become slowly aware, the belt buckle of a man who, it turns out, was probably hewn rather than born.

Or a little car runs into the back of yours and you rush out to show a bunch of fives to the driver who, it becomes apparent as he goes on unfolding more body like some horrible conjuring trick, must have been sitting on the back seat.

Or you might be leading your mutinous colleagues to the captain's cabin and you hammer on the door and he sticks his great head out with a cutlass in either hand and you say "We're taking over the ship, you scum, and the lads are right with me!" and he says "What lads?" and you suddenly feel a great emptiness behind you and you say "Um . . ."

In other words, it's the familiar hot sinking feeling experienced by everyone who has let the waves of their own anger throw them far up on the beach of retribution, leaving them, in the poetic language of the everyday, up shit creek.

Rincewind was still angry and humiliated and so forth, but these emotions had died down a bit and something of his normal character had reasserted itself. It was not very pleased to find itself on a few threads of blue and gold wool high above the phosphorescent waves.

He'd been heading for Ankh-Morpork. He tried to remember why.

Of course, it was where it had all started. Perhaps it was the presence of the University, which was so heavy with magic it lay like a cannonball on the incontinence blanket of the Universe, stretching reality very thin. Ankh was where things started, and finished.

It was also his home, such as it was, and it called to him.

It has already been indicated that Rincewind appeared to have a certain amount of rodent in his ancestry, and in times of stress he felt an overpowering urge to make a run for his burrow.

He let the carpet drift for a while on the air currents while dawn, which Creosote would probably have referred to as pink-fingered, made a ring of fire around the edge of the Disc. It spread its lazy light over a world that was subtly different.

Rincewind blinked. There was a weird light. No, now he came to think about it, not weird but wyrd, which was much weirder. It was like looking at the world through a heat haze, but a haze that had a sort of life of its own. It danced and stretched, and gave more than a hint that it wasn't just an optical illusion but that it was reality itself that was being tensed and distended, like a rubber balloon trying to contain too much gas.

The wavering was greatest in the direction of Ankh-Morpork, where flashes and fountains of tortured air indicated that the struggle hadn't abated. A similar column hung over Al Khali, and then Rincewind realized that it wasn't the only one.

Wasn't that a tower over in Quirm, where the

Circle Sea opened onto the great Rim Ocean? And there were others.

It had all gone critical. Wizardry was breaking up. Goodbye to the University, the levels, the Orders; deep in his heart, every wizard knew that the natural unit of wizardry was one wizard. The towers would multiply and fight until there was one tower left, and then the wizards would fight until there was one wizard.

By then, he'd probably fight himself.

The whole edifice that operated as the balance wheel of magic was falling to bits. Rincewind resented that, deeply. He'd never been any good at magic, but that wasn't the point. He knew where he fitted. It was right at the bottom, but at least he fitted. He could look up and see the whole delicate machine ticking away, gently, browsing off the natural magic generated by the turning of the Disc.

All he had was nothing, but that was something, and now it had been taken away.

Rincewind turned the carpet until it was facing the distant gleam that was Ankh-Morpork, which was a brilliant speck in the early morning light, and a part of his mind that wasn't doing anything else wondered why it was so bright. There also seemed to be a full moon, and even Rincewind, whose grasp of natural philosophy was pretty vague, was sure there had been one of those only the other day.

Well, it didn't matter. He'd had enough. He wasn't going to try to understand anything anymore. He was going home.

Except that wizards can never go home.

This is one of the ancient and deeply meaningful

sayings about wizards and it says something about most of them that they have never been able to work out what it means. Wizards aren't allowed to have wives but they are allowed to have parents, and many of them go back to the old home town for Hogswatch Night or Soul Cake Thursday, for a bit of a singsong and the heart-warming sight of all their boyhood bullies hurriedly avoiding them in the street.

It's rather like the other saying they've never been able to understand, which is that you can't cross the same river twice. Experiments with a long-legged wizard and a small river say you can cross the same river thirty, thirty-five times a minute.

Wizards don't like philosophy very much. As far as they are concerned, one hand clapping makes a noise like "cl."

In this particular case, though, Rincewind couldn't go home because it actually wasn't there anymore. There was a city straddling the river Ankh, but it wasn't one he'd ever seen before; it was white and clean and didn't smell like a privy full of dead herrings.

He landed in what had once been the Plaza of Broken Moons, and also in a state of some shock. There were *fountains*. There had been fountains before, of course, but they had oozed rather than played and they had looked like thin soup. There were milky flagstones underfoot, with little glittery bits in them. And, although the sun was sitting on the horizon like half a breakfast grapefruit, there was hardly anyone around. Normally Ankh was permanently crowded, the actual shade of the sky being a mere background detail.

Smoke drifted over the city in long greasy coils from the crown of boiling air above the University. It was the only movement, apart from the fountains.

Rincewind had always been rather proud of the fact that he always felt alone, even in the teeming city, but it was even worse being alone when he was by himself.

He rolled up the carpet and slung it over one shoulder and padded through the haunted streets toward the University.

The gates hung open to the wind. Most of the building looked half ruined by misses and ricochets. The tower of sourcery, far too high to be real, seemed to be unscathed. Not so the old Tower of Art. Half the magic aimed at the tower next door seemed to have rebounded on it. Parts of it had melted and started to run; some parts glowed, some parts had crystalized, a few parts seemed to have twisted partly out of the normal three dimensions. It made you feel sorry even for stone that it should have to undergo such treatment. In fact nearly everything had happened to the tower except actual collapse. It looked so beaten that possibly even gravity had given up on it.

Rincewind sighed, and padded around the base of the tower toward the Library.

Towards where the Library had been.

There was the arch of the doorway, and most of the walls were still standing, but a lot of the roof had fallen in and everything was blackened by soot.

Rincewind stood and stared for a long time.

Then he dropped the carpet and ran, stumbling and sliding through the rubble that half-blocked the doorway. The stones were still warm underfoot. Here and there the wreckage of a bookcase still smouldered.

Anyone watching would have seen Rincewind dart backward and forward across the shimmering heaps, scrabbling desperately among them, throwing aside charred furniture, pulling aside lumps of fallen roof with less than superhuman strength.

They would have seen him pause once or twice to get his breath back, then dive in again, cutting his hands on shards of half-molten glass from the dome of the roof. They would have noticed that he seemed to be sobbing.

Eventually his questing fingers touched something warm and soft.

The frantic wizard heaved a charred roof beam aside, scrabbled through a drift of fallen tiles and peered down.

There, half squashed by the beam and baked brown by the fire, was a large bunch of overripe, squashy bananas.

He picked one up, very carefully, and sat and watched it for some time until the end fell off.

Then he ate it.

"We shouldn't have let him go like that," said Conina.

"How could we have stopped him, oh, beauteous doe-eyed eaglet?"

"But he may do something stupid!"

"I should think that is very likely," said Creosote primly.

"While we do something clever and sit on a baking beach with nothing to eat or drink, is that it?"

"You could tell me a story," said Creosote, trembling slightly.

"Shut up."

The Seriph ran his tongue over his lips.

"I suppose a quick anecdote is out of the question?" he croaked.

Conina sighed. "There's more to life than narrative, you know."

"Sorry. I lost control a little, there."

Now that the sun was well up the crushed-shell beach glowed like a salt flat. The sea didn't look any better by daylight. It moved like thin oil.

Away on either side the beach stretched in long, excruciatingly flat curves, supporting nothing but a few clumps of withered dune grass which lived off the moisture in the spray. There was no sign of any shade.

"The way I see it," said Conina, "this is a beach, and that means sooner or later we'll come to a river, so all we have to do is keep walking in one direction."

"And yet, delightful snow on the slopes of Mount Eritor, we do not know which one."

Nijel sighed, and reached into his bag.

"Erm," he said, "excuse me. Would this be any good? I stole it. Sorry."

He held out the lamp that had been in the treasury.

"It's magic, isn't it?" he said hopefully. "I've heard about them, isn't it worth a try?"

Creosote shook his head.

"But you said your grandfather used it to make his fortune!" said Conina.

"*A* lamp," said the Seriph, "he used *a* lamp. Not

this lamp. No, the real lamp was a battered old thing, and one day this wicked pedlar came around offering new lamps for old and my great-grandmother gave it to him for this one. The family kept it in the vault as a sort of memorial to her. A truly stupid woman. It doesn't work, of course."

"You tried it?"

"No, but he wouldn't have given it away if it was any good, would he?"

"Give it a rub," said Conina. "It can't do any harm."

"I wouldn't," warned Creosote.

Nijel held the lamp gingerly. It had a strangely sleek look, as if someone had set out to make a lamp that could go fast.

He rubbed it.

The effects were curiously unimpressive. There was a halfhearted pop and a puff of wispy smoke near Nijel's feet. A line appeared in the beach several feet away from the smoke. It spread quickly to outline a square of sand, which vanished.

A figure barrelled out of the beach, jerked to a stop, and groaned.

It was wearing a turban, an expensive tan, a small gold medallion, shiny shorts and advanced running shoes with curly toes.

It said, "I want to get this absolutely straight. Where am I?"

Conina recovered first.

"It's a beach," she said.

"Yah," said the genie. "What I mean was, which lamp? What world?"

"Don't you know?"

The creature took the lamp out of Nijel's unresisting grasp.

"Oh, this old thing," he said. "I'm on time share. Two weeks every August but, of course, usually one can never get away."

"Got a lot of lamps, have you?" said Nijel.

"I am somewhat over-committed on lamps," the genie agreed. "In fact I am thinking of diversifying into rings. Rings are looking big at the moment. There's a lot of movement in rings. Sorry, people; what can I do you for?" The last phrase was turned in that special voice which people use for humorous self-parody, in the mistaken hope that it will make them sound less like a prat.

"We—" Conina began.

"I want a drink," snapped Creosote. "And you are *supposed* to say that my wish is your command."

"Oh, absolutely no one says that sort of thing anymore," said the genie, and produced a glass out of nowhere. He treated Creosote to a brilliant smile lasting a small percentage of one second.

"We want you to take us across the sea to Ankh-Morpork," said Conina firmly.

The genie looked blank. Then he pulled a very thick book* from the empty air and consulted it.

---

* It was a Fullomyth, an invaluable aid for all whose business is with the arcane and hermetic. It contained lists of things that didn't exist and, in a very significant way, weren't important. Some of its pages could only be read after midnight, or by strange and improbable illuminations. There were descriptions of underground constellations and wines as yet unfermented. For the really up-to-the-epoch occultist, who could afford the version bound in spider skin, there was even an insert showing the London Underground with the three stations they never dare show on the public maps.

"It sounds a really neat concept," he said eventually. "Let's do lunch next Tuesday, okay?"

"Do what?"

"I'm a little energetic right now."

"*You're a little*—?" Conina began.

"Great," said the genie, sincerely, and glanced at his wrist. "Hey, is that the time?" He vanished.

The three of them looked at the lamp in thoughtful silence, and then Nijel said, "Whatever happened to, you know, the fat guys with the baggy trousers and I Hear And Obey O Master?"

Creosote snarled. He'd just drunk his drink. It had turned out to be water with bubbles in it and a taste like warm flatirons.

"I'm bloody well not standing for it," snarled Conina. She snatched the lamp from his hand and rubbed it as if she was sorry she wasn't holding a handful of emery cloth.

The genie reappeared at a different spot, which still managed to be several feet away from the weak explosion and obligatory cloud of smoke.

He was now holding something curved and shiny to his ear, and listening intently. He looked hurriedly at Conina's angry face and contrived to suggest, by waggling his eyebrows and waving his free hand urgently, that he was currently and inconveniently tied up by irksome matters which, regretfully, prevented him giving her his full attention as of now but, as soon as he had disentangled himself from this importunate person, she could rest assured that her wish, which was certainly a wish of tone and brilliance, would be his command.

"I shall smash the lamp," she said quietly.

The genie flashed her a smile and spoke hastily into the thing he was cradling between his chin and his shoulder.

"Fine," he said. "Great. It's a slice, believe me. Have your people call my people. Stay beyond, okay? Bye." He lowered the instrument. "Bastard," he said vaguely.

"I really shall smash the lamp," said Conina.

"Which lamp is this?" said the genie hurriedly.

"How many have you got?" said Nijel. "I always thought genies had just the one."

The genie explained wearily that in fact he had several lamps. There was a small but well-appointed lamp where he lived during the week, another rather unique lamp in the country, a carefully restored peasant rushlight in an unspoilt wine-growing district near Quirm, and just recently a set of derelict lamps in the docks area of Ankh-Morpork that had great potential, once the smart crowd got there, to become the occult equivalent of a suite of offices and a wine bar.

They listened in awe, like fish who had inadvertently swum into a lecture on how to fly.

"Who are your people the other people have got to call?" said Nijel, who was impressed, although he didn't know why or by what.

"Actually, I don't have any people yet," said the genie, and gave a grimace that was definitely upwardly-mobile at the corners. "But I will."

"Everyone shut up," said Conina firmly, "and *you*, take us to Ankh-Morpork."

"I should, if I were you," said Creosote. "When the young lady's mouth looks like a letter box, it's best to do what she says."

The genie hesitated.

"I'm not very deep on transport," he said.

"Learn," said Conina. She was tossing the lamp from hand to hand.

"Teleportation is a major headache," said the genie, looking desperate. "Why don't we do lun—"

"Right, that's it," said Conina. "Now I just need a couple of big flat rocks—"

"Okay, okay. Just hold hands, will you? I'll give it my best shot, but this could be one big mistake—"

The astro-philosophers of Krull once succeeded in proving conclusively that all places are one place and that the distance between them is an illusion, and this news was an embarrassment to all thinking philosophers because it did not explain, among other things, signposts. After years of wrangling the whole thing was then turned over to Ly Tin Wheedle, arguably the Disc's greatest philosopher* who after some thought proclaimed that although it was indeed true that all places were one place, that place was *very large*.

And so psychic order was restored. Distance is, however, an entirely subjective phenomenon and creatures of magic can adjust it to suit themselves.

They are not necessarily very good at it.

---

* He always argued that he was.

* * *

Rincewind sat dejectedly in the blackened ruins of the Library, trying to put his finger on what was wrong with them.

Well, everything, for a start. It was unthinkable that the Library should be burned. It was the largest accumulation of magic on the Disc. It underpinned wizardry. Every spell ever used was written down in it somewhere. Burning them was, was, was . . .

There weren't any ashes. Plenty of wood ashes, lots of chains, lots of blackened stone, lots of mess. But thousands of books don't burn easily. They would leave bits of cover and piles of feathery ash. And there wasn't any.

Rincewind stirred the rubble with his toe.

There was only the one door into the Library. Then there were the cellars—he could see the stairs down to them, choked with garbage—but you couldn't hide all the books down there. You couldn't teleport them out either, they would be resistant to such magic; anyone who tried something like that would end up wearing his brains outside his hat.

There was an explosion overhead. A ring of orange fire formed about halfway up the tower of sourcery, ascended quickly and soared off toward Quirm.

Rincewind slid around on his makeshift seat and stared up at the Tower of Art. He got the distinct impression that it was looking back at him. It was totally without windows, but for a moment he thought he saw a movement up among the crumbling turrets.

He wondered how old the tower really was. Older than the University, certainly. Older than the city, which had formed about it like screen around a mountain. Maybe older than geography. There had been a time when the continents were different, Rincewind understood, and then they'd sort of shuffled more comfortably together like puppies in a basket. Perhaps the tower had been washed up on the waves of rock, from somewhere else. Maybe it had been there before the Disc itself, but Rincewind didn't like to consider that, because it raised uncomfortable questions about who built it and what for.

He examined his conscience.

It said: I'm out of options. Please yourself.

Rincewind stood up and brushed the dust and ash off his robe, removing quite a lot of the moulting red plush as well. He removed his hat, made a preoccupied attempt at straightening the point, and replaced it on his head.

Then he walked unsteadily toward the Tower of Art.

There was a very old and quite small door at the base. He wasn't at all surprised when it opened as he approached.

"Strange place," said Nijel. "Funny curve to the walls."

"Where are we?" said Conina.

"And is there any alcohol?" said Creosote. "Probably not," he added.

"And why is it rocking?" said Conina. "I've never been anywhere with metal walls before." She sniffed. "Can you smell oil?" she added, suspiciously.

The genie reappeared, although this time without the smoke and erratic trapdoor effects. It was noticeable that he tried to keep as far away from Conina as politely possible.

"Everyone okay?" he said.

"Is this Ankh?" she said. "Only when we wanted to go there, we rather hoped you'd put us somewhere with a door."

"You're on your way," said the genie.

"In what?"

Something about the way in which the spirit hesitated caused Nijel's mind to leap a tall conclusion from a standing start. He looked down at the lamp in his hands.

He gave it an experimental jerk. The floor shook.

"Oh, no," he said. "It's physically impossible."

"We're in the *lamp*?" said Conina.

The room trembled again as Nijel tried to look down the spout.

"Don't worry about it," said the genie. "In fact, don't think about it if possible."

He explained—although "explained" is probably too positive a word, and in this case really means failed to explain but at some length—that it was perfectly possible to travel across the world in a small lamp being carried by one of the party, the lamp itself moving because it was being carried by one of the people inside it, because of a) the fractal nature of reality, which meant that everything could be thought of as being inside everything else and b) creative public relations. The trick relied on the laws of physics failing to spot the flaw until the journey was complete.

"In the circumstances it is best not to think about it, yuh?" said the genie.

"Like not thinking about pink rhinoceroses," said Nijel, and gave an embarrassed laugh as they stared at him.

"It was a sort of game we had," he said. "You had to avoid thinking of pink rhinoceroses." He coughed. "I didn't say it was a particularly good game."

He squinted down the spout again.

"No," said Conina, "not very."

"Uh," said the genie, "Would anyone like coffee? Some sounds? A quick game of Significant Quest?*

"Drink?" said Creosote.

"White wine?"

"Foul muck."

The genie looked shocked.

"Red is bad for—" it began.

"—but any port in a storm," said Creosote hurriedly. "Or sauterne, even. But no umbrella in it." It dawned on the Seriph that this wasn't the way to talk to the genie. He pulled himself together a bit. "No umbrella, by the Five Moons of Nasreem. Or bits of fruit salad or olives or curly straws or ornamental monkeys, I command thee by the Seventeen Siderites of Sarudin."

"I'm not an umbrella person," said the genie sulkily.

"It's pretty sparse in here," said Conina, "Why don't you furnish it."

---

* Very popular among gods, demi-gods, daemons and other supernatural creatures, who feel at home with questions like "What is It all About?" and "Where will It all End?"

"What I don't understand," said Nijel, "is, if we're all in the lamp I'm holding, then the me in the lamp is holding a smaller lamp and in *that* lamp—"

The genie waved his hands urgently.

"Don't talk about it!" he commanded. "Please!"

Nijel's honest brow wrinkled. "Yes, but," he said, "is there a lot of me, or what?"

"It's all cyclic, but stop drawing attention to it, yuh? . . . Oh, shit."

There was the subtle, unpleasant sound of the universe suddenly catching on.

It was dark in the tower, a solid core of antique darkness that had been there since the dawn of time and resented the intrusion of the upstart daylight that nipped in around Rincewind.

He felt the air move as the door shut behind him and the dark poured back, filling up the space where the light had been so neatly that you couldn't have seen the join even if the light had still been there.

The interior of the tower smelled of antiquity, with a slight suspicion of raven droppings.

It took a great deal of courage to stand there in that dark. Rincewind didn't have that much, but stood there anyway.

Something started to snuffle around his feet, and Rincewind stood very still. The only reason he didn't move was for fear of treading on something worse.

Then a hand like an old leather glove touched his, very gently, and a voice said: "Oook."

Rincewind looked up.

The dark yielded, just once, to a vivid flash of light. And Rincewind saw.

The whole tower was lined with books. They were squeezed on every step of the rotting spiral staircase that wound up inside. They were piled up on the floor, although something about the way in which they were piled suggested that the word "huddled" would be more appropriate. They had lodged—all right, they had perched—on every crumbling ledge.

They were observing him, in some covert way that had nothing to do with the normal six senses. Books are pretty good at conveying meaning, not necessarily their own personal meanings of course, and Rincewind grasped the fact that they were trying to tell him something.

There was another flash. He realized that it was magic from the sourcerer's tower, reflected down from the distant hole that led onto the roof.

At least it enabled him to identify Wuffles, who was wheezing at his right foot. That was a bit of a relief. Now if he could just put a name to the soft, repetitive slithering noise near his left ear . . .

There was a further obliging flash, which found him looking directly into the little yellow eyes of the Patrician, who was clawing patiently at the side of his glass jar. It was a gentle, mindless scrabbling, as if the little lizard wasn't particularly trying to get out but was just vaguely interested in seeing how long it would take to wear the glass away.

Rincewind looked down at the pear-shaped bulk of the Librarian.

"There's thousands of them," he whispered, his voice being sucked away and silenced by the massed ranks of books. "How did you get them all in here?"

"Oook oook."

"They what?"

"Oook," repeated the Librarian, making vigorous flapping motions with his bald elbows.

"Fly?"

"Oook."

"Can they do that?"

"Oook," nodded the Librarian.

"That must have been pretty impressive. I'd like to see that one day."

"Oook."

Not every book had made it. Most of the important grimoires had got out but a seven-volume herbal had lost its index to the flames and many a trilogy was mourning for its lost volume. Quite a few books had scorch marks on their bindings; some had lost their covers and trailed their stitching unpleasantly on the floor.

A match flared, and pages rippled uneasily around the walls. But it was only the Librarian, who lit a candle and shambled across the floor at the base of a menacing shadow big enough to climb skyscrapers. He had set up a rough table against one wall and it was covered with arcane tools, pots of rare adhesives and a bookbinder's vice which was already holding a stricken folio. A few weak lines of magic fire crawled across it.

The ape pushed the candlestick into Rincewind's hand, picked up a scalpel and a pair of tweezers, and bent low over the trembling book. Rincewind went pale.

"Um," he said, "er, do you mind if I go away? I faint at the sight of glue."

The Librarian shook his head and jerked a preoccupied thumb toward a tray of tools.

"Oook," he commanded. Rincewind nodded miserably and obediently handed him a pair of long-nosed scissors. The wizard winced as a couple of damaged pages were snipped free and dropped to the floor.

"What are you doing to it?" he managed.

"Oook."

"An appendectomy? Oh."

The ape jerked his thumb again, without looking up. Rincewind fished a needle and thread out of the ranks on the tray and handed them over. There was silence broken only by the scritching sound of thread being pulled through paper until the Librarian straightened up and said:

"Oook."

Rincewind pulled out his handkerchief and mopped the ape's brow.

"Oook."

"Don't mention it. Is it—going to be all right?"

The Librarian nodded. There was also a general, almost inaudible sigh of relief from the tier of books above them.

Rincewind sat down. The books were frightened. In fact they were terrified. The presence of the sourcerer made their spines creep, and the pressure of their attention closed in around him like a vise.

"All right," he mumbled, "but what can I do about it?"

"Oook." The Librarian gave Rincewind a look that would have been exactly like a quizzical look over the top of a pair of half-moon spectacles, if he had been wearing any, and reached for another broken book.

"I mean, you know I'm no good at magic."

"Oook."

"The sourcery that's about now, it's terrible stuff. I mean, it's the original stuff, from right back in the dawn of time. Or around breakfast, at any rate."

"Oook."

"It'll destroy everything eventually, won't it?"

"Oook."

"It's about time someone put a stop to this sourcery, right?"

"Oook."

"Only it can't be me, you see. When I came here I thought I could do something, but that tower! It's so big! It must be proof against all magic! If really powerful wizards won't do anything about it, how can I?"

"Oook," agreed the Librarian, sewing a ruptured spine.

"So, you see, I think someone else can save the world this time. I'm no good at it."

The ape nodded, reached across and lifted Rincewind's hat from his head.

"Hey!"

The Librarian ignored him, picked up a pair of shears.

"Look, that's my hat, if you don't mind *don't you dare do that to my—*"

He leapt across the floor and was rewarded with a thump across the side of the head, which would have astonished him if he'd had time to think about it; the Librarian might shuffle around the place like a good-natured wobbly balloon, but underneath that oversized skin was a framework of superbly-cantilevered bone and muscle that could drive a fistful of calloused knuckles through a thick oak plank. Running into the Librarian's arm was like hitting a hairy iron bar.

Wuffles started to bounce up and down, yelping with excitement.

Rincewind screamed a hoarse, untranslatable yell of fury, bounced off the wall, snatched up a fallen rock as a crude club, kicked forward and stopped dead.

The Librarian was crouched in the center of the floor with the shears touching—but not yet cutting—the hat.

And he was grinning at Rincewind.

They stood like a frozen tableau for some seconds. Then the ape dropped the shears, flicked several imaginary flecks of dust off the hat, straightened the point, and placed it on Rincewind's head.

A few shocked moments after this Rincewind realized that he was holding up, at arm's length, a very large and extremely heavy rock. He managed to force it away on one side before it recovered from the shock and remembered to fall on him.

"I see," he said, sinking back against the wall and rubbing his elbows. "And all that's supposed to tell me something, is it? A moral lesson, let Rincewind confront his true self, let him work out what he's really prepared to fight for. Eh? Well, it was a very cheap trick. And I've news for you. If you think it worked—" he snatched the hat brim—"if you think it worked. If you think I've. You've got another thought. Listen, it's. If you think."

His voice stuttered into silence. Then he shrugged.

"All right. But when you get down to it, what can I actually do?"

The Librarian replied with an expansive gesture that indicated, as clearly as if he had said "oook," that Rincewind was a wizard with a hat, a library of magical books and a tower. This could be regarded as everything a magical practitioner could need. An ape, a small terrier with halitosis and a lizard in a jar were optional extras.

Rincewind felt a slight pressure on his foot. Wuffles, who was extremely slow on the uptake, had fastened his toothless gums on the toe of Rincewind's boot and was giving it a vicious suck.

He picked the little dog up by the scruff of its neck and the bristly stub that, for the want of a better word, it called its tail, and gently lifted it sideways.

"Okay," he said. "You'd better tell me what's been happening here."

From the Carrack Mountains, overlooking the vast cold Sto Plain in the middle of which Ankh-Morpork sprawled like a bag of dropped groceries, the view was particularly impressive. Mishits and ricochets from the magical battle were expanding outward and upwards, in a bowl-shaped cloud of curdled air at the heart of which strange lights flashed and sparkled.

The roads leading away from it were packed with refugees, and every inn and wayside tavern was crowded out. Or nearly every one.

No one seemed to want to stop at the rather pleasant little pub nestling among trees just off the road to Quirm. It wasn't that they were frightened to go inside, it was just that, for the moment, they weren't being allowed to notice it.

There was a disturbance in the air about half a mile away and three figures dropped out of nowhere into a thicket of lavender.

They lay supine in the sunshine among the broken, fragrant branches, until their sanity came back. Then Creosote said, "Where are we, do you suppose?"

"It smells like someone's underwear drawer," said Conina.

"Not mine," said Nijel, firmly.

He eased himself up gently and added, "Has anyone seen the lamp?"

"Forget it. It's probably been sold to build a winebar," said Conina.

Nijel scrabbled around among the lavender stems until his hands found something small and metallic.

"Got it!" he declared.

"Don't rub it!" said the other two, in harmony. They were too late anyway, but that didn't much matter, because all that happened when Nijel gave it a cautious buff was the appearance of some small smoking red letters in mid-air.

"'Hi,'" Nijel read aloud. "'Do not put down the lamp, because your custom is important to us. Please leave a wish after the tone and, very shortly, it will be our command. In the meantime, have a nice eternity.'" He added, "You know, I think he's a bit over-committed."

Conina said nothing. She was staring out across the plains to the broiling storm of magic. Occasionally some of it would detach and soar away to some distant tower. She shivered, despite the growing heat of the day.

"We ought to get down there as soon as possible," she said. "It's very important."

"Why?" said Creosote. One glass of wine hadn't really restored him to his former easygoing nature.

Conina opened her mouth, and—quite unusually for her—shut it again. There was no way to explain that every gene in her body was dragging her onward, telling her that she should get involved; visions of swords and spiky balls on chains kept invading the hairdressing salons of her consciousness.

Nijel, on the other hand, felt no such pounding. All he had to drive him onward was imagination, but he did have enough of that to float a medium-sized war galley. He looked toward the city with what would have been, but for his lack of chin, an expression of set-jawed determination.

Creosote realized that he was outnumbered.

"Do they have any drink down there?" he said.

"Lots," said Nijel.

"That might do for a start," the Seriph conceded. "All right, lead on, O peach-breasted daughter of—"

"And no poetry."

They untangled themselves from the thicket and walked down the hillside until they reached the road which, before very long, went past the afore-mentioned tavern or, as Creosote persisted in call-ing it, caravanserai.

They hesitated about going in. It didn't seem to welcome visitors. But Conina, who by breeding and upbringing tended to skulk around the back of buildings, found four horses tethered in the yard.

They considered them carefully.

"It would be stealing," said Nijel, slowly.

Conina opened her mouth to agree and the words "Why not?" slid past her lips. She shrugged.

"Perhaps we should leave some money—" Nijel suggested.

"Don't look at me," said Creosote.

"—or maybe write a note and leave it under the bridle. Or something. Don't you think?"

By way of an answer Conina vaulted up onto the largest horse, which by the look of it belonged to a soldier. Weaponry was slung all over it.

Creosote hoisted himself uneasily onto the sec-ond horse, a rather skittish bay, and sighed.

"She's got that letter-box look," he said. "I should do what she says."

Nijel regarded the other two horses suspiciously. One of them was very large and extremely white, not the offwhite which was all that most horses could manage, but a translucent, ivory white tone which Nijel felt an unconscious urge to describe as "shroud." It also gave him a distinct impression that it was more intelligent than he was.

He selected the other one. It was a bit thin, but docile, and he managed to get on after only two tries.

They set off.

The sound of their hoofbeats barely penetrated the gloom inside the tavern. The innkeeper moved like someone in a dream. He knew he had customers, he'd even spoken to them, he could even see them sitting around a table by the fire, but if asked to describe *who* he'd talked to and *what* he had seen he'd have been at a loss. This is because the human brain is remarkably good at shutting out things it doesn't want to know. His could currently have shielded a bank vault.

And the drinks! Most of them he'd never heard of, but strange bottles kept appearing on the shelves above the beer barrels. The trouble was that whenever he tried to think about it, his thoughts just slid away . . .

The figures around the table looked up from their cards.

One of them raised a hand. It's stuck on the end of his arm and it's got five fingers, the innkeeper's mind said. It must be a hand.

One thing the innkeeper's brain couldn't shut out was the sound of the voices. This one sounded as though someone was hitting a rock with a roll of sheet lead.

BAR PERSON.

The innkeeper groaned faintly. The thermic lances of horror were melting their way steadily through the steel door of his mind.

LET ME SEE, NOW. THAT'S A—WHAT WAS IT AGAIN?

"A Bloody Mary." *This* voice made a simple drinks order sound like the opening of hostilities.

OH, YES. AND—

"Mine was a small egg nog," said Pestilence.

AN EGG NOG.

"With a cherry in it."

GOOD, lied the heavy voice. AND THAT'LL BE A SMALL PORT WINE FOR ME AND, the speaker glanced across the table at the fourth member of the quartet and sighed, YOU'D BETTER BRING ANOTHER BOWL OF PEANUTS.

About three hundred yards down the road the horse thieves were trying to come to terms with a new experience.

"Certainly a smooth ride," Nijel managed eventually.

"And a lovely—a lovely view," said Creosote, his voice lost in the slipstream.

"But I wonder," said Nijel, "if we have done exactly the right thing."

"We're moving, aren't we?" demanded Conina. "Don't be petty."

"It's just that, well, looking at cumulus clouds from *above* is—"

"Shut up."

"Sorry."

"Anyway, they're stratus. Strato-cumulus at most."

"Right," said Nijel miserably.

"Does it make any difference?" said Creosote, who was lying flat on his horse's neck with his eyes shut.

"About a thousand feet."

"Oh."

"Could be seven hundred and fifty," conceded Conina.

"Ah."

The tower of sourcery trembled. Colored smoke rolled through its vaulted rooms and shining corridors. In the big room at the very tip, where the air was thick and greasy and tasted of burning tin, many wizards had passed out with the sheer mental effort of the battle. But enough remained. They sat in a wide circle, locked in concentration.

It was just possible to see the shimmering in the air as the raw sourcery swirled out of the staff in Coin's hand and into the center of the octogram.

Outlandish shapes appeared for a brief instant and vanished. The very fabric of reality was being put through the wringer in there.

Carding shuddered and turned away in case he saw anything he really couldn't ignore.

The surviving senior wizards had a simulacrum of the Disc hovering in front of them. As Carding looked at it again the little red glow over the city of Quirm flared and went out.

The air creaked.

"There goes Quirm," murmured Carding.

"That just leaves Al Khali," said one of the others. "There's some clever power there."

Carding nodded glumly. He'd quite liked Quirm, which was a—had been a pleasant little city overlooking the Rim Ocean.

He dimly recalled being taken there, once, when he was small. For a moment he gazed sadly into the past. It had wild geraniums, he recalled, filling the sloping cobbled streets with their musky fragrance.

"Growing out of the walls," he said out loud. "Pink. They were pink."

The other wizards looked at him oddly. One or two, of a particularly paranoid frame of mind even for wizards, glanced suspiciously at the walls.

"Are you all right?" said one of them.

"Um?" said Carding. "Oh. Yes, Sorry. Miles away."

He turned back to look at Coin, who was sitting off to one side of the circle with the staff across his knees. The boy appeared to be asleep. Perhaps he was. But Carding knew in the tormented pit of his soul that the staff didn't sleep. It was watching him, testing his mind.

It knew. It even knew about the pink geraniums.

"I never wanted it to be like this," he said softly. "All we really wanted was a bit of respect."

"Are you *sure* you're all right?"

Carding nodded vaguely. As his colleagues resumed their concentration he glanced sideways at them.

Somehow, all his old friends had gone. Well, not friends. A wizard never had friends, at least not friends who were wizards. It needed a different word. Ah yes, that was it. *Enemies*. But a very decent class of enemies. Gentlemen. The cream of their profession. Not like these people, for all that they seemed to have risen in the craft since the sourcerer had arrived.

Other things besides the cream floated to the top, he reflected sourly.

He turned his attention to Al Khali, probing with his mind, knowing that the wizards there were almost certainly doing the same, seeking constantly for a point of weakness.

He thought: Am I a point of weakness? Spelter tried to tell me something. It was about the staff. A man should lean on his staff, not the other way around . . . it's steering him, leading him . . . I wish I'd listened to Spelter . . . this is wrong, I'm a point of weakness . . .

He tried again, riding the surges of power, letting them carry his mind into the enemy tower. Even Abrim was making use of sourcery, and Carding let himself modulate the wave, insinuating himself past the defenses erected against him.

The image of the interior of the Al Khali tower appeared, focused . . .

. . . *the Luggage trundled along the glowing corridors. It was exceedingly angry now. It had been awoken from hibernation, it had been scorned, it had been briefly attacked by a variety of mythological and now extinct lifeforms, it had a headache and now, as it entered the Great Hall, it detected the hat. The horrible hat, the cause of everything it was currently suffering. It advanced purposefully . . .*

Carding, testing the resistance of Abrim's mind, felt the man's attention waver. For a moment he saw through the enemy's eyes, saw the squat oblong cantering across the stone. For a moment Abrim attempted to shift his concentration and then, no more able to help himself than is a cat when it sees something small and squeaky run across the floor, Carding struck.

Not much. It didn't need much. Abrim's mind was attempting to balance and channel huge forces, and it needed hardly any pressure to topple it from its position.

Abrim extended his hands to blast the Luggage, gave the merest beginnings of a scream, and imploded.

The wizards around him thought they saw him grow impossibly small in a fraction of a second and vanish, leaving a black after-image . . .

The more intelligent of them started to run . . .

And the magic he had been controlling surged back out and flooded free in one great, randomized burst that blew the hat to bits, took out the entire lower levels of the tower and quite a large part of what remained of the city.

So many wizards in Ankh had been concentrating on the hall that the sympathetic resonance blew them across the room. Carding ended up on his back, his hat over his eyes.

They hauled him out and dusted him off and carried him to Coin and the staff, amid cheers—although some of the older wizards forbore to cheer. But he didn't seem to pay any attention.

He stared sightlessly down at the boy, and then slowly raised his hands to his ears.

"Can't you hear them?" he said.

The wizards fell silent. Carding still had power, and the tone of his voice would have quelled a thunderstorm.

Coin's eyes glowed.

"I hear nothing," he said.

Carding turned to the rest of the wizards.

"Can't *you* hear them?"

They shook their heads. One of them said, "Hear what, brother?"

Carding smiled, and it was a wide, mad smile. Even Coin took a step backwards.

"You'll hear them soon enough," he said. "You've made a beacon. You'll all hear them. But you won't hear them for long." He pushed aside the younger wizards who were holding his arms and advanced on Coin.

"You're pouring sourcery into the world and other things are coming with it," he said. "Others have given them a pathway but you've given them an *avenue*!"

He sprang forward and snatched the black staff out of Coin's hands and swung it up in the air to smash it against the wall.

Carding went rigid as the staff struck back. Then his skin began to blister . . .

Most of the wizards managed to turn their heads away. A few—and there are always a few like that—watched in obscene fascination.

Coin watched, too. His eyes widened in wonder. One hand went to his mouth. He tried to back away. He couldn't.

"*They're* cumulus."

"Marvelous," said Nijel weakly.

WEIGHT DOESN'T COME INTO IT. MY STEED HAS CARRIED ARMIES. MY STEED HAS CARRIED CITIES. YEA, HE HATH CARRIED ALL THINGS IN THEIR DUE TIME, said Death. BUT HE'S NOT GOING TO CARRY YOU THREE.

"Why not?"

IT'S A MATTER OF THE LOOK OF THE THING.

"It's going to look pretty good, then, isn't it," said War testily, "the One Horseman and Three Pedestrians of the Apocralypse."

"Perhaps you could ask them to wait for us?" said Pestilence, his voice sounding like something dripping out of the bottom of a coffin.

I HAVE THINGS TO ATTEND TO, said Death. He made a little clicking noise with his teeth. I'M SURE YOU'LL MANAGE. YOU NORMALLY DO.

War watched the retreating horse.

"Sometimes he really gets on my nerves. Why is he always so keen to have the last word?" he said.

"Force of habit, I suppose."

They turned back to the tavern. Neither spoke for some time, and then War said, "Where's Famine?"

"Went to find the kitchen."

"Oh." War scuffed one armored foot in the dust, and thought about the distance to Ankh. It was a very hot afternoon. The Apocralypse could jolly well wait.

"One for the road?" he suggested.

"Should we?" said Pestilence, doubtfully. *"I thought we were expected. I mean, I wouldn't like to disappoint people."*

"We've got time for a quick one, I'm sure," War insisted. "Pub clocks are never right. We've got bags of time. All the time in the world."

Carding slumped forward and thudded on the shining white floor. The staff rolled out of his hands and upended itself.

Coin prodded the limp body with his foot.

"I did warn him," he said. "I told him what would happen if he touched it again. What did he mean, *them*?"

There was an outbreak of coughing and a considerable inspection of fingernails.

"What did he mean?" Coin demanded.

Ovin Hakardly, lecturer in Lore, once again found that the wizards around him were parting like morning mist. Without moving he appeared to have stepped forward. His eyes swivelled backwards and forward like trapped animals.

"Er," he said. He waved his thin hands vaguely. "The world, you see, that is, the reality in which we live, in fact, it can be thought of as, in a manner of speaking, a rubber sheet." He hesitated, aware that the sentence was not going to appear in anyone's book of quotable quotes.

"In that," he added hurriedly, "it is distorted, uh, *distended* by the presence of magic in any degree and, if I may make a point here, too much magical potentiality, if foregathered in one spot, forces our reality, um, downwards, although of course one should not take the term literally (because in no sense do I seek to suggest a physical dimension) and it has been postulated that a sufficient exercise of magic can, shall we say, um, break through the actuality at its lowest point and offer, perhaps, a pathway to the inhabitants or, if I may use a more correct term, *denizens* of the lower plane (which is called by the loose-tongued the Dungeon Dimensions) who, because perhaps of the difference in energy levels, are naturally attracted to the brightness of this world. Our world."

There was the typical long pause which usually followed Hakardly's speeches, while everybody mentally inserted commas and stitched the fractured clauses together.

Coin's lips moved silently for a while. "Do you mean magic attracts these creatures?" he said eventually.

His voice was quite different now. It lacked its former edge. The staff hung in the air above the prone body of Carding, rotating slowly. The eyes of every wizard in the place were on it.

"So it appears," said Hakardly. "Students of such things say their presence is heralded by a coarse susurration."

Coin looked uncertain.

"They buzz," said one of the other wizards helpfully.

The boy knelt down and peered closely at Carding.

"He's very still," he said cautiously. "Is anything bad happening to him?"

"It may be," said Hakardly, guardedly. "He's dead."

"I wish he wasn't."

"It is a view, I suspect, which he shares."

"But I can help him," said Coin. He held out his hands and the staff glided into them. If it had a face, it would have smirked.

When he spoke next his voice once again had the cold distant tones of someone speaking in a steel room.

"If failure had no penalty success would not be a prize," he said.

"Sorry?" said Hakardly. "You've lost me there."

Coin turned on his heel and strode back to his chair.

"We can fear nothing," he said, and it sounded more like a command. "What of these Dungeon Dimensions? If they should trouble us, away with them! A true wizard will fear nothing! Nothing!"

He jerked to his feet again and strode to the simulacrum of the world. The image was perfect in every detail, down to a ghost of Great A'Tuin paddling slowly through the interstellar deeps a few inches above the floor.

Coin waved his hand through it disdainfully.

"Ours is a world of magic," he said. "And what can be found in it that can stand against us?"

Hakardly thought that something was expected of him.

"Absolutely no one," he said. "Except for the gods, of course."

There was a dead silence.

"The gods?" said Coin quietly.

"Well, yes. Certainly. We don't challenge the gods. They do their job, we do ours. No sense in—"

"Who rules the Disc? Wizards or gods?"

Hakardly thought quickly.

"Oh, wizards. Of course. But, as it were, *under* the gods."

When one accidentally puts one boot in a swamp it is quite unpleasant. But not as unpleasant as pushing down with the other boot and hearing that, too, disappear with a soft sucking noise. Hakardly pressed on.

"You see, wizardry is more—"

"Are we not more powerful than the gods, then?" said Coin.

Some of the wizards at the back of the crowd began to shuffle their feet.

"Well. Yes and no," said Hakardly, up to his knees in it now.

The truth was that wizards tended to be somewhat nervous about the gods. The beings who dwelt on Cori Celesti had never made their feelings plain on the subject of ceremonial magic, which after all had a certain godness about it, and wizards tended to avoid the whole subject. The trouble with gods was that if they didn't like something they didn't just drop hints, so common sense suggested that it was unwise to put the gods in a position where they had to decide.

"There seems to be some uncertainty?" said Coin.

"If I may counsel—" Hakardly began.

Coin waved a hand. The walls vanished. The wizards stood at the top of the tower of sourcery, and as one man their eyes turned to the distant pinnacle of Cori Celesti, home of the gods.

"When you've beaten everyone else, there's only the gods left to fight," said Coin. "Have any of you seen the gods?"

There was a chorus of hesitant denials.

"I will show them to you."

"You've got room for another one in there, old son," said War.

Pestilence swayed unsteadily. *"I'm sure we should be getting along,"* he muttered, without much conviction.

"Oh, go on."

"Just a half, then. And then we really must be going."
War slapped him on the back and glared at Famine.
"And we'd better have another fifteen bags of peanuts," he added.

"Oook," the Librarian concluded.

"Oh," said Rincewind. "It's the staff that's the problem, then."

"Oook."

"Hasn't anyone tried to take it away from him?"

"Oook."

"What happened to them, then?"

"Eeek."

Rincewind groaned.

The Librarian had put his candle out because the presence of the naked flame was unsettling the books, but now that Rincewind had grown accustomed to the dark, he realized it wasn't dark at all. The soft octarine glow from the books filled the inside of the tower with something that, while it wasn't exactly light, was a blackness you could see by. Now and again the ruffle of stiff pages floated down from the gloom.

"So, basically, there's no way our magic could defeat him, isn't that right?"

The Librarian oooked disconsolate agreement and continued to spin around gently on his bottom.

"Pretty pointless, then. It may have struck you that I am not exactly gifted in the magical department. I mean, any duel is going to go on the lines of 'Hallo, I'm Rincewind' closely followed by bazaam!"

"Oook."

"Basically, what you're saying is that I'm on my own."

"Oook."

"Thanks."

By their own faint glow Rincewind regarded the books that had stacked themselves around the inner walls of the ancient tower.

He sighed and marched briskly to the door, but slowed down noticeably as he reached it.

"I'll be off, then," he said.

"Oook."

"To face who knows what dreadful perils," Rincewind added. "To lay down my life in the service of mankind—"

"Eeek."

"All right, bipeds—"

"Woof."

"—and quadrapeds, all right." He glanced at the Patrician's jamjar, a beaten man.

"And lizards," he added. "Can I go now?"

A gale was howling down out of a clear sky as Rincewind toiled toward the tower of sourcery. Its high white doors were shut so tightly it was barely possible to see their outline in the milky surface of the stone.

He hammered on it for a bit, but nothing much happened. The doors seemed to absorb the sound.

"Fine thing," he muttered to himself, and remembered the carpet. It was lying where he had left it, which was another sign that Ankh had changed. In the thieving days before the sourcerer nothing stayed for long where you left it. Nothing printable, anyway.

He rolled it out on the cobbles so that the golden dragons writhed against the blue ground, unless of course the blue dragons were flying against a golden sky.

He sat down.

He stood up.

He sat down again and hitched up his robe and, with some effort, unrolled one of his socks. Then he replaced his boot and wandered around for a bit until he found, among the rubble, a half-brick. He inserted the half-brick into the sock and gave the sock a few thoughtful swings.

Rincewind had grown up in Morpork. What a Morpork citizen liked to have on his side in a fight was odds of about twenty to one, but failing that a sockful of half-brick and a dark alley to lurk in was generally considered a better bet than any two magic swords you cared to name.

He sat down again.

"Up," he commanded.

The carpet did not respond. Rincewind peered at the pattern, then lifted a corner of the carpet and tried to make out if the underside was any better.

"All right," he conceded, "down. Very, very carefully. Down."

"Sheep," slurred War. "It was sheep." His helmeted head hit the bar with a clang. He raised it again. "Sheep."

"Nonono," said Famine, raising a thin finger unsteadily. "Some other domess . . . dummist . . . tame animal. Like pig. Heifer. Kitten? Like that. Not sheep."

"*Bees,*" said Pestilence, and slid gently out of his seat.

"Okay," said War, ignoring him, "right. Once again, then. From the top." He rapped the side of his glass for the note.

"We are poor little . . . unidentified domesticated animals . . . that have lost our way . . ." he quavered.

"*Baabaabaa,*" muttered Pestilence, from the floor.

War shook his head. "It isn't the same, you know," he said. "Not without him. He used to come in beautifully on the bass."

"*Baabaabaa,*" Pestilence repeated.

"Oh, shut up," said War, and reached uncertainly for a bottle.

The gale buffeted the top of the tower, a hot, unpleasant wind that whispered with strange voices and rubbed the skin like fine sandpaper.

In the center of it Coin stood with the staff over his head. As dust filled the air the wizards saw the lines of magic force pouring from it.

They curved up to form a vast bubble that expanded until it must have been larger than the city. And shapes appeared in it. They were shifting and indistinct, wavering horribly like visions in a distorting mirror, no more substantial than smoke rings or pictures in the clouds, but they were dreadfully familiar.

There, for a moment, was the fanged snout of Offler. There, clear for an instant in the writhing storm, was Blind Io, chief of the gods, with his orbiting eyes.

Coin muttered soundlessly and the bubble began

to contract. It bulged and jerked obscenely as the things inside fought to get out, but they could not stop the contraction.

Now it was bigger than the University grounds.

Now it was taller than the tower.

Now it was twice the height of a man, and smoke gray.

Now it was an iridescent pearl, the size of . . . well, the size of a large pearl.

The gale had gone, replaced by a heavy, silent calm. The very air groaned with the strain. Most of the wizards were flat on the floor, pressed there by the unleashed forces that thickened the air and deadened sound like a universe of feathers, but every one of them could hear his own heart beating loud enough to smash the tower.

"Look at me," Coin commanded.

They turned their eyes upwards. There was no way they could disobey.

He held the glistening thing in one hand. The other held the staff, which had smoke pouring from its ends.

"The gods," he said. "Imprisoned in a thought. And perhaps they were never more than a dream."

His voice become older, deeper. "Wizards of Unseen University," it said, "have I not given you absolute dominion?"

Behind them the carpet rose slowly over the side of the tower, with Rincewind trying hard to keep his balance. His eyes were wide with the sort of terror that comes naturally to anyone standing on a few threads and several hundred feet of empty air.

He lurched off the hovering thing and onto the

tower, swinging the loaded sock around his head in wide, dangerous sweeps.

Coin saw him reflected in the astonished stares of the assembled wizards. He turned carefully and watched the wizard stagger erratically toward him.

"Who are you?" he said.

"I have come," said Rincewind thickly, "to challenge the sourcerer. Which one is he?"

He surveyed the prostrate wizardry, hefting the half-brick in one hand.

Hakardly risked a glance upwards and made frantic eyebrow movements at Rincewind who, even at the best of times, wasn't much good at interpreting non-verbal communication. This wasn't the best of times.

"With a sock?" said Coin. "What good is a sock?"

The arm holding the staff rose. Coin looked down at it in mild astonishment.

"No, stop," he said. "I want to talk to this man." He stared at Rincewind, who was swaying back and forth under the influence of sleeplessness, horror and the after-effects of an adrenaline overdose.

"Is it magical?" he said, curiously. "Perhaps it is the sock of an Archchancellor? A sock of force?"

Rincewind focused on it.

"I don't think so," he said. "I think I bought it in a shop or something. Um. I've got another one somewhere."

"But in the end it has something heavy?"

"Um. Yes," said Rincewind. He added, "It's a half-brick."

"But it has great power."

"Er. You can hold things up with it. If you had

another one, you'd have a brick." Rincewind spoke slowly. He was assimilating the situation by a kind of awful osmosis, and watching the staff turn ominously in the boy's hand.

"So. It is a brick of ordinariness, within a sock. The whole becoming a weapon."

"Um. Yes."

"How does it work?"

"Um. You swing it, and then you. Hit something with it. Or sometimes the back of your hand, sometimes."

"And then perhaps it destroys a whole city?" said Coin.

Rincewind stared into Coin's golden eyes, and then at his sock. He had pulled it on and off several times a year for years. It had darns he'd grown to know and lo—well, know. Some of them had whole families of darns of their own. There were a number of descriptions that could be applied to the sock, but slayer-of-cities wasn't among them.

"Not really," he said at last. "It sort of kills people but leaves buildings standing."

Rincewind's mind was operating at the speed of continental drift. Parts of it were telling him that he was confronting the sourcerer, but they were in direct conflict with other parts. Rincewind had heard quite a lot about the power of the sourcerer, the staff of the sourcerer, the wickedness of the sourcerer and so on. The only thing no one had mentioned was the age of the sourcerer.

He glanced toward the staff.

"And what does *that* do?" he said slowly.

And the staff said, *You must kill this man.*

The wizards, who had been cautiously struggling upright, flung themselves flat again.

The voice of the hat had been bad enough, but the voice of the staff was metallic and precise; it didn't sound as though it was offering advice but simply stating the way the future had to be. It sounded quite impossible to ignore.

Coin half-raised his arm, and hesitated.

"Why?" he said.

You do not disobey me.

"You don't have to," said Rincewind hurriedly. "It's only a thing."

"I do not see why I should hurt him," said Coin. "He looks so harmless. Like an angry rabbit."

He defies us.

"Not me," said Rincewind, thrusting the arm with the sock behind his back and trying to ignore the bit about the rabbit.

"Why should I do everything you tell me?" said Coin to the staff. "I always do everything you tell me, and it doesn't help people at all."

People must fear you. Have I taught you nothing?

"But he looks so funny. He's got a sock," said Coin.

He screamed, and his arm jerked oddly. Rincewind's hair stood on end.

You will do as you are commanded.

"I won't."

You know what happens to boys who are bad.

There was a crackle and a smell of scorched flesh. Coin dropped to his knees.

"Here, hang on a minute—" Rincewind began.

Coin opened his eyes. They were gold still, but flecked with brown.

Rincewind swung his sock around in a wide humming arc that connected with the staff halfway along its length. There was a brief explosion of brick dust and burnt wool and the staff spun out of the boy's hand. Wizards scattered as it tumbled end over end across the floor.

It reached the parapet, bounced upwards and shot over the edge.

But, instead of falling, it steadied itself in the air, spun in its own length and sped back again trailing octarine sparks and making a noise like a buzzsaw.

Rincewind pushed the stunned boy behind him, threw away the ravaged sock and whipped his hat off, flailing wildly as the staff bored toward him. It caught him on the side of the head, delivering a shock that almost welded his teeth together and toppled him like a thin and ragged tree.

The staff turned again in mid-air, glowing red-hot now, and swept back for another and quite definitely final run.

Rincewind struggled up on his elbows and watched in horrified fascination as it swooped through the chilly air which, for some reason he didn't understand, seemed to be full of snowflakes.

And became tinged with purple, blotched with blue. Time slowed and ground to a halt like an underwound phonograph.

Rincewind looked up at the tall black figure that had appeared a few feet away.

It was, of course, Death.

He turned his glowing eyesockets toward Rincewind and said, in a voice like the collapse of undersea chasms, GOOD AFTERNOON.

He turned away as if he had completed all necessary business for the time being, stared at the horizon for a while, and started to tap one foot idly. It sounded like a bagful of maracas.

"Er," said Rincewind.

Death appeared to remember him. I'M SORRY? he said politely.

"I always wondered how it was going to be," said Rincewind.

Death took an hourglass out from the mysterious folds of his ebon robes and peered at it.

DID YOU? he said, vaguely.

"I suppose I can't complain," said Rincewind virtuously. "I've had a good life. Well, quite good." He hesitated. "Well, not all that good. I suppose most people would call it pretty awful." He considered it further. "*I* would," he added, half to himself.

WHAT ARE YOU TALKING ABOUT, MAN?

Rincewind was nonplussed. "Don't you make an appearance when a wizard is about to die?"

OF COURSE. AND I MUST SAY YOU PEOPLE ARE GIVING ME A BUSY DAY.

"How do you manage to be in so many places at the same time?"

GOOD ORGANIZATION.

Time returned. The staff, which had been hanging in the air a few feet away from Rincewind, started to scream forward again.

And there was a metallic thud as Coin caught it one-handedly in mid-flight.

The staff uttered a noise like a thousand fingernails dragging across glass. It thrashed wildly up and down, flailing at the arm that held it, and bloomed into evil green flame along its entire length.

So. At the last, you fail me.

Coin groaned but held on as the metal under his fingertips went red, then white.

He thrust the arm out in front of him, and the force streaming from the staff roared past him and drew sparks from his hair and whipped his robe up into weird and unpleasant shapes. He screamed and whirled the staff around and smashed it on the parapet, leaving a long bubbling line in the stone.

Then he threw it away. It clattered against the stones and rolled to a halt, wizards scattering out of its path.

Coin sagged to his knees, shaking.

"I don't like killing people," he said. "I'm sure it can't be right."

"Hold onto that thought," said Rincewind fervently.

"What happens to people after they're dead?" said Coin.

Rincewind glanced up at Death.

"I think this one's for you," he said.

HE CANNOT SEE OR HEAR ME, said Death, UNTIL HE WANTS TO.

There was a little clinking noise. The staff was rolling back toward Coin, who looked down at it in horror.

Pick me up.

"You don't have to," said Rincewind again.

You cannot resist me. You cannot defeat yourself, said the staff.

Coin reached out very slowly, and picked it up.

Rincewind glanced at his sock. It was a stub of burnt wool, its brief career as a weapon of war having sent it beyond the help of any darning needle.

Now kill him.

Rincewind held his breath. The watching wizards held their breath. Even Death, who had nothing to hold but his scythe, held it tensely.

"No," said Coin.

You know what happens to boys who are bad.

Rincewind saw the sourcerer's face go pale.

The staff's voice changed. Now it wheedled.

Without me, who would there be to tell you what to do?

"That is true," said Coin slowly.

See what you have achieved.

Coin stared slowly around at the frightened faces.

"I am seeing," he said.

I taught you everything I know.

"I am thinking," said Coin, "that you do not know enough."

Ingrate! Who gave you your destiny?

"You did," said the boy. He raised his head.

"I realize that I was wrong," he added, quietly.

Good—

"I did not throw you far enough!"

Coin got to his feet in one movement and swung the staff over his head. He stood still as a statue, his hand lost in a ball of light that was the color of molten copper. It turned green, ascended through shades of blue, hovered in the violet and then seared into pure octarine.

Rincewind shaded his eyes against the glare and saw Coin's hand, still whole, still gripping tight, with beads of molten metal glittering between his fingers.

He slithered away, and bumped into Hakardly. The old wizard was standing like a statue, with his mouth open.

"What'll happen?" said Rincewind.

"He'll never beat it," said Hakardly hoarsely. "It's his. It's as strong as him. He's got the power, but *it* knows how to channel it."

"You mean they'll cancel each other out?"

"Hopefully."

The battle was hidden in its own infernal glow. Then the floor began to tremble.

"They're drawing on everything magical," said Hakardly. "We'd better leave the tower."

"Why?"

"I imagine it will vanish soon enough."

And, indeed, the white flagstones around the glow looked as though they were unravelling and disappearing into it.

Rincewind hesitated.

"Aren't we going to help him?" he said.

Hakardly stared at him, and then at the iridescent tableau. His mouth opened and shut once or twice.

"I'm sorry," he said.

"Yes, but just a bit of help on his side, you've seen what that *thing* is like—"

"I'm sorry."

"He helped *you*." Rincewind turned on the other wizards, who were scurrying away. "All of you. He gave you what you wanted, didn't he?"

"We may never forgive him," said Hakardly.

Rincewind groaned.

"What will be left when it's all over?" he said. "What will be left?"

Hakardly looked down.

"I'm sorry," he repeated.

The octarine light had grown brighter and was beginning to turn black around the edge. It wasn't the black that is merely the opposite of light, though; it was the grainy, shifting blackness that glows beyond the glare and has no business in any decent reality. And it buzzed.

Rincewind did a little dance of uncertainty as his feet, legs, instincts and incredibly well-developed sense of self-preservation overloaded his nervous system to the point where, just as it was on the point of fusing, his conscience finally got its way.

He leapt into the fire and reached the staff.

The wizards fled. Several of them levitated down from the tower.

They were a lot more perspicacious than those that used the stairs because, about thirty seconds later, the tower vanished.

The snow continued to fall around a column of blackness, which buzzed.

And the surviving wizards who dared to look back saw, tumbling slowly down the sky, a small object trailing flames behind it. It crashed into the cobbles, where it smouldered for a bit before the thickening snow put it out.

Pretty soon it became just a small mound.

A little while later a squat figure swung itself across the courtyard on its knuckles, scrabbled in the snow, and hauled the thing out.

It was, or rather it had been, a hat. Life had not been kind to it. A large part of the wide brim had been burned off, the point was entirely gone, and the tarnished silver letters were almost unreadable. Some of them had been torn off in any case. Those that were left spelled out: WIZD.

The Librarian turned around slowly. He was entirely alone, except for the towering column of burning blackness and the steadily falling flakes.

The ravaged campus was empty. There were a few other pointy hats that had been trampled by terrified feet, and no other sign that people had been there.

All the wizards were wazards.

"War?"

"Wazzat?"

"Wasn't there," Pestilence groped for his glass, *"something?"*

"Wazzat?"

"We ought to be . . . there's something we ought to be doing," said Famine.

"S'right. Got an appointment."

"The—" Pestilence gazed reflectively into his drink. *"Thingy."*

They stared gloomily at the bar counter. The innkeeper had long ago fled. There were several bottles still unopened.

"Okra," said Famine, eventually. "That was it."

"Nah."

"The Apos . . . the Apostrophe," said War, vaguely.

They shook their heads. There was a lengthy pause.

"What does 'apocrustic' mean?" said Pestilence, gazing intently into some inner world.

"Astringent," said War, "I think."

"It's not that, then?"

"Shouldn't think so," said Famine, glumly.

There was another long, embarrassed silence.

"Better have 'nother drink," said War, pulling himself together.

"S'right."

About fifty miles away and several thousand feet up, Conina at last managed to control her stolen horse and brought it to a gentle trot on the empty air, displaying some of the most determined nonchalance the Disc had ever seen.

"Snow?" she said.

Clouds were roaring soundlessly from the direction of the Hub. They were fat and heavy and shouldn't be moving so fast. Blizzards trailed beneath them, covering the landscape like a sheet.

It didn't look like the kind of snow that whispers down gently in the pit of the night and in the morning turns the landscape into a glittering wonderland of uncommon and ethereal beauty. It looked like the kind of snow that intends to make the world as bloody cold as possible.

"Bit late in the year," said Nijel. He glanced downwards, and then immediately closed his eyes.

Creosote watched in delighted astonishment. "Is that how it happens?" he said. "I've only heard about it in stories. I thought it sprouted out of the ground somehow. Bit like mushrooms, I thought."

"Those clouds aren't right," said Conina.

"Do you mind if we go down now?" said Nijel weakly. "Somehow it didn't look so bad when we were moving."

Conina ignored this. "Try the lamp," she commanded. "I want to know about this."

Nijel fumbled in his pack and produced the lamp.

The voice of the genie sounded rather tinny and far off, and said: "If you would care to relax a little . . . trying to connect you." There then followed some tinkly little music, the kind that perhaps a Swiss chalet would make if you could play it, before a trapdoor outlined itself in the air and the genie himself appeared. He looked around him, and then at them.

"Oh, wow," he said.

"Something's happening to the weather," said Conina. "Why?"

"You mean you don't know?" said the genie.

"We're asking you, aren't we?"

"Well, I'm no judge, but it rather looks like the Apocralypse, yuh?"

"*What?*"

The genie shrugged. "The gods have vanished, okay?" he said. "And according to, you know, legend, that means—"

"The Ice Giants," said Nijel, in a horrified whisper.

"Speak up," said Creosote.

"The Ice Giants," Nijel repeated loudly, with a trace of irritation. "The gods keep them imprisoned, see. At the Hub. But at the end of the world they'll break free at last, and ride out on their dreadful glaciers and regain their ancient domination, crushing out the flames of civilization until the world lies naked and frozen under the terrible cold stars until Time itself freezes over. Or something like that, apparently."

"But it isn't *time* for the Apocralypse," said Conina desperately. "I mean, a dreadful ruler has to arise, there must be a terrible war, the four dreadful horsemen have to ride, and then the Dungeon Dimensions will break into the world—" She stopped, her face nearly as white as the snow.

"Being buried under a thousand-foot ice sheet sounds awfully like it, anyway," said the genie. He reached forward and snatched his lamp out of Nijel's hands.

"Mucho apologies," he said, "but it's time to liquidize my assets in this reality. See you around. Or something." He vanished up to the waist, and then with a faint last cry of "Shame about lunch," disappeared entirely.

The three riders peered through the veils of driving snow toward the Hub.

"It may be my imagination," said Creosote, "but can either of you hear a sort of creaking and groaning?"

"Shut up," said Conina distractedly.

Creosote leaned over and patted her hand.

"Cheer up," he said, "it's not the end of the world." He thought about this statement for a bit, and then added, "Sorry. Just a figure of speech."

"What are we going to *do*?" she wailed.

Nijel drew himself up.

"I think," he said, "that we should go and explain."

They turned toward him with the kind of expression normally reserved for messiahs or extreme idiots.

"Yes," he said, with a shade more confidence. "We should explain."

"Explain to the Ice Giants?" said Conina.

"Yes."

"Sorry," said Conina, "have I got this right? You think we should go and find the terrifying Ice Giants and sort of tell them that there are a lot of warm people out here who would rather they didn't sweep across the world crushing everyone under mountains of ice, and could they sort of reconsider things? Is that what you think we should do?"

"Yes. That's right. You've got it exactly."

Conina and Creosote exchanged glances. Nijel remained sitting proudly in the saddle, a faint smile on his face.

"Is your geese giving you trouble?" said the Seriph.

"Geas," said Nijel calmly. "It's not giving me trouble, it's just that I must do something brave before I die."

"That's it though," said Creosote. "That's the whole rather sad point. You'll do something brave, and then you'll die."

"What alternative have we got?" said Nijel.

They considered this.

"I don't think I'm much good at explaining," said Conina, in a small voice.

"I am," said Nijel, firmly. "I'm always having to explain."

The scattered particles of what had been Rincewind's mind pulled themselves together and drifted up through the layers of dark unconsciousness like a three-day corpse rising to the surface.

It probed its most recent memories, in much the same way that one might scratch a fresh scab.

He could recall something about a staff, and a pain so intense that it appeared to insert a chisel between every cell in his body and hammer on it repeatedly.

He remembered the staff fleeing, dragging him after it. And then there had been that dreadful bit where Death had appeared and reached *past* him, and the staff had twisted and become suddenly alive and Death had said, IPSLORE THE RED, I HAVE YOU NOW.

And now there was this.

By the feel of it Rincewind was lying on sand. It was very cold.

He took the risk of seeing something horrible and opened his eyes.

The first thing he saw was his left arm and, surprisingly, his hand. It was its normal grubby self. He had expected to see a stump.

It seemed to be nighttime. The beach, or whatever it was, stretched on toward a line of distant low mountains, under night sky frosted with a million stars.

A little closer to him there was a rough line in the silvery sand. He lifted his head slightly and saw the scatter of molten droplets. They were octiron, a metal so intrinsically magical that no forge on the Disc could even warm it up.

"Oh," he said. "We won, then."

He flopped down again.

After a while his right hand came up automatically and patted the top of his head. Then it patted the sides of his head. Then it began to grope, with increasing urgency, in the sand around him.

Eventually it must have communicated its concern to the rest of Rincewind, because he pulled himself upright and said, "Oh, bugger."

There seemed to be no hat anywhere. But he could see a small white shape lying very still in the sand a little way away and, further off—

A column of daylight.

It hummed and swayed in the air, a three-dimensional hole into somewhere else. Occasional flurries of snow blew out of it. He could see skewed images in the light, that might be buildings or landscapes warped by the weird curvature. But he couldn't see them very clearly, because of the tall, brooding shadows that surrounded it.

The human mind is an astonishing thing. It can operate on several levels at once. And, in fact, while Rincewind had been wasting his intellect in groaning and looking for his hat, an inner part of his brain had been observing, assessing, analyzing and comparing.

Now it crept up to his cerebellum, tapped it on the shoulder, thrust a message into its hand and ran for it.

The message ran something like this: I hope I find me well. The last trial of magic has been too much for the tortured fabric of reality. It has opened a hole. I am in the Dungeon Dimensions. And the things in front of me are . . . the Things. It has been nice knowing me.

The particular thing nearest Rincewind was at least twenty feet high. It looked like a dead horse that had been dug up after three months and then introduced to a range of new experiences, at least one of which had included an octopus.

It hadn't noticed Rincewind. It was too busy concentrating on the light.

Rincewind crawled back to the still body of Coin and nudged it gently.

"Are you alive?" he said. "If you're not, I'd prefer it if you didn't answer."

Coin rolled over and stared up at him with puzzled eyes. After a while he said, "I remember—"

"Best not to," said Rincewind.

The boy's hand groped vaguely in the sand beside him.

"It isn't here anymore," said Rincewind, quietly. The hand stopped its searching.

Rincewind helped Coin to sit up. He looked blankly at the cold silver sand, then at the sky, then at the distant Things, and then at Rincewind.

"I don't know what to do," he said.

"No harm in that. I've never known what to do," said Rincewind with hollow cheerfulness. "Been completely at a loss my whole life." He hesitated. "I think it's called being human, or something."

"But I've *always* known what to do!"

Rincewind opened his mouth to say that he'd seen some of it, but changed his mind. Instead he said, "Chin up. Look on the bright side. It could be worse."

Coin took another look around.

"In what respect, exactly?" he said, his voice a shade more normal.

"Um."

"What is this place?"

"It's a sort of other dimension. The magic broke through and we went with it, I think."

"And those things?"

They regarded the Things.

"I think they're Things. They're trying to get back through the hole," said Rincewind. "It isn't easy. Energy levels, or something. I remember we had a lecture on them once. Er."

Coin nodded, and reached out a thin pale hand toward Rincewind's forehead.

"Do you mind—?" he began.

Rincewind shuddered at the touch. "Mind what?" he said.

—if I have a look in your head?

"Aargh."

It's rather a mess in here. No wonder you can't find things.

"Ergh."

You ought to have a clear out.

"Oogh."

"Ah."

Rincewind felt the presence retreat. Coin frowned.

"We can't let them get through," he announced. "They have horrible powers. They're trying to will the hole bigger, and they can do it. They've been waiting to break into our world for—" he frowned— "*ians?*"

"Aeons," said Rincewind.

Coin opened his other hand, which had been tightly clenched, and showed Rincewind the small gray pearl.

"Do you know what this is?" he said.

"No. What is it?"

"I—can't remember. But we should put it back."

"Okay. Just use sourcery. Blow them to bits and let's go home."

"No. They live on magic. It'd only make them worse. I can't use magic."

"Are you sure?" said Rincewind.

"I'm afraid your memory was very clear on the subject."

"Then what shall we do?"

"I don't know!"

Rincewind thought about this and then, with an air of finality, started to take off his last sock.

"No half-bricks," he said, to no one in particular. "Have to use sand."

"You're going to attack them with a sockful of sand?"

"No. I'm going to run away from them. The sockful of sand is for when they follow."

People were returning to Al Khali, where the ruined tower was a smoking heap of stones. A few brave souls turned their attention to the wreckage, on the basis that there might be survivors who could be rescued or looted or both.

And, among the rubble, the following conversation might have been heard:

"There's something moving under here!"

"Under that? By the two beards of Imtal, you are mishearing. It must weigh a ton."

"Over here, brothers!"

And then sounds of much heaving would have been heard, and then:

"It's a box!"

"It could be treasure, do you think?"

"It's growing legs, by the Seven Moons of Nas-reem!"

"*Five* moons—"

"Where'd it go? Where'd it go?"

"Never mind about that, it's not important. Let's get this straight, according to the legend it was *five* moons—"

In Klatch they take their mythology seriously. It's only real life they don't believe.

The three horsepersons sensed the change as they descended through the heavy snowclouds at the Hub end of the Sto Plain. There was a sharp scent in the air.

"Can't you smell it?" said Nijel, "I remember it when I was a boy, when you lay in bed on that first morning in winter, and you could sort of taste it in the air and—"

The clouds parted below them and there, filling the high plains country from end to end, were the herds of the Ice Giants.

They stretched for miles in every direction, and the thunder of their stampede filled the air.

The bull glaciers were in the lead, bellowing their vast creaky calls and throwing up great sheets of earth as they plowed relentlessly forward. Behind them pressed the great mass of cows and their calves, skimming over land already ground down to the bedrock by the leaders.

They bore as much resemblance to the familiar glaciers the world thought it knew as a lion dozing in the shade bears to three hundred pounds of wickedly coordinated muscle bounding toward you with its mouth open.

". . . and . . . and . . . when you went to the window," Nijel's mouth, lacking any further input from his brain, ran down.

Moving, jostling ice packed the plain, roaring forward under a great cloud of clammy steam. The ground shook as the leaders passed below, and it was obvious to the onlookers that whoever was going to stop this would need more than a couple of pounds of rock salt and a shovel.

"Go on, then," said Conina, "explain. I think you'd better shout."

Nijel looked distractedly at the herd.

"I think I can see some figures," said Creosote helpfully. "Look, on top of the leading . . . things."

Nijel peered through the snow. There were indeed beings moving around on the backs of the glaciers. They were human, or humanoid, or at least humanish. They didn't look very big.

That turned out to be because the glaciers themselves were very big, and Nijel wasn't very good at perspective. As the horses flew lower over the leading glacier, a huge bull heavily crevassed and scarred by moraine, it became apparent that one reason why the Ice Giants were known as the Ice Giants was because they were, well, giants.

The other was that they were made of ice.

A figure the size of a large house was crouched at the crest of the bull, urging it to greater efforts by means of a spike on a long pole. It was craggy, in fact it was more nearly faceted, and glinted green and blue in the light; there was a thin band of silver in its snowy locks, and its eyes were tiny and black and deep set, like lumps of coal.*

There was a splintering crash ahead as the leading glaciers smacked into a forest. Birds rattled up in panic. Snow and splinters rained down around Nijel as he galloped on the air alongside the giant.

He cleared his throat.

"Erm," he said, "excuse me?"

Ahead of the boiling surf of earth, snow and smashed timber a herd of caribou was running in blind panic, their rear hooves a few feet from the tumbling mess.

Nijel tried again.

"I say?" he shouted.

The giant's head turned toward him.

"Vot you vant?" it said. "Go avay, hot person."

"Sorry, but is this really necessary?"

The giant looked at him in frozen astonishment. It turned around slowly and regarded the rest of the herd, which seemed to stretch all the way to the Hub. It looked at Nijel again.

"Yarss," it said, "I tink so. Othervise, why ve do it?"

"Only there's a lot of people out there who would prefer you not to, you see," said Nijel, desperately. A rock spire loomed briefly ahead of the glacier, rocked for a second and then vanished.

---

* Although this was the only way in which they resembled the idols built, in response to ancient and unacknowledged memories, by children in snowy weather; it was extremely unlikely that this Ice Giant would be a small mound of grubby ice with a carrot in it by the morning.

He added, "Also children and small furry animals."

"They vill suffer in the cause of progress. Now is the time ve reclaim the vorld," rumbled the giant. "Whole vorld of ice. According to inevitability of history and triumph of thermodynamics."

"Yes, but you don't have to," said Nijel.

"Ve *vant* to," said the giant. "The gods are gone, ve throw off shackles of outmoded superstition."

"Freezing the whole world solid doesn't sound very progressive to me," said Nijel.

"*Ve* like it."

"Yes, yes," said Nijel, in the maniacally glazed tones of one who is trying to see all sides of the issue and is certain that a solution will be found if people of goodwill will only sit around a table and discuss things rationally like sensible human beings. "But is this the right time? Is the world ready for the triumph of ice?"

"It bloody vell better be," said the giant, and swung his glacier prod at Nijel. It missed the horse but caught him full in the chest, lifting him clean out of the saddle and flicking him onto the glacier itself. He spun, spreadeagled, down its freezing flanks, was carried some way by the boil of debris, and rolled into the slush of ice and mud between the speeding walls.

He staggered to his feet, and peered hopelessly into the freezing fog. Another glacier bore down directly on him.

So did Conina. She leaned over as her horse swept down out of the fog, caught Nijel by his leather barbarian harness, and swung him up in front of her.

As they rose again he wheezed, "Cold-hearted bastard. I really thought I was getting somewhere for a moment there. You just can't talk to some people."

The herd breasted another hill, scraping off quite a lot of it, and the Sto Plain, studded with cities, lay helpless before it.

Rincewind sidled toward the nearest Thing, holding Coin with one hand and swinging the loaded sock in the other.

"No magic, right?" he said.

"Yes," said the boy.

"Whatever happens, you musn't use magic?"

"That's it. Not here. They haven't got much power here, if you don't use magic. Once they break through, though . . ."

His voice trailed away.

"Pretty awful," Rincewind nodded.

"Terrible," said Coin.

Rincewind sighed. He wished he still had his hat. He'd just have to do without it.

"All right," he said. "When I shout, you make a run for the light. Do you understand? No looking back or anything. No matter what happens."

"No matter what?" said Coin uncertainly.

"No matter what." Rincewind gave a brave little smile. "Especially no matter what you hear."

He was vaguely cheered to see Coin's mouth become an "O" of terror.

"And then," he continued, "when you get back to the other side—"

"What shall I do?"

Rincewind hesitated. "I don't know," he said. "Anything you can. As much magic as you like. Anything. Just stop them. And . . . um . . ."

"Yes?"

Rincewind gazed up at the Thing, which was still staring into the light.

"If it . . . you know . . . if anyone gets out of this, you know, and everything is all right after all, sort of thing, I'd like you to sort of tell people I sort of stayed here. Perhaps they could sort of write it down somewhere. I mean, I wouldn't want a statue or anything," he added virtuously.

After a while he added, "I think you ought to blow your nose."

Coin did so, on the hem of his robe, and then shook Rincewind's hand solemnly.

"If ever you . . ." he began, "that is, you're the first . . . it's been a great . . . you see, I never really . . ." His voice trailed off, and then he said, "I just wanted you to know that."

"There was something else I was trying to say," said Rincewind, letting go of the hand. He looked blank for a moment, and then added, "Oh, yes. It's vital to remember who you really are. It's very important. It isn't a good idea to rely on other people or things to do it for you, you see. They always get it wrong."

"I'll try and remember," said Coin.

"It's very important," Rincewind repeated, almost to himself. "And now I think you'd better run."

Rincewind crept closer to the Thing. This particular one had chicken legs, but most of the rest of it was mercifully hidden in what looked like folded wings.

It was, he thought, time for a few last words. What he said now was likely to be very important. Perhaps they would be words that would be remembered, and handed down, and maybe even carved deeply in slabs of granite.

Words without too many curly letters in, therefore.

"I really wish I wasn't here," he muttered.

He hefted the sock, whirled it once or twice, and smashed the Thing on what he hoped was its kneecap.

It gave a shrill buzz, spun wildly with its wings creaking open, lunged vaguely at Rincewind with its vulture head and got another sockful of sand on the upswing.

Rincewind looked around desperately as the Thing staggered back, and saw Coin still standing where he had left him. To his horror he saw the boy begin to walk toward him, hands raised instinctively to fire the magic which, here, would doom both of them.

"Run away, you idiot!" he screamed, as the Thing began to gather itself for a counter-attack. From out of nowhere he found the words, "You know what happens to boys who are bad!"

Coin went pale, turned and ran toward the light. He moved as though through treacle, fighting against the entropy slope. The distorted image of the world turned inside out hovered a few feet away, then inches, wavering uncertainly . . .

A tentacle curled around his leg, tumbling him forward.

He flung his hands out as he fell, and one of them touched snow. It was immediately grabbed by something else that felt like a warm, soft leather glove, but under the gentle touch was a grip as tough as tempered steel and it tugged him forward, also dragging whatever it was that had caught him.

Light and grainy dark flicked around him and suddenly he was sliding over cobbles slicked with ice.

The Librarian let go his hold and stood over Coin with a length of heavy wooden beam in his hand. For a moment the ape reared against the darkness, the shoulder, elbow and wrist of his right arm unfolding in a poem of applied leverage, and in a movement as unstoppable as the dawn of intelligence brought it down very heavily. There was a squashy noise and an offended screech, and the burning pressure on Coin's leg vanished.

The dark column wavered. There were squeals and thumps coming from it, distorted by distance.

Coin struggled to his feet and started to run back into the dark, but this time the Librarian's arm blocked his path.

"We can't just leave him in there!"

The ape shrugged.

There was another crackle from the dark, and then a moment of almost complete silence.

But only almost complete. Both of them thought they heard, a long way off but very distinct, the sound of running feet fading into the distance.

They found an echo in the outside world. The ape

glanced around, and then pushed Coin hurriedly to one side as something squat and battered and with hundreds of little legs barrelled across the stricken courtyard and, without so much as pausing in its stride, leapt into the disappearing darkness, which flickered for one last time and vanished.

There was a sudden flurry of snow across the air where it had been.

Coin wrenched free of the Librarian's grip and ran into the circle, which was already turning white. His feet scuffed up a sprinkle of fine sand.

"He didn't come out!" he said.

"Oook," said the Librarian, in a philosophic manner.

"I thought he'd come out. You know, just at the last minute."

"Oook?"

Coin looked closely at the cobbles, as if by mere concentration he could change what he saw. "Is he dead?"

"Oook," observed the Librarian, contriving to imply that Rincewind was in a region where even things like time and space were a bit iffy, and that it was probably not very useful to speculate as to his exact state at this point in time, if indeed he was at any point in time at all, and that, all in all, he might even turn up tomorrow or, for that matter, yesterday, and finally that if there was any chance at all of surviving then Rincewind almost certainly would.

"Oh," said Coin.

He watched the Librarian shuffle around and head back for the Tower of Art, and a desperate loneliness overcame him.

"I say!" he yelled.

"Oook?"

"What should I do now?"

"Oook?"

Coin waved vaguely at the desolation.

"You know, perhaps I could do something about all this?" he said in a voice tilting on the edge of terror. "Do you think that would be a good idea? I mean, I could help people. I'm sure you'd like to be human again, wouldn't you?"

The Librarian's everlasting smile hoisted itself a little further up his face, just enough to reveal his teeth.

"Okay, perhaps not," said Coin hurriedly, "but there's other things I could do, isn't there?"

The Librarian gazed at him for some time, then dropped his eyes to the boy's hand. Coin gave a guilty start, and opened his fingers.

The ape caught the little silver ball neatly before it hit the ground and held it up to one eye. He sniffed it, shook it gently, and listened to it for a while.

Then he wound up his arm and flung it away as hard as possible.

"What—" Coin began, and landed full length in the snow when the Librarian pushed him over and dived on top of him.

The ball curved over at the top of its arc and tumbled down, its perfect path interrupted suddenly by the ground. There was a sound like a harp string breaking, a brief babble of incomprehensible voices, a rush of hot wind, and the gods of the Disc were free.

The were *very* angry.

* * *

"There is nothing we can do, is there?" said Creosote.

"No," said Conina.

"The ice is going to win, isn't it?" said Creosote.

"Yes," said Conina.

"No," said Nijel.

He was trembling with rage, or possibly with cold, and was nearly as pale as the glaciers that rumbled past below them.

Conina sighed. "Well, just how do you think—" she began.

"Take me down somewhere a few minutes ahead of them," said Nijel.

"I really don't see how that would help."

"I wasn't asking your opinion," said Nijel, quietly. "Just do it. Put me down a little way ahead of them so I've got a while to get sorted out."

"Get what sorted out?"

Nijel didn't answer.

"I *said*," said Conina, "get what—"

"Shut up!"

"I don't see why—"

"Look," said Nijel, with the patience that lies just short of axe-murdering. "The ice is going to cover the whole world, right? Everyone's going to die, okay? Except for us for a little while, I suppose, until these horses want their, their, their oats or the lavatory or whatever, which isn't much use to us except maybe Creosote will just about have time to write a sonnet or something about how cold it is all of a sudden, and the whole of human history is about to be scraped up and in these circumstances I would like very much to make it completely clear that I am not about to be argued with, is that absolutely understood?"

He paused for breath, trembling like a harpstring.

Conina hesitated. Her mouth opened and shut a few times, as though she was considering arguing, and then she thought better of it.

They found a small clearing in a pine forest a mile or two ahead of the herd, although the sound of it was clearly audible and there was a line of steam above the trees and the ground was dancing like a drumtop.

Nijel strolled to the middle of the clearing and made a few practice swings with his sword. The others watched him thoughtfully.

"If you don't mind," whispered Creosote to Conina, "I'll be off. It's at times like this that sobriety loses its attractions and I'm sure the end of the world will look a lot better through the bottom of a glass, if it's all the same to you. Do you believe in Paradise, o peach-cheeked blossom?"

"Not as such, no."

"Oh," said Creosote. "Well, in that case we probably won't be seeing each other again." He sighed. "What a waste. All this was just because of a geas. Um. Of course, if by some unthinkable chance—"

"Goodbye," said Conina.

Creosote nodded miserably, wheeled the horse and disappeared over the treetops.

Snow was shaking down from the branches around the clearing. The thunder of the approaching glaciers filled the air.

Nijel started when she tapped him on the shoulder, and dropped his sword.

"What are you doing here?" he snapped, fumbling desperately in the snow.

"Look, I'm not prying or anything," said Conina meekly, "but what exactly do you have in mind?"

She could see a rolling heap of bulldozed snow and soil bearing down on them through the forest, the mind-numbing sound of the leading glaciers now overlaid with the rhythmic snapping of tree trunks. And, advancing implacably above the treeline, so high that the eye mistook them at first for sky, the blue-green prows.

"Nothing," said Nijel, "nothing at all. We've just got to resist them, that's all there is to it. That's what we're here for."

"But it won't make any difference," she said.

"It will to me. If we're going to die anyway, I'd rather die like this. Heroically."

"Is it heroic to die like this?" said Conina.

"*I* think it is," he said, "and when it comes to dying, there's only one opinion that matters."

"Oh."

A couple of deer blundered into the clearing, ignored the humans in their blind panic, and rocketed away.

"You don't have to stay," said Nijel. "I've got this geas, you see."

Conina looked at the backs of her hands.

"I think I should," she said, and added, "You know, I thought maybe, you know, if we could just get to know one another better—"

"Mr. and Mrs. Harebut, was that what you had in mind?" he said bluntly.

Her eyes widened. "Well—" she began.

"Which one did you intend to be?" he said.

The leading glacier smashed into the clearing just behind its bow wave, its top lost in a cloud of its own creation.

At exactly the same time the trees opposite it bent low as a hot wind blew from the Rim. It was loaded with voices—petulant, bickering voices—and tore into the clouds like a hot iron into water.

Conina and Nijel threw themselves down into snow which turned to warm slush under them. Something like a thunderstorm crashed overhead, filled with shouting and what they at first thought were screams although, thinking about them later, they seemed more like angry arguments. It went on for a long time, and then began to fade in the direction of the Hub.

Warm water flooded down the front of Nijel's vest. He lifted himself cautiously, and then nudged Conina.

Together they scrambled through the slush and mud to the top of the slope, climbed through a log-jam of smashed timber and boulders, and stared at the scene.

The glaciers were retreating, under a cloud stuffed with lightning. Behind them the landscape was a network of lakes and pools.

"Did we do that?" said Conina.

"It would be nice to think so, wouldn't it?" said Nijel.

"Yes, but *did*—" she began.

"Probably not. Who knows? Let's just find a horse," he said.

"The Apogee," said War, "or something. I'm pretty sure."

They had staggered out of the inn and were sitting on a bench in the afternoon sunshine. Even War had been persuaded to take off some of his armor.

"Dunno," said Famine. "Don't think so."

Pestilence shut his crusted eyes and leaned back against the warm stones.

"*I think*," he said, "*it was something about the end of the world*."

War sat and thoughtfully scratched his chin. He hiccuped.

"What, the whole world?" he said.

"*I reckon*."

War gave this some further consideration. "I reckon we're well out of it, then," he said.

People were returning to Ankh-Morpork, which was no longer a city of empty marble but was once again its old self, sprawling as randomly and colorfully as a pool of vomit outside the all-night takeaway of History.

And the University had been rebuilt, or had rebuilt itself, or in some strange way had never been unbuilt; every strand of ivy, every rotting casement, was back in place. The sourcerer had offered to replace everything as good as new, all wood sparkling, all stone unstained, but the Librarian had been very firm on the subject. He wanted everything replaced as good as old.

The wizards came creeping back with the dawn, in ones or twos, scuttling for their old rooms, trying to avoid one another's gaze, trying to remember a recent past that was already becoming unreal and dream-like.

Conina and Nijel arrived around breakfast time and, out of kindness, found a livery stable for War's horse.* It was Conina who insisted that they look for Rincewind at the University, and who, therefore, first saw the books.

They were flying out of the Tower of Art, spiraling around the University buildings and swooping through the door of the reincarnated Library. One or two of the more impudent grimoires were chasing sparrows, or hovering hawk-like over the quad.

The Librarian was leaning against the doorway, watching his charges with a benevolent eye. He waggled his eyebrows at Conina, the nearest he ever got to a conventional greeting.

"Is Rincewind here?" she said.

"Oook."

"Sorry?"

The ape didn't answer but took them both by the hand and, walking between them like a sack between two poles, led them across the cobbles to the tower.

---

* Which wisely decided not to fly again, was never claimed, and lived out the rest of its days as the carriage horse of an elderly lady. What War did about this is unrecorded; it is pretty certain that he got another one.

There were a few candles alight inside, and they saw Coin seated on a stool. The Librarian bowed them into his presence like an ancient retainer in the oldest family of all, and withdrew.

Coin nodded at them. "He knows when people don't understand him," he said. "Remarkable, isn't he?"

"Who are you?" said Conina.

"Coin," said Coin.

"Are you a student here?"

"I'm learning quite a lot, I think."

Nijel was wandering around the walls, giving them the occasional prod. There had to be some good reason why they didn't fall down, but if there was it didn't lie in the realms of civil engineering.

"Are you looking for Rincewind?" said Coin.

Conina frowned. "How did you guess that?"

"He told me some people would come looking for him."

Conina relaxed. "Sorry," she said, "we've had a bit of a trying time. I thought perhaps it was magic, or something. He's all right, isn't he? I mean, what's been happening? Did he fight the sourcerer?"

"Oh, yes. And he won. It was very . . . interesting. I saw it all. But then he had to go," said Coin, as though reciting.

"What, just like that?" said Nijel.

"Yes."

"I don't believe it," said Conina. She was beginning to crouch, her knuckles whitening.

"It is true," said Coin. "Everything I say is true. It has to be."

"I want to—" Conina began, and Coin stood up, extended a hand and said, "Stop."

She froze. Nijel stiffened in mid-frown.

"You will leave," said Coin, in a pleasant, level voice, "and you will ask no more questions. You will be totally satisfied. You have all your answers. You will live happily ever after. You will forget hearing these words. You will go now."

They turned slowly and woodenly, like puppets, and trooped to the door. The Librarian opened it for them, ushered them through and shut it behind them.

Then he stared at Coin, who sagged back onto the stool.

"All right, all right," said the boy, "but it was only a little magic. I had to. You said yourself people had to forget."

"Oook?"

"I can't help it! It's too easy to change things!" He clutched his head. "I've only got to *think* of something! I can't stay, everything I touch goes wrong, it's like trying to sleep on a heap of eggs! This world is too thin! *Please tell me what to do!*"

The Librarian spun around on his bottom a few times, a sure sign of deep thought.

Exactly what he said is not recorded, but Coin smiled, nodded, shook the Librarian's hand, and opened his own hands and drew them up and around him and stepped into another world. It had a lake in, and some distant mountains, and a few pheasants watching him suspiciously from under the trees. It was the magic all sourcerers learned, eventually.

Sourcerers never become part of the world. They merely wear it for a while.

He looked back, halfway across the turf, and waved at the Librarian. The ape gave him an encouraging nod.

And then the bubble shrank inside itself, and the last sourcerer vanished from this world and into a world of his own.

Although it has nothing much to do with the story, it is an interesting fact that, about five hundred miles away, a small flock, or rather in this case a herd, of birds were picking their way cautiously through the trees. They had heads like a flamingo, bodies like a turkey, and legs like a Sumo wrestler; they walked in a jerky, bobbing fashion, as though their heads were attached to their feet by elastic bands. They belonged to a species unique even among Disc fauna, in that their prime means of defense was to cause a predator to laugh so much that they could run away before it recovered.

Rincewind would have been vaguely satisfied to know that they were geas.

Custom was slow in the Mended Drum. The troll chained to the doorpost sat in the shade and reflectively picked someone out of his teeth.

Creosote was singing softly to himself. He had discovered beer and wasn't having to pay for it, because the coinage of compliments—rarely employed by the swains of Ankh—was having an astonishing effect on the landlord's daughter. She was a large, good-natured girl, with a figure that was the color and, not to put too fine a point on it, the same shape as unbaked bread. She was intrigued. No one had ever referred to her breasts as jewelled melons before.

"Absolutely," said the Seriph, sliding peacefully off his bench, "no doubt about it." Either the big yellow sort or the small green ones with huge warty veins, he told himself virtuously.

"And what was that about my hair?" she said encouragingly, hauling him back and refiling his glass.

"Oh." The Seriph's brow wrinkled. "Like a goat of flocks that grazes on the slopes of Mount Wossname, and no mistake. And as for your ears," he added quickly, "no pink-hued shells that grace the sea-kissed sands of—"

"Exactly *how* like a flock of goats?" she said.

The Seriph hesitated. He'd always considered it one of his best lines. Now it was meeting Ankh-Morpork's famous literal-mindedness head-on for the first time. Strangely enough, he felt rather impressed.

"I mean, in size, shape or smell?" she went on.

"I think," said the Seriph, "that perhaps the phrase I had in mind was exactly *not* like a flog of gits."

"Ah?" The girl pulled the flagon toward her.

"And I think perhaps I would like another drink," he said indistinctly, "and then—and then—" He looked sideways at the girl, and took the plunge. "Are you much of a raconteur?"

"What?"

He licked his suddenly dry lips. "I mean, do you know many stories?" he croaked.

"Oh, yes. Lots."

"Lots?" whispered Creosote. Most of his concubines only knew the same old one or two.

"Hundreds. Why, do you want to hear one?"

"What, now?"

"If you like. It's not very busy in here."

Perhaps I did die, Creosote thought. Perhaps this is Paradise. He took her hands. "You know," he said, "it's ages since I've had a good narrative. But I wouldn't want you to do anything you don't want to."

She patted his arm. What a nice old gentleman, she thought. Compared to some we get in here.

"There's one my granny used to tell me. I know it backwards," she said.

Creosote sipped his beer and watched the wall in a warm glow. Hundreds, he thought. And she knows some of them *backwards*.

She cleared her throat, and said, in a sing-song voice that made Creosote's pulse fuse. "There was a man and he had eight sons—"

The Patrician sat by his window, writing. His mind was full of fluff as far as the last week or two was concerned, and he didn't like that much.

A servant had lit a lamp to dispel the twilight, and a few early evening moths were orbiting it. The Patrician watched them carefully. For some reason he felt very uneasy in the presence of glass but that, as he stared fixedly at the insects, wasn't what bothered him most.

What bothered him was that he was fighting a terrible urge to catch them with his tongue.

And Wuffles lay on his back at his master's feet, and barked in his dreams.

Lights were going on all over the city, but the last few strands of sunset illuminated the gargoyles as they helped one another up the long climb to the roof.

The Librarian watched them from the open door, while giving himself a philosophic scratch. Then he turned and shut out the night.

It was warm in the Library. It was *always* warm in the Library, because the scatter of magic that produced the glow also gently cooked the air.

The Librarian looked at his charges approvingly, made his last rounds of the slumbering shelves, and then dragged his blanket underneath his desk, ate a goodnight banana, and fell asleep.

Silence gradually reclaimed the Library. Silence drifted around the remains of a hat, heavily battered and frayed and charred around the edges, that had been placed with some ceremony in a niche in the wall. No matter how far a wizard goes, he will always come back for his hat.

Silence filled the University in the same way that air fills a hole. Night spread across the Disk like plum jam, or possibly blackberry preserve.

But there would be a morning. There would always be another morning.